An Uncertain Justice

by Marnie L. Pehrson

An Uncertain Justice

By Marnie L. Pehrson
marnie@marniepehrson.com
www.AnUncertainJustice.com
www.MarniePehrson.com

Published by
Spirit Tree Publishing
www.SpiritTreePublishing.com

Cover Design by Tamara Ingram, TheArtPad@digis.net

Library of Congress: 2009911762

Printed in the United States of America
ISBN 978-0-9825878-0-5

In loving memory of

My grandmother, Edna Jane Springfield, whose smiling face, twinkling eyes and warm hugs will forever remain sweet memories. Whether she was serving her delicious fried apple pies or Neapolitan ice cream from her "Frigidaire," or letting me play the upper octave notes as she pounded out "Redwing" on her piano, she always made me feel important and loved. For many years after her passing her presence seemed so near, I knew she served as my guardian angel.

To Mamaw… until we meet again…

Acknowledgments

Researching *An Uncertain Justice* was like trying to solve an 87-year-old mystery. Piecing together records, newspaper clippings, and accounts of people who were alive at the time became a major undertaking. Fortunately, I was able to speak to Mr. John Puryear and Monteen Moore, descendents of Tom Tarvin, one of the deputies assigned to the hanging. They were able to give me insights into Tom's feelings as an unwilling participant in the whole affair.

I received the full story of the trial through the assistance of Walker County lawyer, Steven Rodham Esq. A special thanks to Steve for helping me obtain the Georgia Supreme Court Decision which contained transcripts of the trial. Walker County Sheriff Steve Wilson was also kind enough to take time from his busy schedule to answer questions regarding the murder.

Information on the characters, the time period, and living conditions were critical to set the tone for the novel. I couldn't have done this without research compiled by Donna Morton Morgan in *The Lookout Mountain Mortons* and assistance from Carolyn Jirlds, Jack and Betty Morton, Joanne Crutchfield, Ruby Hale, and interviews with Thadda Springfield Moody before her passing.

Most importantly, no project of this magnitude could ever be possible without someone who has faith in you and believes in what you are doing. This book would never have been possible without the content editing and constant encouragement of Kerry Blair. Kerry has believed in and encouraged me in this project since day one. I am so grateful for her faith that buoyed me when I didn't have it myself.

Special thanks also goes to my line editor, Meredith Dias for her eagle eye. Others who have been instrumental in editing, offering suggestions, and critiquing the manuscript include Jennifer Youngblood, Rachael Crook, Marcia Lynn McClure, Shawna Jones, Jeri Gilchrist, and Lisa Rae Preston. Thank you all for your help! I couldn't have done it without you!

Prologue

Walker County Jail, Lafayette, Georgia
April 27, 1923
11:50 a.m.

"I hope it's a good, easy death," the prisoner said as he approached the gallows inside the Walker County Jail.

Deputy Tom Tarvin looked at the condemned man. He was young and clean-shaved with good posture and a well-cut suit and tie. If Tom had encountered him on the street, he'd have taken him for a fine man; he never suspected he might be a murderer. But then, Tom had always doubted this boy's guilt.

Tom's eyes met those of big-city reporter Rupert Merewether. If he hadn't gotten involved, probably none of them would be there. That man had stirred the pot so much that Tom feared they were hanging an innocent man while the guilty one looked on. If only Merewether had found another way to make a name for himself, justice would have likely run its course with different results.

Tom pressed his fingers to his graying temples and rubbed, trying to soothe the ache that throbbed within. He reminded himself—again—that he was only doing his job. His duty.

"How far's the drop?" the prisoner asked, his voice so calm he could have been inquiring about the weather on an ordinary day. But this was no ordinary day. It was the day—the hour—he would die.

"Six feet, eight inches," Tom's partner, Deputy Aknow, answered.

A wave of nausea washed over Tom. His eyes riveted on the trap door beneath the prisoner's boots. He hoped it was the right height—

prayed it was. None of them had ever hanged a man. Sheriff Harmon had a book on the subject explaining that the drop from the trap had to be just right. If it was too far, or the man was too heavy, the rope could snap the head clean off.

Bile rose in the back of Tom's throat. He swallowed hard, forcing it down.

Never would he have agreed to spring the trap, not for anything in the world. Bringing this man to the gallows would haunt him all his days.

His eyes shifted toward Sheriff Harmon's closed office door. The man had been sequestered all morning, refusing to talk to reporters, letting Tom and the other deputy handle things until the final moment.

When the jailhouse door opened to allow the exit of family members unwilling, unable, to watch the final act, Tom heard the subdued voices of several hundred people waiting outside. With a lump in his throat, he watched the prisoner's family cling to one another, dabbing at bloodshot eyes with torn and crumpled handkerchiefs. At last, the prisoner's father draped his arms around the group and ushered them outside.

The poor parents! Tom thought. What would it be like to know that in moments your son would die horribly, declaring his innocence to the bitter end?

After the family exited and the doors closed once again, Deputy Aknow asked the prisoner for his final words.

The man straightened even though his arms were tied behind his back and his feet bound together. "Boys," he said, "I'm going to leave here grinning. A body would like to stay on this earth awhile longer, but when you've got to go, there's no use in crying." His forced smile faltered, belying the brave words. Nervously he added, "Would someone please comb my hair?"

Tom and Aknow patted their pockets but found no comb. Tom used his fingers to rake the prisoner's dark hair as best he could until someone in the small audience, perhaps a reporter, produced a comb. Tom used it, then straightened the prisoner's black tie. He avoided the man's eyes as he buttoned his burial suit. At last, he patted the man's shoulder and reluctantly accepted the noose from Aknow's hand.

His own hands trembled as Tom looped the rope around the young man's neck. It slid through his fingers as he drew it tight, giving him a slight burn across one palm. Tom flinched, knowing it was nothing compared to what this man would soon feel, nothing compared to the fire that seared his soul for the part he was playing in this hanging.

Deputy Aknow held up the black hood and moved to place it over the young man's head.

The prisoner said, "Before you do that, tell Mrs. Harmon I said good-bye."

Tom nodded. The sheriff's wife had been kind to the prisoner when she brought in his meals.

"How should I stand to make it spring easier?" the young man asked, as if death were an afterthought.

"Just put your feet right there on the trap," Tom managed, pointing down at the wood. He placed a reassuring hand on the boy's upper arm to help settle him into place.

Deputy Aknow covered the prisoner's head with the black cloth. Only then did Sheriff Harmon leave his office, stepping into an adjoining room to spring the trap.

An eerie silence filled the chamber as the two deputies stepped back. Tom held his breath. Everyone in the room seemed to do the same. The only sound Tom heard in the ensuing silence was the hammering of his heart.

Suddenly, as if no one had expected it to happen, the trap snapped open, a loud creak and thud slicing through the silence.

The body dropped six feet, eight inches.

There were a few gasps and tears, but mostly the onlookers were frozen in horror. Even the ever-ready fingers of reporters were still, hovered over pads of paper, their owners forgetting for the moment what they had meant to record. Everyone in the room had come knowing what he would see, yet every one was unprepared for what he saw.

The bile in Tom's throat overwhelmed him at last as he looked downward. The drop hadn't been far enough! The man dangled—struggling, writhing, choking.

Eleven interminable minutes passed until at last the body fell still.

The Chattanooga Times - April 28, 1923:

"At [eleven] minutes after 12, the prisoner had paid the inexorable penalty of the law for those who violate the sacred commandment, 'Thou Shalt not Kill.'"

The true story behind the last legal hanging in the state of Georgia began thirteen months earlier…

Chapter 1: The Apple Doesn't Fall Far

Hinkle, Lookout Mountain, Georgia
Friday, March 3, 1922

"I sure dread movin', Grandpa." Sherman Morton shook his head, then reared back and let the ax crack against the log in front of him. The steam from his sigh lingered in the crisp air like the fog that encircled the mountain.

Sherman let the ax dangle from his hand as he inhaled the familiar scent of wood, hay, and frying bacon. His shoulders slumped and his blue eyes fixed on his grandfather. Lookout Mountain had been Sherman's home all seventeen years of his life. He'd always been a hop-skip-and-jump from his grandparents, but now he'd be an hour's drive away, clear off on a different mountain—another state, even!

"I know it's gonna be rough. Your grandma and I are gonna miss y'all somethin' fierce, but I guess that's the way the wood chips splinter sometimes." Grandpa Joe shrugged his shoulders. "It's not like your Pa has much of a choice."

"I know." Sherman pushed his hat down a little lower on his brow, lifted the ax, and let it descend. A swell of satisfaction surged through his body as he felt the log split beneath the tool's weight. A slight smile curled the corner of his lips.

"You're gonna do well for yourself," Joe said.

"You mean at the Mowbray Mine?" Sherman picked up another log and set it on the stump. "I suppose one mine's about the same as another. If Durham wasn't runnin' out of coal, we'd've done well here, too."

"I ain't talkin' about coal minin'." When Sherman's eyes lifted, his grandfather continued, "I'm talkin' about the man you are and the man you'll yet become."

Sherman straightened under his grandfather's admiring gaze.

"Look atcha!" Joe waved a hand in Sherman's direction. "Hard workin', a willin' heart." Sherman's eyes lowered to the log again, embarrassed, yet honored by his grandfather's appraisal. "God can do a lot with a willin' heart and an obedient hand."

Sherman didn't know what to say, but his grandfather's confidence meant everything.

"This move," Joe continued, "it's just the beginnin' of bigger things for you, Sherman. It's your chance to be the man you were born to be. The trick is lookin' at it as an opportunity instead of a trial." Grandpa Joe pulled a sheriff's star from his pocket and pinned it in place on his own coat.

"I'll try to remember that, Grandpa," Sherman said.

"You do that." Joe put a hand on the younger man's shoulder. "Guess I'll leave you to your chopping. I've got a still to locate."

"Still lookin' for the same one?" Sherman asked.

"Yep. Can't seem to track it down, but we will."

"Nothing stops you when you've set your mind to something. Right, Grandpa?"

"I do my best," Joe said. His expression grew somber. "The sad part about these stills is the havoc they wreak on young lives. We had two boys, barely fourteen, get hold of some bad moonshine last night and pert near die from it."

"Do I know 'em?"

"The Randall and the McLean boys." Joe ran his hand along his mustache.

Sherman shook his head in disgust. "Those boys know better."

"I know, comin' from good church-goin' families. Good parents. Just got mixed up with a bad crowd and a worse batch of moonshine." One corner of Joe's mouth turned up beneath the mustache. "Doc says they should be fine. Let's hope they've learned their lesson." He took a few steps toward Sherman's house before turning back. "Any chance you could plow Grandma's garden today?"

"I'd be happy to," Sherman said, glad for the chance to help his grandmother before he had to leave and to see his grandfather yet again. He returned to chopping with new enthusiasm.

Sherman's little sisters, Edna Mae and Ruby, played marbles on the front porch. A loud crack indicated a clean shot as an aggie rolled across the wooden planks. Ruby hung her blonde head in defeat while Edna Mae celebrated her victory by jumping up and down, her little dress and dark hair blowing in the March morning breeze.

"Ouch!" Ruby exclaimed. In the next moment the fair-haired child broke into giggles. "Grandpa!" She hopped up from the porch and ran into the yard to greet Joe.

Sherman caught the encounter from the corner of his eye and shook his head with a chuckle. Grandpa Morton and his rocks. He didn't greet his grandchildren the way normal grandfathers did. Instead of a hug, he'd pelt them with a small rock or two.

The girls ran toward Grandpa Joe, who tossed one tiny pebble after another at their skirts. He darted this way and that as they came at him with stones of their own.

Sherman took a few more swings with the ax until the log split. He tossed the log on the pile then leaned the ax against the barn. He gathered an armful of logs and headed toward the house.

"Whoa, now, Edna Mae!" Grandpa exclaimed. Edna Mae held up a rock the size of a man's fist. Grandpa raised open palms and his pebbles fell into the grass. "I surrender. You win, little 'un!"

Edna Mae dropped her rock and both girls ran toward their grandfather and jumped into his arms. He kissed each child on the cheek and hugged them both—one in each arm. He tickled the girls, and they broke into delighted giggles.

About that time, Sherman's father, who'd been working in the house, stepped out on the porch. "What's all the ruckus?" he called. "Ah, rock wars with Grandpa, eh?

Edna Mae strutted like a peacock. "I won!"

"She was gonna hit him with that big ol' rock." Eight-year-old Ruby pointed at the limestone weapon.

"I wasn't really goin' to, Grandpa." Edna Mae looked up at him with big chocolate eyes, and Sherman could see his grandfather melt.

Joe gathered Edna Mae in his arms and rose to his feet, kissing her cheek once more. The little girl reached for her grandfather's deputy sheriff's badge, fingering the silver star.

"How's the packin' going, Will?" Grandpa Joe asked his son.

"Good, we're almost done here. Should be ready to go in the mornin'." Will nudged a tuft of grass with one well-worn boot.

"You think you can spare a youngin or two to go over and help your Ma plow her garden?" Grandpa asked. "Sherman's already said he'll help."

Will nodded. "He can take Little Gordon and Ruby with 'im. They can help pick up rocks."

Sherman set the armful of split wood on the porch. He looked up and saw his brother Gordon scowling in the doorway. The fifteen-year-old hated being called "little." Ever since Aunt Mary Ann married Gordon Phillips, Sherman's brother had been designated "little Gordon" to dispel confusion.

"I wanna go!" Edna Mae exclaimed.

"Nah, baby, you stay here with your mama and Bonnie," their father replied.

"Why can't I go?" Edna Mae whined.

"You're too little for workin' in the garden and nobody has the time to keep an eye on you," their father explained.

Edna Mae buried her head in her grandfather's shoulder.

"Don't suppose we could talk you into stayin'?" Joe asked his son.

Sherman smiled, glad his grandfather asked one more time, even if it wouldn't do any good.

"Papa, I know you want every last youngin to stay here in Hinkle with you and Mama, but we've gotta go." Will's exasperation was evident in his blue eyes.

"I know. It's just that our family's been on Lookout Mountain since right after the War Between the States. It's a shame to see things change."

Will was too busy rolling his eyes to notice Joe wink at Sherman.

"You could help me with the sawmill or in buildin' the shanties out to the mine," Joe continued.

"Papa, you know good and well with the mine slowin' down the way it is, they won't be needin' a bunch of new shanties."

Sherman knew it was true. The mine wasn't producing much. There was too little work for too many men. When Will had learned about the need for miners out at Montlake, he and Sherman had taken the long trip down the mountain into Daisy and back up Mowbray Mountain to sign on. Both of them working full-time would be good money for their family.

Edna Mae wiggled free of her grandfather's arms and ran inside the house in search of her mama. "Well, we sure are gonna miss y'all," Grandpa Joe said, putting his brown derby back on his head.

"We'll miss you too, Papa." Will's expression softened as Joe gave up the battle.

Grandpa Joe shoved his hand in his pocket. "What time you figurin' on leavin' in the mornin'?"

"Real early—first light," Will answered.

"Ya'll stop on by this evenin' and say good-bye," Joe suggested.

"We'll do that."

Sherman watched his grandfather walk away until his white shirt was only a speck amidst the trees.

~*~

Sherman held the reins taut as the mule plowed a straight row across Grandma Josie's garden spot. He'd had a lot of experience, so despite his youth and lanky frame, he could plow a row as straight as any man and split a cord of wood faster than most.

Sherman removed his hat and swiped his sleeve across his brow. Beads of perspiration moistened his brown hair and trickled down his sideburns. He closed his eyes and tilted his head back, reveling in the March breeze on his cheeks and the soothing warmth of the sun on his face. He loved the contrast of warmth and chill that came only in the spring.

He put his hat back on his head and continued plowing. After turning the mule to begin another row, he faced Gordon and Ruby, who worked alongside Grandma Josie. The old woman leaned on her cane and pointed toward rocks the children should remove.

Gordon reached for a heavy limestone slab.

"Bend yer knees, Gordon!" Sherman called across the field.

Minding his older brother, Gordon straightened his back and squatted down. He lifted the rock, waddled a few feet into the grass, and let it drop. Ruby picked up smaller stones and tossed them in a pile outside the garden while Grandma Josie hobbled through the freshly tilled earth, periodically bending over to remove a stone herself.

Sherman admired his grandmother. She had been partially paralyzed on her right side for nearly twenty-two years, but she never let that stop her from getting out in her garden. Nothing took precedence over that. Grandpa Joe often took workers out of his fields to see that Grandma Josie's garden was well tended. Spending his last day on Lookout Mountain plowing that garden suited Sherman just fine. It seemed fitting, in fact.

Sherman thought back on the times he had spent with his grandmother. More than once she'd grabbed one end of a crosscut saw and told Sherman to get the other. Together they'd felled a tree to make the garden a bit bigger. Nothing stopped Grandma Josie, nor was she one to wait around for help. She hobbled out to work every day. She and Joe had taught Sherman by example the value of hard work.

Grandpa Joe's enterprising nature had also rubbed off on his grandson. As he tilled the field, Sherman couldn't help but think about the job he'd start the following week at the Montlake coalmines. Although he didn't relish the thought of working underground rather than out in the fresh mountain air, he did look forward to the money he would earn.

Sherman had plans: find a pretty girl to marry and build a nice home for her and the passel of children they'd have. Family was the heart of the Mortons. Sherman had been raised to believe that a good man was a good provider. Turning the mule to start another row, he continued to devise ways to earn money. He could buy and develop land. Perhaps one day he would build houses like Grandpa Joe. But not shanties, he thought—real houses with plenty of room for growing families.

"I'm gonna go start dinner." Grandma Josie's voice broke into Sherman's thoughts. He looked over his shoulder and waved to indicate he had heard. With her hair slicked back in a bun on her small head, she looked like a little gray bird. No one would suspect the strength that filled her tiny frame.

Grandma wiggled her cane in farewell and hobbled back toward the house.

Sometime later, when Sherman was about two-thirds through his chore, he looked around and noticed Gordon and Ruby were no longer tossing rocks from the furrowed earth. He scanned the property until he spotted them. Gordon stood at the apex of the barn roof with an outstretched hand toward Ruby. She grasped it and, with his help, scrambled to the top.

The two sat, straddling the roof. Sherman had done his share of "riding the barn," but he knew by the sun that Grandpa Joe would be home for dinner any minute—and fit to be tied if he found those two atop the barn.

Sherman hollered up at the children, but they either pretended they didn't hear or were too engrossed in play to pay him any mind. He shrugged and went back to the plow. The job needed to be done. If those two wanted to ride the barn right when Grandpa was due home, then they'd just have to risk the consequences.

Sure enough, Sherman had just started his final row when Grandpa Joe appeared on the path toward the house. Sherman held his breath, almost hoping his younger siblings wouldn't get caught.

Grandpa headed toward the front door. Just when Sherman was sure he hadn't seen them, the old man turned and stepped back onto the porch. As if reacting to a sixth sense—or years of experience—he lifted his gaze to the roof.

Gordon and Ruby had hunkered down, trying to make themselves smaller so as not to be seen.

"What do you two think you're doin'?" Joe called.

The two flattened themselves on the roof.

"Little Gordon, you get yourself and your sister down from that barn right this instant."

The children obeyed, of course, shimmying down a pole that leaned against the outer wall. They landed at Grandpa's feet.

Joe stood with his hands in his pockets, his eyebrows furrowed, and his expression stern. At last he took Gordon by the arm and started toward the woodshed. "What have I told ya about climbin' atop that barn?"

Gordon dragged his feet and whined, "You said not ta do it."

"That's right. You know better. And then to take your little sister up there with you. It's dangerous, boy. Both of ya could've been killed. I'm ashamed ya'd put your little sister in such danger."

Gordon didn't say another word as Grandpa marched him into the woodshed and shut the door. Ruby stood in shock and horror for a moment, then ran inside the barn to cower, certain she'd be next.

A short while later, Joe emerged from the shed and strode into the house. Sherman wasn't surprised he didn't look for Ruby. Grandpa tended to be softer on the girls, so he probably held Gordon responsible for initiating the rash act.

When Gordon emerged from the woodshed he had red splotches on his face and one hand held to his backside. He rubbed vigorously, shook his leg a little, then stepped around the back of the shed and slid down to the ground.

Sherman reined in the mule and watched in amazement as Gordon removed a pouch of tobacco and paper from the bib pocket of his overalls and rolled a cigarette. The boy had evidently lost his mind. He'd already set off Grandpa; now he seemed bound and determined to light a fire under Grandma as well. Everyone knew Grandma wouldn't tolerate smoking. Sherman shook his head, jiggled the reins, and resumed his task. Sometimes he wondered if that brother of his had a lick of sense at all. Maybe it was Gordon's brain that deserved the nickname "Little".

By the time Sherman finished the row, Grandma stood at the door, waving him in for dinner. He unhitched the mule from the plow and led the animal toward the water trough. Removing his hat, he wiped his forehead with a handkerchief and stopped at the door to the barn. "Come along, Ruby. Grandma's got dinner ready."

Ruby, who'd been huddled in a corner, put down a kitten and brushed the hay from her dress. "You think Grandpa'll swat me for ridin' the barn?"

Sherman shrugged. "Seems he'd've already done it if he was aimin' to." He reached over and removed a piece of straw from Ruby's blonde hair.

Ruby followed her big brother timidly into the house. Grandpa was already seated at the table reading a newspaper. Before him was a big bowl of mashed potatoes and a round of cornbread on a plate. The house smelled of coffee, burning firewood, and cornbread, but there was also a hint of mothballs and the musty odor that comes from humidity settling into wood. All of it came together to form the unique aroma of his grandparents' home. Sherman made a point of committing the well-loved smell to memory.

Grandma leaned on her cane and set a plate on the table. "Where's Gordon?"

"I'll get him." Sherman went back outside toward the woodshed.

He found Gordon sitting against the barn stuffing pine needles in his mouth, chewing furiously. He reeked of tobacco. Sherman shook his head at the foolishness.

"Come along, Gordon. Grandma's got dinner ready."

Gordon rose and swiped the dirt and hay from the back of his pants. Sherman thought about scolding his brother, but figured he'd get his due shortly.

Inside, Sherman pulled out a chair between Ruby and Gordon. His brother was still chomping on pine needles—and fooling no one. Before he could sit down, Grandma's cane swished through the air and cracked against Gordon's hip.

"Ouch!" Gordon exclaimed and rubbed the spot. "What's that for?"

Storm clouds had gathered in Grandma Josie's dark eyes. Her glare could have pinned him to the floor. "You've been smoking!"

"Nah, Grandma. I—"

"Don't lie to me, boy! You know lies aren't tolerated 'round here."

Grandpa looked up from his paper to offer his unspoken support.

Gordon's countenance fell with his chin. "Yes'm, I won't do it no more."

"You'd better not," she retorted. Then, her voice softened. "Now have a seat so Grandpa can say grace."

Sherman couldn't help but notice the way Gordon eased onto the chair. Not too bright, he thought, setting off both Grandpa and Grandma in the very same hour.

Grandpa Joe blessed the food, and then each child took turns passing their plates to Grandma to fill. She gave Sherman and Grandpa the biggest helpings. Sherman suppressed a sigh. If his mother or Aunt Josephine had cooked the food he'd have been thrilled at the larger portion, but Grandma Josie was not a good cook. In fact, she was terrible.

Sherman sliced open his cornbread and added a slab of butter while his little sister dove into the potatoes. Immediately Ruby's blue eyes widened with dismay and she snatched up her glass of milk and guzzled it down.

Sherman was glad he'd decided to eat his cornbread first. But even with butter, the dry crumbs caught in his throat, so he broke it up into his milk and ate it with a spoon. It tasted pretty good that way, and he'd devoured it in no time.

That was a mistake. It left him nothing to kill the taste of the potatoes. After one nibble he knew why Ruby had reacted as she had.

Goat! The hideous taste was goat. Grandma had seasoned the potatoes with tallow. The nasty-tasting grease clung to the top of his mouth, making him want to retch. He reached for the pitcher of milk, poured another glass, and guzzled it as Ruby had. It did little to remove the thin layer of lard caked on the roof of his mouth.

Sherman eyed his plate in dismay. Why had he gobbled that slab of cornbread? As dry as it was, it was delicious in comparison, especially with milk. He regretted finishing the job outside. He'd rather plow nine more rows than eat another bite of Grandma's potatoes.

Postponing the inevitable as long as he could, Sherman watched his grandparents eat as normal. He couldn't understand how anyone could grow accustomed to the texture or flavor, even after dozens of years. Maybe old age had affected their taste buds.

Gordon's eyes met Sherman's, begging silently, *"Surely you can figure some way out of eating this stuff."*

Sherman racked his brain for something that could distract Grandma's attention from their plates. Then, as if heaven had taken pity on him, a stroke of inspiration hit. "Grandma," he said, "tell us about the panther."

Relieved, Gordon played along. "Yeah, Grandma! Tell us!"

"Oh, you've heard it a dozen times." Grandma Josie waved her fork in the air as if to dismiss them.

"Please, Grandma," Ruby pleaded. "I love that story."

Grandma put her napkin on her lap and cleared her throat. Grandpa Joe lowered his newspaper to listen.

"Well, I'd been up tending poor ol' Betty Lou McAllister. She's passed now, but she was ailin' at the time. Her son fetched me to bring my herbs and see what could be done for his mama. So I packed up my satchel and walked over there with the boy."

Grandma's eyes were alight as she warmed to her story. "When I got there, poor Betty was plumb green, so I mixed her up some ginger tea and other herbs for achin' bellies. Then I sat up with her into the night. It was dark by the time Betty Lou's stomach settled down enough for her to sleep, so I borrowed one of the McAllisters' lanterns and set out for home."

She looked to her husband. "You remember, Joe. The McAllisters lived 'bout three miles up the road—quite a jaunt in the dark. There weren't no moon, but the stars were out." Josie took a sip of milk. "I'd gotten pretty good at listening for a rustle near the path, announcing the presence of a rattlesnake. So this time I heard a rustlin'—about a mile from home—but I knew it weren't no snake, it was too loud for that. Then I heard this cry. It sounded like a woman screamin' with childbirth. I lifted my lantern and there to my left was a panther—as black as coal, its white fangs a-glowin' in the dark."

Sherman was so engaged in Grandma's story that he shoveled a scoop of potatoes into his mouth without thinking. Shocked by what he'd done, he held his breath and forced them down with milk. He hoped Grandma thought his wide eyes were in response to her story.

"What did you do?" Ruby prodded.

Grandma shook her head. "I was terrified. The only thing I could think to do was to try to scare it off with my lantern. I held it up higher and the panther moved in front of me. It wailed again. I jiggled my lantern in its direction and it started stalkin' around me until it paused at my right. Its fangs were white, almost sparkling in the lantern light."

Sherman held his breath and shoveled another scoop of potatoes into his mouth. Somehow Grandma's story was helping the nasty food go down a little easier.

Grandma held up her hand to demonstrate how she'd held the lantern to keep the panther at bay. "It kept pacing, and sometimes it got so close I knew I'd be torn to shreds. But I just kept turning with it until I was facing the way I'd come. I started backin' my way down the path with that panther followin' me. I just kept easin' backwards, making my way home. That's how I went the whole way—with that panther a-circlin' me, and me easin' down the path whenever it wasn't blockin' my way. Finally, when it saw the lights of the house, it ran off into the woods."

Ruby's blue eyes were huge. "Grandma, you're so brave!"

When Sherman looked back down at his plate, he was relieved to see a single bite of potato left. Holding his breath, he shoveled it into his mouth. If Grandma could face a panther, surely he could conquer this last bite of goat tallow potatoes.

Chapter 2: Premonitions and Remembrances

Hinkle, Lookout Mountain, Georgia
Sunday, March 12, 1922

Mary Ann Phillips rolled over in bed and draped an arm across her husband's chest. She loved to watch him sleep. He was a handsome man in her estimation.

"Wake up, hon," she said as she kissed his cheek.

He groaned in response, his eyes fluttering open. Gordon raked a hand through his black hair and rested his head on his palm. "I could use another hour," he muttered, closing his eyes.

Mary Ann knew how hard her husband worked on the railroad and how exhausted he was from it. "You could nap after church," she suggested.

"And where would I get a decent nap at your parents' house?"

Mary Ann chuckled. "Guess you're right about that." Her parents' home swarmed with grandchildren on Sunday afternoons. "Will and his youngins won't be there. That'll diminish the crowd a mite."

"Will's youngins are the well-behaved ones." Gordon rolled on his side, facing his wife. He put a hand on her waist and kissed her lips.

"True," Mary Ann agreed and looked across the room at their three little ones piled in a bed. Christeen and Evie lay curled up next to each other like kittens while Junior slept sideways at the foot of the bed. His small bare feet stuck out of the covers, dangling over the edge. Mary Ann smiled. She loved that little boy as if he were her own. And even though Christeen wasn't his, Gordon doted on her every bit as much as he did on Evie. Mary Ann had been widowed and met Gordon not long after his wife died giving birth to stillborn twins. Much to Joseph and Josie Morton's chagrin, their daughter dived headfirst into a second marriage.

Two years had passed when little Evie came along. Mary Ann's parents finally accepted Gordon and his namesake as part of the family.

Mary Ann yawned. "Guess I better get up and get the youngins ready for church."

She rolled out of bed and pulled a robe around her shoulders. Mornings were chilly on the mountain. She slipped on her shoes and crossed into the cabin's only other room. She stepped around the boxes that served as additional chairs, passed the kitchen table, and paused in front of the stove.

Knowing how much Gordon liked to sleep in on Sundays, Mary Ann didn't get up early to cook. She made extra biscuits on Saturday nights and they ate those with butter and honey on Sunday mornings. She lit the stove and started a pot of coffee.

Gordon put on his shoes and headed for the outhouse while Mary Ann returned to the bedroom and dressed the children. After breakfast, the family walked the mile to Payne's Chapel Methodist Church, where the Mortons had long attended. Mary Ann held Junior and Christeen's hands while Gordon carried little Evie in his arms.

Soon Mary Ann's brother Howard and his family joined them. Howard and Rannie Morton had three children of their own and two nephews. The group entered the chapel and found Grandma Josie and Grandpa Joe seated alone on a long pew. It was common knowledge that the Mortons took up the front two rows. Before Will and his family moved, they had taken three.

The children greeted their grandparents with a kiss and took a seat. After the service they split into groups. The children went to smaller rooms for Sunday school while the adults remained in the sanctuary.

Joseph Morton had taught Sunday school for years. He was not flowery like many preachers, and well-liked for his ability to cut to the heart of a matter.

"'To everything there is a season,'" Joe began his lesson, "'and a time to every purpose under the heaven: a time to be born, and a time to die; a time to plant, and a time to pluck up that which is planted.'" He straightened his black tie against his starched white shirt. "'A time to kill, and a time to heal; a time to break down, and a time to build up; a time to weep, and a time to laugh; a time to mourn, and a time to dance.'"

He set his Bible on the podium and marked the place with a ribbon. "This here's saying we have to learn to take the good with the bad and see the hope in the hopeless."

Joe's eyes traveled from one adult child to the next before lingering on his wife. "None of us knows when it'll be our time to go." He paused. "I can't say the hour that I might not be with you anymore."

His eyes misted and Mary Ann felt a chill ascend her spine. Surely he wasn't predicting anything, she told herself. It was just Papa's way of driving home his message.

Chilled still, she bowed her head and prayed that was the truth of things.

~*~

Mary Ann stood at the counter of her mother's kitchen cutting potatoes. The air smelled delicious. Josephine was making fried chicken while Grandma Josie sat at her kitchen table peeling carrots. The menfolk relaxed on the front porch like a pack of hounds. Mary Ann paused from her task to check on her little ones. She opened the front door a crack to see little Evie asleep on Gordon's belly.

"Any luck trackin' down that still, yet, Papa?" Howard leaned back in his rocking chair and stretched his long arms high above his head.

"Nope, not yet. Still followin' up on some leads."

Mary Ann looked across the lawn where her sister-in-law, Rannie, entertained the younger children. The older cousins were nowhere in sight, which was just as well. They tended to run off to smoke or pick fights with one another, and she didn't want her little ones caught in the middle of their meanness.

She stepped back into the kitchen and returned to peeling potatoes.

"Have you heard anything from Will and Nancy?" Josephine asked her mother.

"We got a letter from 'em yesterday," she replied. "They've settled in. Said the little two-room shanty they're in isn't as nice as the ones Papa builds."

"I bet Nancy sure is missin' the homeplace." Josephine rotated a piece of chicken and then wiped her hand on a towel.

"You gotta know she is," Mary Ann agreed.

"Imagine all them youngin's crammed in a two-room shanty!" Josephine shook her head at the shame of it.

Mary Ann thought about her own cabin. They were crowded enough with their three little ones. She'd hate to be like her brother's family and have grown boys and girls along with little ones stuffed like sardines in a can.

Gordon had big plans for advancement on the railroad. He'd promised Mary Ann a better house soon. She'd hate to be ten years down the road like Will and Nancy and still living in a two-room shanty. But it wasn't her brother's fault the Durham mine was going under. He was a hard worker and a good provider. He had to go where the work was. If that meant making do for a time, he'd do it, and have Nancy's and the children's support in the process.

"Put it up!" Mary Ann heard Grandpa yell. "Put it up this minute!" he repeated in his stern deputy sheriff voice.

"Uh, oh." Josephine's eyes met Mary Ann's with a twinkle.

"Them boys is out to the croquet course." Grandma shook her head.

"Will they ever learn Grandpa can hear the crack of a mallet a mile away?" Josephine sighed.

"You boys know better than playin' croquet on the Sabbath!" Grandpa scolded. Through the back window, Mary Ann and Josephine watched him climb the hill in the back, motioning for the children to get down from the course.

"That big ol' thing is just too much of a temptation," Mary Ann muttered. Her sister nodded her agreement.

Mary Ann thought about the many times she and her siblings had been caught back there on Sundays. It was as if that croquet course was the Tree of Knowledge of Good and Evil planted in the middle of the Garden of Eden. Like the Father of mankind, their father had built the temptation and then commanded them not to touch it on the Sabbath. If the tree had tempted Adam and Eve half as much as the croquet course tempted every Morton youngster, it was no wonder the pair had sampled the fruit. What was a body to do when there was no work to keep him busy?

A child with no chores on Sunday couldn't resist running up that hill. It was unfair to place the biggest and best croquet course in the county right behind the house as a constant Sabbath temptation.

Mary Ann pitied the four nephews who descended the hill with shoulders slumped and heads hanging. She didn't know what was worse – listening to Grandpa preach the importance of Sabbath day observance for the next half hour or knowing they'd lost their chance at a good game of croquet.

~*~

Joe sat on the front porch with only the crickets and bullfrogs to keep him company. The moon was a sliver shy of being full. He looked at it, pondering the majesty of God's creations and feeling blessed to live in such a beautiful world. Joe loved the Sabbath. It gave him time to reflect and relax with his family. He sighed, thinking back on the years he and Josie had spent together.

They'd been married almost forty-three years, would celebrate their anniversary on the twentieth of April. Thinking of that reminded Joe of Josie's birthday coming up the next week, March twentieth. He'd ordered a pretty blue hat from the mine's commissary, because Josie deserved a pretty new hat for Sundays. He withdrew a small pad of paper from his shirt pocket and made a note to pick it up on Thursday. Satisfied, he slipped the pad back into his pocket.

Joe stood and stretched his arms high above his head with a loud, long yawn, then entered the house smiling. Josie slept on the couch, her feet propped up on the coffee table, her cane leaning against the arm of the couch.

He hated that she had to use a cane, despised the memory of the frightening day on which she'd had the stroke. She was expecting their youngest at the time, and it had nearly scared Joe out of his mind. He feared losing them both, but Josie and the baby had lived. She'd been partially paralyzed on one side ever since, but at least she was alive. He couldn't imagine how he would have coped without her.

Joe's eyes misted at the memory of the doctor handing him their youngest son. Granville turned out as healthy as the rest, even more rambunctious and carousing. Putting thoughts of Granville's disturbing ways from his mind, Joe leaned over Josie and lifted her from the couch.

She stirred as he carried her to their bedroom. She slipped her arms around his neck and nestled her head into his shoulder. He laid her on the bed and covered her with a quilt.

"Love you, Joe," Josie mumbled, only semi-conscious.

"I love you too, sweetheart." He brushed a stray strand of hair from her brow, then bent and pressed a kiss to her forehead.

Chapter 3: Little Brown Jug

Lookout Mountain, Georgia
Monday, March 13, 1922

Ralph Baker held a jug up to the still, letting corn liquor drizzle into it. A pungent odor filled the cave, and the torches mounted on the cavern walls flickered and reflected off the brown glass. When the jug was full, Ralph shut off the spigot and handed the gallon jug to his older brother. George, in turn, pounded a cork into place with the heel of his hand, and passed it on to Travis Iverson. Travis removed the cork and guzzled down a swig.

"Hey," George grumbled, "no samples."

"Just makin' sure it's good stuff." Travis glared at the brothers, corked the container, and set it on a nearby workbench. "Besides, this one's mine for my time." He raked a hand through his greasy brown hair, his eyes daring them to argue.

"Your time?" Ralph grumbled. "You're already gettin' a cut for sellin' the stuff."

"You can't expect me to peddle what I ain't tasted, can ya?" Travis snorted. "What if it's bad? That'd ruin my reputation." He removed a pinch of tobacco from a pouch and shoved it between his teeth and gums. A dark stain trailed from the corner of his mouth and down his stubbled chin.

"Tastin's one thing, takin' a whole jug's another." Ralph stepped menacingly toward Travis. Unfazed, Travis spit tobacco juice on Ralph's boot.

"I oughta—" Ralph's hands clenched into fists, but George stepped between the two before he could raise them.

George put a hand to his brother's chest. "Settle down, Ralph. There's plenty here. We can spare a jug."

Ralph glared at Travis for several moments more. At last he snatched up another empty jug from a pile on the floor, shoved it under the still, and released the spigot.

"How many is that?" George asked.

Travis counted the jugs of whisky. "Eleven. I need one more."

When Ralph muttered about Travis already having a dozen George elbowed him in the ribs. "Just keep him happy," he whispered.

The last thing they needed, George thought, was Travis getting sore. He knew the right people and kept his customers from figuring out—or caring—where he got the moonshine. He tried to massage the ache from his head with his fingers. He needed a good stiff drink, but he'd hold off until they finished with Travis.

"You boys remember now," Travis continued, "I'm the one who has folks keeping a jug o' your corn liquor on their kitchen table next to the salt and pepper."

George knew he was right. Knew, too, that the man sold it at a tidy markup. While Ralph couldn't stand the thought of anyone else making a dime off their work, George recognized the value of the arrangement when he was sober. It was when he'd had a swig or two that things got a little fuzzy. He reminded himself of this when his head continued to throb and the cravings grew worse.

Travis couldn't let it go. "You know good 'n' well you wouldn't be runnin' moonshine from this cave for nigh onto six months now if it wasn't for me."

"He's right, Ralph," George inserted when Ralph grimaced. "That's the longest we've ever stayed hid."

Travis laughed. "What those lawmen don't get is that their making moonshine agin the law just lines our pockets with more money."

George slapped Travis on the back, "You're right about that. Moonshine's a staple on the mountain. We're just seein' to it folks have what they need."

"That's right!"

Ralph filled another jug. George corked it and passed it to Travis. Ralph rose and wiggled his fingers, indicating he expected payment on the spot.

Travis tucked the jug under his arm and pulled his wallet from his back pocket. Ignoring Ralph, he counted several bills into George's palm. "That oughta cover it."

"We'll help you carry 'em out," George offered. He reached for three jugs. Travis got two more. George followed their best customer out of the cave, expecting Ralph to be behind them with the rest. After a few feet he turned and looked back. Ralph was guzzling from the jug Travis had left on the bench.

George motioned impatiently for his brother to hurry up. Instead, Ralph spit a wad of tobacco into the jug, swiped his sleeve around the mouth, and corked it. Chuckling, he set it back on the bench and picked up the remaining four jugs from the cave floor.

George wanted to whack his younger brother upside the head. The boy was always up to some kind of nonsense bound to cause trouble. They were making too much money from Travis to risk messing up such a good thing.

George helped Travis load the moonshine into his Buick. When he turned back, Ralph was there, smiling like a weasel. George stepped around him. "I'll get the rest," he muttered.

"Don't forget mine," Travis called.

"Yeah, be sure you don't forget that one," Ralph said.

George shook his head and passed the jug on the bench on his way deeper into the cavern. Retrieving a jug from his personal stash, he returned to the Buick and handed Travis the replacement. The rest of the purchase was already tucked safely away, covered with a quilt.

"Remember, I need forty more on Friday for a big party," Travis said.

"We'll have it ready," George assured him.

"Good, and don't make me wait next time." Travis uncorked his jug and guzzled. With a sigh and a burp, he complimented the quality of the moonshine.

Ralph snorted, but George shot him a warning glance before he could laugh out loud.

"What?" Travis looked from Ralph to George.

"Nothin'." George shook his head. "Ralph's been samplin' too much of the product hisself."

Travis climbed into the car and started the engine. When he was a few yards down the road, George backhanded the side of his brother's head. He had to reach up to do it. Ralph was only fourteen, but already inches taller than George. "Sometimes I swear you've got rocks for brains!"

Ralph slapped his brother's hand away. "He had it comin'. I hate that fella. I'd just as soon put a bullet through his head as look at his ugly mug."

George rolled his eyes. "We need him and you know it."

"I don't know it. We could make more money without him." Ralph marched back into the cave with George trailing.

"If we want to stay hid from the law we need somebody to make the sales," George explained for what seemed like the fiftieth time.

Ralph swore and spit a wad of tobacco against a cavern wall. "None of our customers is gonna go runnin' to the law. They know if they did they'd be out of the good stuff."

"All it takes is one slip. One loose lip and we're cooked. Besides, that big Buick of his can outrun everything the law has."

"You worry like an old lady." Ralph's patronizing laugh made George want to slap the smirk off his brother's face.

Ralph thrust a jug into his older brother's hand. "You need a drink, George. You're spineless when you're sober."

George stared at the liquor. He'd been trying not to drink so much. It didn't make good sense to drink up their only source of income. Besides, he didn't like himself when he was drunk.

"Come on! You know you've gotta go home and face Lulu's naggin'. You can't do that without a good stiff drink. She runs all over you when you're sober."

The thought of going home to Lulu made George press the jug to his lips. He loved that girl, but every time she reminded him of the leaky roof and mounting debts, he felt as if he were drowning. She wanted a nicer home, a respectable living. She didn't seem to understand that he'd lost his job now that the Durham mine was going under. Running moonshine was his best chance to provide for her and the family they hoped to have. Probably his only chance. Just that morning a revenuer had come calling, saying if he didn't pay his property taxes he and Lulu would lose the house. He hoped the big sale to Travis on Friday would be enough to cover it all.

George took another drink and burped. Ralph reached for another swig.

"You best not drink too much or Ma and Pa'll smell it on ya," George warned.

"Ma stays so busy with the little 'uns she don't pay me no mind. And Pa's so busy tryin' to earn a livin' he's hardly home." Still, Ralph took another sip and handed the jug back to his brother.

"Too bad Pa's such a stickler," George said. "There's easier ways to earn a living. We could cut him in on the business."

Ralph chuckled. "Yeah, right...Pa runnin' moonshine. That'll never happen. He'd rather work six jobs."

George knew it would break their parents' hearts to know he and Ralph were running moonshine. It was just as well they were too busy to notice that—and all the foolishness Ralph was up to.

George took another drink. It hit the spot. After a few more swallows, he was sorry he hadn't let Travis take that jug of tobacco spittle after all. It would've been a hoot.

Chapter 4: A Chance Encounter

Mowbray Mountain, Daisy, Tennessee
Tuesday, March 14, 1922

Sherman swiped perspiration from his blackened brow and stepped onto the dumbwaiter with five other men. The pulley squeaked as a conveyer pulled the workers from the mine. Sherman squinted when the first rays of sun hit his eyes. As they approached the surface, he drank in fresh air as if it were his first taste of water after a long summer drought.

He opened his eyes when the conveyance jolted to a halt. It rattled and swayed a little before its iron doors drew open. Sherman waited for the men in front to exit and at last stepped with coal-covered boots out into the dusty streets of the mining community.

Walking home with tools in hand, Sherman scanned the horizon, enjoying the unseasonably warm afternoon. When he looked down at his black hands and arms, he decided what he would do with the rest of the day. He increased his pace toward the shanties.

After greeting his mother and putting away his tools, Sherman went straight to the little chest in which he kept his belongings. He retrieved a change of clothes, a bar of soap, and a bleached feed sack that would serve as his towel.

"I'm off to clean up and get some fresh air, Mama," Sherman said. "I'll be back before dark."

Nancy paused in her dough kneading, gave her son a wistful smile, and told him to enjoy himself. Sherman knew she meant it. She thought he worked too hard and had grown up too fast. She often wished aloud that he could relax more and enjoy life. Today, he would.

There was a spring in Sherman's step as he approached the Blue Hole. Three boys swam in the deep cerulean reservoir nestled halfway down the mountainside. Sherman set his clean clothes and soap on a rock by the edge of the water. He removed his filthy clothes and left them in a heap as he dived headfirst into the water. As warm as the day had felt, the frigid water was a shock. Rising to the surface, he exclaimed, "Whoohoo!" The other boys laughed.

"Cold, ain't it?" a chubby redhead called from across the swimming hole.

"Sure is, but it feels good!" Sherman swam to the rock for his soap.

The water loosened his tired muscles as he bathed and swam. Dressed in a fresh pair of clothes, he felt like a new man.

"Where can I get a drink of spring water?" Sherman asked the redhead.

"There's a spring just down the mountain," he was told. "You can't miss it. There's always someone from Daisy there gettin' water."

Sherman thanked the boy and set off down the mountain. He relished fresh air as never before. Mining might be good money, but he vowed not to spend his life in a hole in the ground. In the mine he felt like a bird trapped in a cave, unable to fly, scarcely able to breathe. He spread his arms wide and enjoyed the gentle breeze on his face.

He soon spotted a young woman carrying two buckets. Her long shapely legs and slender waist caught his attention. He followed her to the spring, where a brook had long gurgled off the mountain, polishing stones until they were almost as smooth as glass. The water was as clear and fresh as the sparkle in the young woman's eyes when she turned.

"Oh!" Her lips drew into a perfect circle. "You startled me."

"Sorry about that, Miss. I was lookin' for a place to get a cool drink. I saw your buckets, and figured you'd lead me to water."

The young woman bent to the stream, letting the water flow into one bucket. When it was full Sherman took the bucket from her and set it on the ground while she reached for the empty one.

She smiled up at him, thanking him for his help. This was the prettiest woman Sherman had ever seen. Her wavy golden hair had a hint of strawberry coloring that made him want to take it between his fingers and see if it smelled as sweet as it looked.

"You don't have anything to get water in," she noted.

"No, I'll use my hands." he shifted his roll of work clothes under his left arm and knelt by the spring.

"Here, have some of this." She sat down on a rock, pulled a dipperful of water from one of her buckets and held it up for him.

Sherman put down his bundle and cupped his hands around the ladle while she held the handle. She offered another scoop and he accepted it.

"Thank you, Miss—or is it Mrs.?" Sherman still knelt in front of the young woman.

"Miss. Miss Edna Springfield," she answered and drew a sip for herself. "And you are?"

He extended his hand, "Sherman Morton." She dropped the dipper and shook his hand with a smile that sparkled in her eyes. "Nice to meet you, Mr. Morton. You work at the mines, then?" Edna straightened her skirt over her knees and laced her fingers together.

"How'd you know?" Sherman's eyebrows lowered a little.

"Your clothes." She pointed to his belongings. "Coal dust."

"Oh." He chuckled. "Right." Sherman felt himself perspire not from the temperature of the air, but from an odd nervousness that had suddenly swept over him. He worked to find something to say to this pretty woman, but his mind had gone as blank as a slate dunked in dishwater.

Several moments passed before Sherman realized he'd been staring. His nervous gaze shifted to the grass by his boots. He picked a blade and twirled it in his fingers.

Edna put her hands on the bucket handles and prepared to rise. Sherman reached out to take them from her. In his haste, his hands covered hers. Rather than drawing back at having touched her, he let his hands remain on hers. His blue eyes met Edna's for several moments before he spoke. "Here, let me carry those for you."

"Are you sure?" she asked.

"I've got it."

She looked down at his roll of clothes. "What about your things?"

When she reached for them, Sherman said, "No, they're dirty, just leave 'em, and I'll come back for 'em on my way back up the mountain." He stepped onto the path. "Do you live nearby?"

"At the foot of the mountain." Edna rose and pointed toward a trail.

As they walked side-by-side, Sherman tried to think of something intelligent to say. This wasn't a silly school girl who tagged along with him on Lookout Mountain. This was a grown woman. He figured her to be in her early twenties, and here he was six months shy of eighteen.

He sighed in relief when she broke the silence. "One of my girlfriends had a beau who worked in the mine. He'd come to visit covered in coal dust, nothing but his eyes and teeth a sparkling white. I told her, 'Blanche, you need to hold out for a man who can take a few steps closer to the washrag.'"

Sherman laughed. "Did she take your advice?"

"Didn't have to. He found another girl closer to home."

"Oh."

"Do you like working at the mines?" Edna stepped over a root that spanned the path.

Sherman shrugged. "It pays well."

Her eyes met his. "But you don't really enjoy it, do you?" She said it as if she'd read something in his face or the tone of his voice.

This surprised him. "Not really," he admitted.

"I don't suppose there are many men who do."

"I reckon you're right about that."

"Must be awfully dark and dreary working down in that hole all day with the coal dust smothering you."

Edna sized it up about right. Sherman nodded in reply.

"What kind of work do you enjoy?" Edna stepped around a boulder and Sherman followed her.

"Oh, just about anything—plowing, lumberjacking, working at my grandpa's sawmill, or building houses with him."

"How come you're working in the mine instead of with your grandpa, then?"

"He lives on Lookout Mountain. We moved so me and Papa could work here. The Durham mine is runnin' out of coal. Papa's the one who pumps the air down into the mine and I do the diggin'." Sherman returned to her side when the path straightened out again.

"I see."

Sherman pushed a tree branch out of their way and held it back until she could pass. "What does your father do?"

"He's a farmer. Always has one of the biggest watermelon patches around."

"I wouldn't mind a slab o' watermelon about now," Sherman mused.

"Wouldn't it be delicious?" She closed her eyes. "I can almost taste it—sweet, cold, and so juicy it runs down your chin." She smiled. "Just what we need on a day like this."

The way she described it made Sherman want a slab of that watermelon all the more, one they would share under a shady tree.

As they came out of the forest, Edna pointed toward the main road. "We live over yonder." She held out her hands. "Here, I can take the water from here. I feel bad you had to carry it all this way and then turn back around to climb the mountain again."

"I don't mind." Sherman shrugged. "I've come this far, may as well finish the task."

The Springfield place was a large two-story home with a porch across the front. The acreage surrounding it had been plowed in neat rows. A large barn and an outbuilding sat beside the house. By the size of the home and the well-kept acreage, it was obvious to Sherman that Edna's father took pride in his property. That's one thing he couldn't say for his own father. Even when they weren't living in a sardine can of a shanty, his father wasn't one to make repairs. He'd let leaks remain in the roof, catching rainwater in pots around the house.

Two young girls playing in the yard ran to greet them, then trailed alongside as they continued toward the house.

"Who's your beau?" the little one asked.

Edna gave the girl a stern look. "This is Mr. Morton. He was kind enough to help me carry the water home. Mr. Morton, these are my little sisters." Edna pointed to the smallest. "This is Thadda."

"I'm six!" Thadda pointed a proud thumb to her chest. She twirled around and her flower print dress flew out with the motion.

"Nice to meet you, Thadda." Sherman nodded at the little blonde. "That's a unique name. I like it."

"I'm named after my daddy. His name is Thaddeus, but everybody calls him Thad."

"And this is Dot." Edna pointed to the older girl.

"I'm ten," Dot said. "Can you believe how hot it is today? I declare, it's hotter than a fritter poppin' in a fryin' pan."

Sherman chuckled. "It is that."

"Here, Dot." Edna took a bucket from Sherman and handed it to her sister. "Why don't you carry this into the house? Mama probably needs it."

"I can get the other one!" Thadda reached for the second bucket and Sherman helped her take it.

"Are you sure you can manage that?" he asked the little girl.

"Oh, yes! I'm six, remember? I'm strong!"

"I'm sure you are." Sherman winked.

Thadda waddled away with the bucket, following her older sister into the house.

Just as she reached the front door, Dot hollered back over her shoulder. "Did you tell him how smart you are, Edna? Tell him about grad-jee-atin' high school."

Sherman watched the rosy glow rise on Edna's cheeks. She shook her head. "Never mind them."

"They're cute." He smiled. Edna's embarrassment gave him courage. Maybe she found him attractive despite his youth. "So, you went all the way to the twelfth grade?"

She nodded, putting her hands in the pockets of her skirt.

"You must be really smart."

"She grad-jee-ated valley dict-or-i-an!" Dot hollered from the front door.

"Oh?" Sherman's eyes widened. This woman was out of his league.

Edna's face turned a deeper shade of crimson, "There were only five people in my class." Edna said, trying to minimize her accomplishment.

"Still, you graduated." Sherman suspected his admiration showed. "That's somethin' to be proud of."

"Well, I can't build houses, work in a coalmine, or cut lumber." The crimson started to fade from her high cheekbones. "Everybody is good at different things."

"I suppose." Sherman wondered if she was trying to make him feel better. Then again, she didn't know he had a fourth grade education and didn't know anyone else who'd gone past the eighth grade.

Edna looked toward the horizon, "I'd invite you in for supper, Mr. Morton, but the sun's close to setting and you better get up that mountain before dark. There are too many foxes and coyotes to travel safely up Mowbray at night."

Sherman nodded. "Guess you're right about that. Next time I'll bring my rifle. Then it won't matter if it's dark." Sherman paused for a moment and then decided to be bold. "Would you like for there to be a next time, Miss Springfield?"

"I'd like that very much, Mr. Morton." Her smile made her eyes twinkle as she extended her hand.

Instead of shaking it, he pressed it to his lips.

"Then I'll be seeing you again." With a nod, he turned and started back up the mountain, an even livelier spring in his step than when he'd descended.

~*~

From the porch Edna watched Sherman saunter down the road. She hoped he would return.

"He's a handsome one!" A delighted grin spread across Dot's cheeks as Edna entered the kitchen.

Edna could only nod and blush. She hadn't had much attention from men. At six feet tall, all legs and no body, there'd been *nobody* who'd have her. Her older sister Thelma and younger sister Lucille found their mates years earlier. Edna felt like an old maid with no prospects.

"Who's a handsome one?" Maude Springfield asked her daughters, her voice slightly garbled from the snuff she kept under her lip. She crossed to the corner of the kitchen and spit a stream of brown juice into a spittoon.

"Just a fella who walked me home from the spring."

"Sherman's his name." Dot picked up a potato to peel. "Sherman Morton."

"Is he from around here? I don't recognize the name." Maude too grabbed a potato.

"No." Edna shook her head. "He's from Georgia—Lookout Mountain originally. He and his family moved here so he and his father could work at the mine."

"Sherman..." Maude scratched her head beneath her gray bun. "His family must've been Union supporters." Maude's eyebrows lifted. "Not too many of us 'round these parts, especially not in Georgia."

Edna thought about her grandfathers, Pearson and Springfield, both of whom had fought for the Union. While Tennesseans picked their sides, supporting the Union in Georgia was unpopular.

"He sure is handsome," Dot cooed. "Don't you just love that dimple in his chin?"

"I like his pretty blue eyes," Thadda interjected as she dug in a drawer for silverware.

"You two are too young to be noticing things like that," Edna scolded, but she couldn't say she hadn't noticed those characteristics herself.

"I'm ten years old, for pity's sake!" Dot retorted. "I could be married five years from now. Lucille was."

"Don't remind me," Edna muttered under her breath. Here she was, twenty-three years old, her ship long since sailed, and Dot was reminding her she should've been married nearly a decade earlier.

"You will not," Maude interjected. "Neither of y'all are gettin' married until you're eighteen."

Dot shrugged off her mother's comment. "Hey, Edna, wouldn't it be a wonderful present if you ended up marrying Mr. Morton?" Dot's eyes widened. "After all, it is your birthday today and all! Imagine meeting your future husband on your birthday!"

Edna shook her head and sliced carrots into the stew pot. "I'll probably never see him again."

"I saw him kiss your hand," Thadda informed the family as she carried silverware to the dining room.

"He did?" Dot's eyes widened. "Oh, my! What a birthday present, indeed!"

"Are you gonna let him kiss ya on the mouth next time?" Thadda called from the dining room.

Edna felt the heat in her cheeks increase. "He's too young for me."

"How old is he?" Maude asked.

"I don't know, but I don't think he could be as old as twenty."

"That don't matter." Maude joined Edna at the stove and raked a plate of diced potatoes into the pot. "What's a few years? Besides, your Daddy's four years older than me."

"That's different. It's customary for the man to be older." Edna reached for another carrot.

"Let custom be hanged! Any man who's handsome, has a job, and is interested is a match in my book." Maude winked at her daughter. "Who cares if he's a little young? In ten years it won't make no difference no way."

Edna giggled at her mother's reasoning.

"Besides, beggars can't be choosers," Thadda observed as she traipsed back through the kitchen for more dishes.

"Thadda!" Maude scolded.

Edna closed her eyes and thought, *Thanks, Thadda, that makes me feel better*. Even though it was a six-year-old who had said it, it still stung because it was true. A six-foot, twenty-three-year-old spinster had to take what she could get. If handsome Sherman Morton ever came again, she'd be ready.

A few minutes later her father, Thad, returned from the fields and came to the sink to wash up. Edna felt a flutter of excitement rise in her. She'd been waiting for the right moment to talk with him about something that had happened to her earlier that morning.

"Daddy," she began.

"Yes," he prompted as he rolled up his sleeves a little higher.

"Mr. McDonald over at the Commissary offered me a job this morning. He wants me to help out as a clerk a few afternoons each week. Isn't that exciting?"

A broad grin swept across Maude's face and Edna could see the snuff blackened around her mother's gums. Edna wished her mother would give up the disgusting habit. It was embarrassing. Edna looked at her father for his approval, but instead found a scowl.

"Daddy," she prodded. "Isn't that exciting? I'll have my own job and can earn my own money for dresses. That way Mama won't have to make them for me. You know how I've never been too good at sewing."

Thad Springfield shook his head, "I don't like it. No daughter of mine is gonna work a job. Ain't right."

"But, Daddy, I've got to start thinking about the future. You and Mama won't always be able to take care of me," Edna reasoned.

"As long as I'm alive, no wife or daughter of mine is gonna get a job. Providin' is man's work, not a woman's." Thad finished rinsing his hands and dried them on a towel.

Edna could feel the tears forming in her eyes. She stepped toward him and lowered her voice, "Please, Daddy, don't you understand.

It's not like my prospects for marriage are bright. I can't cook; I hate housekeeping; I can't sew worth a flip."

"You're bein' too hard on yourself, Edna. You cook right well and you're always goin' to those quilting bees with your Mama. You must be able to sew or they wouldn't invite you."

"The women at the quilting bees only let me come because they enjoy hearing my stories," Edna retorted. She noticed her mother give a wan smile. Her mother knew it was true. Edna's stitches were wide and she had no sense of color coordination. But the ladies loved Edna's storytelling so much they welcomed her for entertainment.

"Any man would be happy to have you, Edna," her father continued, letting one thumb hang on his suspender strap. "You're a right pretty girl with a bright mind. You hold out for a good man to provide for you."

"What good is my high school diploma if I'm not allowed to use the mind God gave me?" Edna retorted.

"If you go gettin' a job, men folk will think you don't need 'em. A man wants a wife he can take care of," Thad reasoned.

Edna brushed the moisture from her eyes. She could hardly believe what she was hearing. She'd gotten her education, and she wanted to use it. She'd been looking for a job for a couple years now, and nothing had been available. Finally Mr. McDonald noticed the way people took to her and offered her this wonderful job. She'd been so excited about being able to talk with people who came into the store and help them with their purchases. It wasn't fair that her father was clipping her wings at her very moment of triumph!

Edna shook her head, holding back the anger that threatened to make her say something she'd regret. She stomped out the front door and started walking. Her mind raced, looking for some option. She could move out, make her own way. Then, he couldn't tell her what to do. But that wouldn't work. The job was only part-time and didn't pay enough to live on. Besides, her family meant too much to her. She didn't want to alienate them. Marriage seemed to be the only door through which her father would allow her to exit, and her prospects had never been good in that department.

Edna thought of Sherman Morton. He looked young, and who could say whether he'd return.

Chapter 5: Pride Goeth Before a Fall

Lookout Mountain, Walker County, Georgia
Wednesday, March 15, 1922

"Oh, George, I'm so glad you're home!" Lulu breathed a sigh of relief and welcomed her husband at the door with a kiss on his cheek.

George looked into his wife's eyes. "You all right, darlin'?"

"That revenuer was by here again today." Lulu clutched her husband's arm. "He said we have to round up that money or they're gonna sell the house."

George gritted his teeth and tossed his hat on the kitchen table. "Can't they cut a fella some slack when they know good 'n' well we're all strugglin' up here on the mountain what with the mine goin' under?"

"I told 'im we're doin' our best, that you're workin' hard to come up with the money."

"Good girl." George kissed his wife and sat down at the table, eyeing the cherry pie.

Lulu went to the cupboard, retrieved a small plate and set it in front of him.

"You are gonna come up with the money. Right, George?"

"Of course I am. I'll have it by the end of the week." George cut a slice of pie and put it on the plate.

"You're not talkin' about runnin' moonshine are ya?"

George licked the pie from his fingers "A man's gotta do what a man's gotta do."

"Oh, George! It's too dangerous! Please tell me you're not involved with Travis and those other goons." Lulu sat down across from her husband.

"It's just for a while—just 'til we can get this bill paid and get back on our feet." George took a bite of pie.

"Then what?"

George shook his head. "I don't know. I'll figure somethin' out…somethin' will turn up. It has to."

"But how can you be sure? If you're off runnin' moonshine you're not looking for a decent job."

George shook his spoon at her. "Look, I'm doin' the best I can. Get off my back about it."

"But…" Lulu began.

George's eyes narrowed with his scowl. "Enough. I don't wanna talk about it no more. I'm doin' what I can and I don't need you naggin' me to do things your way. Your way doesn't work. I've tried lookin' for a job, Lulu, and there ain't none to be had."

Lulu swallowed hard and stood. "Suit yourself, George. I've got laundry to do." She stomped outside and slammed the door behind her.

George shook his head, pulled a flask of whiskey from his jacket, and took another swig.

~*~

Ralph Baker motioned for the coalminer to follow him through the forest, then looked back over his shoulder at the man. "You promise now, promise, promise you won't tell nobody."

The man raised a blackened hand. "I promise."

"Cause if you go waggin' your tongue, you won't be gettin' no more, and you know we've got the best around these parts." Ralph added, "You heard what happened to those two boys who pert near died on the Johnson's whiskey. That'd never happen with ours."

"I know, I know. I ain't tellin' nobody."

"Then come along. It's not far from here." Ralph peered through the trees, making sure no one followed. He was pleased with himself.

George would be pleased, too, when he realized how many customers Ralph had rounded up, customers for whom they wouldn't have to pay Travis a cut

"You wait here while I go get it." Ralph pointed to a log outside the cave. He ventured inside, gathered up three jugs, and brought them out to the coalminer. The man handed him a wad of cash and thanked him. Ralph watched him leave. When he was out of sight, Ralph went back in the cave for a couple jugs for himself. He removed the cork from one and guzzled it down. Sighing with pleasure, he recorked it and set out for home.

On his way, he stopped by George's house. George's wife was hanging clothes out on the line. Ralph tipped his hat at her frown. "George inside?"

"Yeah." LlLu's frown deepened.

Ralph found his brother lying on the couch, his arm curled around a jug of moonshine. Ralph set his two jugs on the kitchen table, walked toward his brother, and slapped a wad of cash on the coffee table.

George sat up a little. "What's this?"

"This is your share of my sales." Ralph stood up proud and straight, thumping a thumb to his chest.

"Your sales?"

"Yep, my sales!"

"I thought I told you not to go messin' around sellin' this stuff yourself." George's eyes narrowed.

Ralph picked up the money and waved it in George's face. "Look at this! We can make twice as much without Travis. We don't need him."

George staggered to his feet. "Did you take anybody to the cave?"

Ralph shrugged. "So what if I did?"

George walked into the coffee table, knocking his shin against it. He cursed and shoved the table aside with his boot, sending it scraping across the wood floor. He grabbed Ralph by the collar.

"I told you not to bring nobody to the cave! Are you outta your cotton-pickin' mind?"

Ralph pushed his brother's hands down. "I told ya, I'm hand-pickin' my customers. These fellas ain't gonna tell nobody nothin'."

"You're an idiot!" George raked both hands through his dark hair.

Ralph had had enough of George's condescending ways. His big brother thought he was so all-fired smart, but Ralph had made more money today than they had in a week with Travis. Ralph grabbed George by his shirt and pulled him up until George stood on his tiptoes. "Take it back!" he growled.

"I won't." George's jaw clenched like granite. "You're a danged blame idiot!"

Ralph pushed George back so hard he staggered and fell onto the couch. Ralph turned to leave, but George charged. He grabbed Ralph from behind and choked his neck.

Ralph struggled and gasped for air. He turned his body to the left and then to the right, finally shaking George off. George staggered toward the kitchen and Ralph came at him, punching him in the face and sending him sailing into the kitchen table. The jugs of liquor and the pie flew onto the floor, busting the glass. The pair continued to fight, slipping and scrambling around in the sloppy mess.

Ralph vaguely registered a woman yelling, but it wasn't until the shot was fired that the brothers stopped fighting. George's wife stood in the doorway with a still-smoking shotgun pointed at the ceiling. Her curly brown hair twirled in all directions.

"Get on home, Ralph," Lulu ordered. "Both of you get out o' here."

Ralph picked himself up off the floor and ate a blob of cherry pie from his shirt.

He could tell by the look in Lulu's eyes she meant business. It wouldn't surprise him if she leveled the gun and fired again.

"All right, all right, Lulu." George wobbled on his knees, but put up a staying hand. "We're just havin' a friendly tussle. Right, Ralph?"

"Yeah, yeah, just a little friendly tussle." Ralph reached out to help his brother to his feet.

Lulu lowered her weapon and stepped into the house. She wrinkled her nose at the powerful stench. "Just look at this mess! I just made that pie, George Baker!" she screeched. "Get out of my kitchen!" She pointed toward the door. "Get out o' here right this minute!"

Ralph put an arm around his brother to keep from sliding on the floor. Together, they eased their way out of the house.

"Don't you dare come back, George Baker! Not until you've sobered up!" Lulu stamped her foot and flung a towel to the floor.

Chapter 6: Tracking Down Trouble

Durham Coalmine, Lookout Mountain, Georgia
Friday, March 17, 1922

Deputy Sheriff Joe Morton sat behind his desk at the Durham mines, doing paperwork. It was so quiet that he heard the ticking of the clock on the wall and the scratches of his pen on paper. Just as he was thinking how nice it was, a scuffle began outside. He looked up when Dave Williams, the mine manager, pushed open the door with one hand, the other hand around Bud Jenkins' arm.

Bud stumbled over his own feet and Mr. Williams pulled him upright. Bud's languid, bloodshot eyes telegraphed his intoxicated state.

"Ya don't have ta help me walk. I kin do it myself." Bud jerked his arm free of Mr. Williams' grasp and staggered toward Joe. He slapped his palms on the desk, bent over, and breathed. "I think I need a wee bit of a drink."

Joe leaned back and turned his head away from Bud's atrocious breath. "I think you'll be needin' a good nap, and I know just the place you can sleep it off."

Mr. Williams pulled over a chair and slipped it behind Bud just before he would have tumbled to the floor. Joe stood and moved Josie's hatbox from the desk to the top of his filing cabinet. He came around and sat on the edge of his desk, facing Bud. "How 'bout you tell us where you got your moonshine?"

"Why? You be needin' a bit of a nip?" Bud snickered and his head bobbed about like a rag doll, his unkempt hair falling in his eyes.

"Yeah, we've been lookin' for a good source, haven't we, Mr. Williams?" Joe winked at the coalmine manager.

"Yeah, Bud, where could we get some o' that 'shine?" Mr. Williams laid a friendly hand on Bud's shoulder.

Bud leaned in and put his forefinger to his lips in a shushing motion. "Well, the best…I mean, the very best 'round these parts comes from—"

At that moment one of the mine supervisors pushed open the door. He panted, "Sheriff, Mr. Williams, I'm so glad you're both here. There's a brawl brewin'. Come directly."

Bud's eyes widened as he momentarily came to his senses. "Sheriff? Why you're Sheriff Morton. You don't drink shine! You're tryin' to trick me."

Joe rolled his eyes and sighed. He gestured for Mr. Williams to go along and break up the fight. "I'll lock him up and be right with ya."

"Who ya gonna lock up, Sheriff?" Bud slurred as he wobbled in his seat.

Joe grabbed Bud's arm and helped him to his feet, "Oh, I'm just gonna give you a nice place for a nap. Don't ya think you need a nap, Bud?"

"A nap does sound mighty fine." The man's eyelids drooped as he stumbled along beside Joe.

The deputy led Bud into a cell, helped him lie down, and covered him with a blanket. Before Joe could lock the cell behind him, Bud was snoring.

By the time Joe reached the commotion outside the mine entrance, the crowd of coal-covered faces was dispersing. Two of the men held dingy handkerchiefs to their bloody noses, but the fighting had stopped.

"Looks like you took care of it." Joe slapped Mr. Williams on the shoulder.

"Some o' these fellas are more work than they're worth."

"Ain't that the truth," Joe agreed as he watched the men walk back to their various posts.

Mr. Williams turned to Joe. "Oh, I was thinkin' since you didn't get anything out of Bud, maybe you ought to talk to his wife. I hear Mable's not too fond of her husband's drinkin'. Maybe she'd shed some light on where he's gettin' the stuff."

"Good idea." Joe knew where Bud and Mable Jenkins lived. He'd repaired a leaky roof on their shanty a couple weeks earlier.

Joe shook Mr. Williams' hand and headed toward the Jenkins' place. The shanties were two-room cabins built side-by-side, not more than fifteen feet apart. One looked pretty much like the other, so Joe counted off as he went. He stopped counting when he saw Mable Jenkins in her doorway, sweeping.

He removed his derby as he approached. "Mornin', Mrs. Jenkins."

"Mornin', Sheriff." She nodded and leaned her broom just inside the house.

"I was wonderin' if I might speak with you for a moment."

"What can I do for ya?" She folded her arms across her chest.

"Ma'am it's about your husband, Bud."

She sighed. "What's he gotten himself into this time?"

"Well, as you know, Ma'am, Walker's a dry county."

She released a sarcastic snort. "If it's such a dry county, how come my Bud's sloshed half the time?"

Joe's eyebrows rose with her forthrightness. "Well, Ma'am, that's what brings me here. Seems Bud's found himself some more corn liquor and is sleepin' it off at the jail."

Mrs. Jenkins' blonde curls tossed as she shook her head in disgust. She was an attractive petite woman in her mid-thirties. Joe marveled that she'd stick with the likes of Bud. His bulldog mug and his affinity for corn liquor didn't seem deserving of a pretty wife.

Joe continued, "I'd really like to find out where he's gettin' it. I tried asking Bud, but he wouldn't tell me."

She chuckled. "Why, of course he wouldn't."

"I don't suppose he's ever told you?" He ran his fingers along the brim of his derby.

"No, he hasn't and, believe me, I've asked." She put a hand on her hip.

"Do you have any idea at all?"

The woman looked to her left and right, noting the people milling around outside their shanties, and motioned him inside. She gestured for Joe to take a seat at a little wooden table then sat down across from him.

Mable put her arms on the table and leaned forward. "If I tell ya where it is, will ya promise not to tell Bud I told ya?"

Joe's pulse accelerated He'd been looking for this still for months. What a stroke of luck! "I promise not to tell Bud a thing."

"And you'll get rid of it and them fellas that're runnin' it, won't cha?"

"Yes, Ma'am," Joe agreed enthusiastically.

"'Cause you know if you bust this one up, they'll just build another and then my poor ol' Bud'll sniff that one out too."

"I'll do my very best to make sure they never build another one, Ma'am." Joe leaned toward her, eager for the location.

She whispered, "Now, I don't know who runs it, couldn't make out the other fella, but last night when Bud slipped off after supper, I followed him." She paused and leaned over the table even farther. Joe waited for her to continue. "It's a couple miles from here, up in the woods."

"Can you remember how to get there?"

"I kin show ya."

"I think it'd be safer if you just drew me a map. Some of these bootleggers are nasty fellas. I wouldn't want anythin' to happen to you."

Mable considered. "I suppose you're right. Plus, like I said, it won't do for Bud to find out I told ya."

Joe pulled a small notepad and pencil from his jacket pocket and placed them on the table in front of Mable. She began drawing a map and explaining to Joe each landmark. She concluded, "I think this'll get ya there, but if you have any trouble, you come back and get me. I'll risk the trip up the hill if it'll keep Bud from findin' that stuff."

Joe took the paper and pencil from her and looked over the map. "I think I can find it. I have an idea where this is." He put the items in his pocket, rose, and extended his hand.

Mable shook it but did not rise from her chair. "You stop 'em now, Sheriff. Folks like that prey on weak men like my Bud."

"I'll take care of it, Mrs. Jenkins. Thank you for your help; and my lips are sealed."

Joe shook his head as he walked away from the Jenkins' place. He'd have to remember to interrogate disgruntled wives more often. Mable Jenkins had managed to find what he'd been hunting for weeks. He chuckled to himself as he went back to his office for an ax. He'd finally hit on a lucky break. Problem was—even if he got these bootleggers, more would crop up to take their place. They always did. His job was never done.

Joe made his way through the forest, along the creek Mable had specified on her map, looking for the next marker. He'd already passed the limestone boulder. It shouldn't be far. As he drew closer, he stepped softly, avoiding twigs and branches, but then he heard the sound of rustling leaves and caught the strong scent of fermentation.

Joe's heart raced and he jerked to his right. He reached for his pistol and stood still, holding his breath.

A few seconds later a brown rabbit hopped through the leaves, its white tail bobbing away from Joe.

A wave of relief settled over him. His hand eased away from his weapon and he continued toward the source of the odor. Sure enough, just where Mable had indicated, there was a cave. Limbs and branches had been placed over the opening. He moved them out of the way and lit his carbide lamp. He pulled his pistol from its holster and eased into the cave.

Joe smiled in satisfaction. He'd located the still. He wrinkled his nose and crept forward, listening for any sound to indicate a human presence.

Finally, in the back recesses of the cave, he found one of the biggest stills he'd ever seen. Its copper coils swirled 'round and 'round. Off to the side were at least forty jugs of moonshine. He saw no sign that might tell him who owned the operation.

He was irritated that no one was here to arrest and yet relieved that he hadn't been confronted by moonshiners. They could be a brutal lot. Some would gun down a man with no more conscience than a farmer eliminating a muskrat.

An uneasy feeling ran along Joe's spine. He looked around again to assure himself he was alone, then set the lamp on a wooden workbench. Holstering his pistol, he retrieved the ax strapped at his side. He reared back and let the ax head fall on the ceramic jugs. Over and over, he raised the ax over the illegal merchandise. He busted every one, spilling liquor onto the cave floor. There was so much of the smelly stuff that it muddied the dirt underfoot. He had to tread carefully so as not to slide in it.

Joe hated the stench of corn liquor. He coughed and pulled his handkerchief from his pocket and held it to his face for a moment, giving himself a slight reprieve from the worst part of his job. Joe leaned on the ax, resting from the exertion. Then, lifting the ax again, he turned to the still, smashing it up until it was not only useless but also unrecognizable. By the time he'd finished he could scarcely breathe, not so much from the work as from the stench.

Satisfied he'd put the bootleggers out of business for a while, he holstered his ax, retrieved his pistol and lamp, and started back out of the cave carrying a large copper coil for evidence. It was a shame he hadn't caught the culprits. At least he'd eliminated the still, and this was one less location in which they could hide.

~*~

The sun's afternoon rays broke through the trees and glistened on the damp grass and underbrush. If one didn't know where he was going, it would be easy to get lost. Ralph and George's boots crunched through the forest on their way to the still.

"Sure am glad we got Travis' order ready yesterday mornin'." George staggered on the path and tipped a jug to his lips.

"Yeah, last thing we need is him gripin' and takin' more payment for waiting," Ralph agreed.

George passed the jug to Ralph who took a swig and corked it.

When they reached the mouth of the cave, George stopped, "Somethin's not right here."

"What?" Ralph looked around.

"Did you cover this back up when you left? I told you to always hide the opening with brush."

"I did! I always do."

"Sure don't look like it," George grumbled as he stomped into the cave. When he reached the still, he let out a loud gasp, then turned and slugged Ralph square in the stomach.

Ralph doubled over, gasping for air and let the jug of moonshine topple to the ground. His mind whirled, trying to figure out what had happened.

"You idiot!" George stomped toward the mangled remains of their still, kicked the coils, and crunched the shards of shattered glass. He screamed, yelled, and cursed. In a violent rage, he raked his arm across the workbench, sending everything crashing to the floor.

Ralph fought for breath and trembled from the shock and fright of his brother's outburst. He shouldn't have encouraged George drink this morning. He wouldn't have if he'd known about…this. Was it his fault? He'd only wanted them to stand up to Travis.

The next thing Ralph knew, George had him by the collar. "You did this!"

"I did not," Ralph choked.

"You caused it! Somebody you brought here did this!" George growled through clenched teeth and pulled Ralph's collar tighter.

"No!" Ralph shook his head, trying to think who might have betrayed him. "Nobody I brought here would've done this."

"Who?" George snarled. "Who did you bring here?"

"Just Marv, Bud, and Fred," Ralph recounted. "That's it. None of them would've told. They're my friends."

George eased up on Ralph's collar as he considered the information.

Ralph hoped his brother would see reason, but George rarely did when he'd been drinking. "They're your friends too, George. They wouldn't have told. They promised me they wouldn't tell."

George released Ralph's shirt and shoved him backwards. "Well, somebody did this! Maybe one of 'em got sloshed and let it slip."

"Maybe it was Travis," Ralph suggested.

George slapped the air. "Travis wouldn't do this. Why ruin somethin' you're making money at?"

Ralph's eyes widened, suddenly remembering why they were there. "Travis! What are we gonna do about Travis's order?"

George raked both hands through his hair and paced the cavern.

"I've got a few gallons at the house," Ralph said.

"I have a couple at mine." George shook his head. "That's not enough." He paced a few more steps and then threw up his hands. "We'll just show him what happened. That's all we can do. He can't expect us to deliver now."

"He's gonna be madder than a hornet," Ralph muttered.

"Yeah, well, I ain't too happy, either," George grumbled. He picked up a twisted coil and flung it into the rock wall. "How in hell am I gonna pay that revenuer now?"

The sound of someone whistling "Dixie" broke into their conversation.

"Oh great." Ralph felt sick. "It's Travis."

"Well, let's get it over with." George folded his arms across his chest. Ralph moved to stand beside him in front of the demolished still.

Travis' whistling came to an abrupt stop. "What the hell's happened here?"

"What does it look like?" George barked.

Travis sauntered in, examining the situation. "So it was ya'll."

"What do you mean it was us?" George's black eyebrows narrowed.

"That got busted up." Travis picked up a mangled coil and tossed it back down. It clanked against the assorted metal littering the cave floor.

"You mean you knew about this?" Ralph stepped forward. "See?" He turned back to George. "I told you he had something to do with this!" Ralph lifted a fist to slam into Travis, but Travis blocked him.

"Explain what you're talkin' about," George ordered.

"I saw that deputy sheriff from the coalmine carrying a copper coil back to his office. He had an ax on him and he reeked of corn liquor." Travis looked toward the corner where all the jugs had been. He kicked at the shards then slammed his fist to the workbench. After uttering an expletive, he yelled, "What in hell am I gonna tell Buster?"

"Just tell him what happened," Ralph said. "It wasn't our fault."

"Did you tell anybody we were here?" George put a hand on Travis's shoulder.

Travis shoved it away. "What do you think I am? A complete idiot?"

George glared at his brother.

Ralph knew he blamed him. But he also knew his friends would never tell. It had to be Travis—that or the law had just been lucky.

"What's that sheriff's name?" George demanded.

"Morton," Travis replied. "Joe Morton. The old man lives in Hinkle and works at the mine."

"Yeah, I remember him." George kicked the debris. "Well, mark my words, he'll pay for this!"

"He sure will!" Ralph vowed, shaking his fist and gritting his teeth. "Just let me get my hands on him!"

"He'll have a warrant out for you two in no time." Travis shook his head. "Ya'll better lay low. Don't go near town until this blows over."

"I ain't runnin' scared," George crowed. "Me and Ralph'll show him. This'll be the last still he gets a hold of."

Chapter 7: Footloose and Fancy Free

Daisy, Tennessee
Friday, March 17, 1922

Edna glanced out her bedroom window to see Sherman Morton coming up the path. Clean-shaven and well dressed, he carried an unlit carbide lamp in one hand and his rifle in the other. Evidently, he hoped to stay a while since it was still several hours before dark.

Her heart accelerated. In his black suit and derby he was even more handsome than she remembered. Edna looked down at her dress. She couldn't be seen in this ratty old thing she'd worked in all day. She hurried to her armoire and found her best dress, a flowery print her mother claimed made the green in her eyes stand out.

She nearly knocked over her dresser lamp in her rush to comb her hair. Although she was as ready as she could get in so little time, Edna cringed when she heard the rap on the door downstairs and Dot's loud voice carrying up the stairwell.

"Edna, your beau's here!"

If she could hear Dot, she knew Mr. Morton could. In fact, the neighbors probably could and they lived nearly a mile away.

Every ounce of blood in her body seemed to rush to her face. There was absolutely no need to pinch her cheeks for color. Taking a deep breath, she opened her bedroom door and straightened her dress, trying to remove the perspiration from her palms in the process. Chiding herself to be calm, she paused outside the door. After all, she told herself, maybe she wouldn't even like him once she got to know him. Why get so worked up this early?

Sherman stood at the foot of the stairs looking up at her with those sparkling blue eyes of his. As she descended, he removed his derby and ran a hand through his brown hair. If good looks were all that mattered in a man, Sherman Morton was the finest catch around.

"Afternoon, Miss Springfield," he said with a smile that caused the dimple in his chin to deepen.

"Good afternoon, Mr. Morton. So nice of you to drop by." When she reached the next-to-the-last step, her ankle turned, causing her to trip and fall forward. Sherman, who'd already put his rifle and lamp in the corner, let his hat drop to the floor. He put out his arms to catch her.

Edna's full weight fell into him. He staggered back a little, putting his hands to her waist to break her fall. With her body flush with his, she looked into his face. How humiliating! This man was her last, best chance at a marriage proposal and she'd just made an utter fool of herself.

Sherman's arms slid around Edna's waist, pulling her closer.

Her mind whirled. Was he trying to help her regain her balance? Supporting her in case her ankle was injured? Or did she sense something more?

His eyes glinted mischievously. "It's mighty nice to be here."

It took a moment before she realized he was responding to her welcome. Gaining her footing, Edna eased away. "I'm so sorry. I'm about as graceful as a goat in a dime store." His chuckle and kind eyes set her at ease.

"Nah, I think your ankle just turned on ya." He loosened his hold but did not remove his hands from her waist. "Are you all right? Can you stand on your ankle?"

Edna shuffled her feet to test the appendage. "It's all right. I'm so sorry for falling for you—I mean on you." If this were baseball, she'd have only one strike left.

"No need to apologize." Sherman grinned. "Glad I could be here to break your fall."

She didn't say she wouldn't have fallen if he hadn't been there. Why was it that she seemed to always make a fool of herself when a handsome man was around?

Sherman released her. "I was wondering if you might like to go for a walk, but if you've hurt your ankle, perhaps we could just sit on the porch."

The last thing Edna wanted to do was stick around the house to be embarrassed by her siblings. She'd done a fine job of that all by herself! She tested her ankle to be sure. "I'm fine. It might do me good to walk on it aways."

"You sure?" He bent down, letting his warm hands slide around her ankle. "It doesn't feel swollen. Not yet anyway."

How unnerving! Worse, her mother entered the room while Sherman still had his hands around her ankle.

"Mama!" Edna exclaimed.

Sherman picked up his hat and stood. "Mrs. Springfield," he said, fumbling with the brim. "Miss Edna tripped. I...I was checking to make sure her ankle wasn't sprained."

"Were you now?" Maude lifted an eyebrow, a smile playing on her lips.

"I'm fine, and we're going for a walk." Edna pushed Sherman toward the door. She kept nudging until they were outside and she'd taken hold of his arm. After rushing several yards up the path, they looked at each other and broke into giggles.

They walked a little way and Edna struck up a conversation. "So, tell me about yourself."

"Ah, not a whole lot to tell really. Just work at the mine, come from a good God-fearin' family. I try to live by the Good Book, but I must admit I've got in a tussle or two in the past. Probably need a little work on my temper," he shrugged. "What about you?"

"Well, if we're gonna be honest," Edna chuckled. "I'm an adequate cook, not really much for housekeeping, but I'll do it. I enjoy sewing, but it's more for the companionship of the other women at the quilting bees. Honestly, I'd rather read a good book, spend time with friends, or sit around tellin' stories as do just about anything."

"You enjoy tellin' stories - eh?" Sherman prompted. "Tell me one."

"Hmmm... let's see. One of my favorites is how my Daddy and Mama eloped. Would you like to hear that one?"

"I'd like that," Sherman nodded.

"Let's sit over here on this big rock," Edna suggested, pointing to a limestone boulder beneath a hickory tree.

They sat down beside each other and Edna straightened her skirt.

She turned to face him. "First it'll be easier if I give you everybody's names so you know who is who. Maude is my mama. Thad is my daddy. Maude's parents were Mary Elizabeth James and William Pearson. Now the James family was very well-to-do. They had money. And William Pearson was a Justice of the Peace. He and his father were affluent lawmen and well known - or I should say downright feared — in the Chattanooga area. So when Thad came courtin' Maude, her parents were none too happy.

"They saw him as an ordinary ol' farmer who had nothing to bring to their daughter. He wasn't rich, and they felt he had no breeding. But Maude fell in love with Thad anyway; and they courted in secret. Her parents practically made her a prisoner in her own home. The time came when Thad asked Maude to marry him. Of course, her Daddy wouldn't give his blessing. Nobody was good enough for his Maude.

"So Thad and Maude set a date for their wedding anyway. They announced that they would be married at nine o'clock Sunday morning no matter whether her family agreed or not. Thad set off for Chattanooga to obtain a marriage license and then arranged for a local preacher to marry them in secret Saturday night. The preacher, of course, thought it an odd request. So Thad offered him five dollars to meet them there and perform the wedding. He agreed."

Sherman chuckled, wrapped up in the story.

"Thad got a couple of his friends to stand as witnesses and Maude snuck out of the house just after dark on Saturday night. She wore a pretty white dress she'd made for herself and had her suitcase in hand. She got in such a hurry, she forgot her hat though, but she met Thad on Highway 27 right in front of her parents' home. There by the light of the moon, they made their vows, and she ran off with Thad."

"What did her daddy do?" Sherman asked.

"It was a whole year before her father would even speak to her again. He wouldn't let her mama come visit her or anything. So Mary Elizabeth and Maude would sneak messages back and forth to each other in the collar of a little dog.

"They did that for full on a year until finally my oldest sister was born. William finally let Mary Elizabeth come visit then. One pinch of Thelma's chubby cheeks and they'd all made their peace and were back to bein' family again. Funny how a baby changes things, don't ya think?"

Sherman smiled, "That's remarkable, makes me feel like I know your folks a bit." Sherman shifted on the rock. "So do you have another one?"

"Oh sure, lots more!" Edna nodded and started into another yarn.

~*~

The sun sank low in the sky by the time Sherman and Edna approached Chickamauga Creek. Things were going well in her estimation. He had laughed at her stories and now he held her hand. Even better, she hadn't blundered since leaving the house.

"Aren't they your little sisters?" Sherman pointed toward several families gathered farther down the creek bank picnicking. The Springfields were easy to spot with their long legs and short torsos.

"Edna! Mr. Morton!" Thadda called, her blonde curls bobbing about her shoulders. Dot trailed along behind. "Come on, Mr. Morton!" Thadda grabbed Sherman's hand and pulled him toward the party.

Edna was forced to begin introductions. "This is my daddy, Thad Springfield." The lanky gentleman rose and, shook Sherman's hand. Mr. Springfield smiled, and his pronounced overbite became even more dramatic.

"This is my brother, Hab," Edna said, pointing out a thirteen-year-old blonde who looked like an older male version of little Thadda.

"Hey." Hab waved, grabbed a friend's arm, and started toward the creek.

"And this is my brother, Frank." It was then Edna realized that Sherman was probably Frank's age. She hadn't had enough nerve to ask yet, but Frank was nineteen and Sherman looked about the same.

Frank waved, then tipped a mason jar of whisky to his lips. He passed the jar to his father and leaned back, resting his head on his hands. "Good night for a picnic."

Edna felt Sherman's hand stiffen She wondered at the suddenly stern expression on his face. His eyes were on her father, who next tipped the jar to his lips.

"Have a seat." Maude motioned to an open spot. "There's fried chicken, mashed potatoes, and corn on the cob."

Sherman removed his hat and they sat down. Edna filled a plate for Sherman and then herself. While they ate, music began on the far side of the creek.

"Where's that coming from?" Sherman asked.

"It's gypsies. They camp down here by the creek and play at night. We like to come here to sing along with them." Edna pointed to a group of people swathed in brightly colored clothes and scarves. Sherman's eyebrows rose.

"Have you never seen gypsies before?" she asked.

"No, can't say that I have," he replied, his eyes still fixed on the band of colorful travelers.

"Then you're in for a treat." Frank slapped Sherman on the shoulder and took another swig of liquor.

"Aren't they supposed to be a dangerous lot?" Sherman asked.

"Oh, they're safe enough. They spice things up a bit around here," Edna assured.

While Sherman and Edna ate, singers joined the instrumentalists.

"It's the *Gypsy Love Song*,"[1] Edna explained.

In the twilight the gypsy voices carried across the creek:

The birds of the forest are calling for thee
And the shades and the glades are lonely
Summer is there with her blossoms fair
And you are absent only.

The picnickers responded:

No bird that nests in the greenwood tree
But sighs to greet you and kiss you
All the violets yearn, yearn for your safe return
But most of all I miss you.

The voices of both groups joined:

Slumber on, my little gypsy sweetheart
Dream of the field and the grove
Can you hear me, hear me in that dreamland
Where your fancies rove?

Gypsies:	*Slumber on*
Picnickers:	*Slumber on*
Gypsies:	*My little gypsy sweetheart*
Picnickers:	*My little gypsy sweetheart*
Gypsies:	*Little gypsy*
Picnickers:	*Wild little woodland dove*
Gypsies:	*All my heart's true love*
Everyone:	*Can you hear the love song that tells you*
	All my heart's true love?

As the song repeated, Frank got up and grabbed a dance partner. Now everyone clapped and sang. They clearly loved to watch Frank dance, and he held nothing back. Soon almost everyone was dancing:

Thad and Maude, Hab with a freckle-faced girl, and Dot and Thadda together. Sherman and Edna alone still sat on the blanket.

Sherman looked as though he'd never seen anything like it.

"Do you want to?" she offered.

He shook his head. "I don't dance."

She rose and held out her hand. "I can teach you."

"I'd rather not."

Edna shrugged and sat back down. "We don't have to." She was glad darkness had settled; it hid the misting in her eyes. The neighbors had started a bonfire, but it wasn't close enough to betray her.

Clearly, she'd taken her last strike, but she didn't know when. Things had gone so well while they were walking, but since they'd joined the picnic Sherman had become stiff and almost sullen. Maybe he didn't like her family? Or maybe he didn't like her. He certainly didn't want to dance. In fact, he'd acted as if she'd suggested he pick up a rattlesnake.

Just as she had decided to give up hope, Sherman's hand covered hers with a gentle squeeze. He'd been watching her while she watched everyone else and now there was a different expression on his face. He stared at her as if admiring a work of art.

"You're beautiful," he whispered before he leaned over and kissed her cheek.

The simple gesture rekindled her hopes almost as high as the nearby bonfire.

~*~

Sherman made his way up the mountain by the light of the carbide lamp. His rifle was ready, for one never knew what lurked in the woods. While he listened to rustling on the path and the babbling creek alongside, his thoughts turned to Edna. She was beautiful and so full of life. She'd made him laugh and feel at ease, but that family! With his staunch religious upbringing, being around them was extremely uncomfortable. Frank had danced shamefully for all to see! The whole family fraternized with gypsies! Disgraceful is what it was.

Disgraceful and...sinful. His family had always taught him that dancing, card-playing and drinking were of the devil.

Sherman was growing fond of Edna, but the thought of how mortified his parents would be by her family made him wonder if he'd have the nerve to introduce her to them. The moonshine topped it all. While his Grandpa Joe spent countless nights tracking down moonshiners, the Springfields not only drank it, but might even make it themselves.

Sherman heard a twig break and gripped his rifle tighter. Turning to his left he lifted his lamp. A pair of raccoon eyes reflected back in the light. He continued as the varmint scurried up a tree.

Sherman hadn't taken three steps before his thoughts returned to Edna's family. He'd had half a mind to walk away from the picnic, but he'd looked at Edna, so happy and serene, apparently oblivious to the sinfulness of her surroundings. She was like an undiscovered diamond stuck amidst the coal. He'd studied her without her notice and decided he could save her, bring her to the light.

Chapter 8: Not Such a Bright Idea

Flintstone, Walker County, Georgia
Friday, March 17, 1922

"How you gonna pay those property taxes now that the still's gone?" Ralph asked in a whisper.

George leaned back in the rocker on his front porch and stared at the night sky while crickets and cicadas seemed to laugh at his predicament. He glanced over his shoulder, through the window at Lulu, who sat knitting by lamplight. "I don't know." He rose and motioned for Ralph to follow him toward a neighbor's field.

"I promised Lulu I'd get the money." George spit a wad of chewing tobacco on the grass near his boot. "If we don't have it next week, we'll lose the house." He raked a hand through his hair.

"What about askin' her folks for money when you're up there tomorrow?"

George shook his head. "They don't have no more to give. And Ma and Pa don't have any to loan either." Ever since he'd lost his job at the mine, George's life had spiraled downward. He needed money and he needed it fast. If only that deputy hadn't busted up their still!

George stared at the neighbor's barn, listening to frogs croak in a nearby pond. A train whistled in the distance, and a scheme began to take form in his mind. He put a hand on Ralph's arm. "I have an idea."

"What?"

"You know how lots of those out-of-town salesmen ride the train up to Durham?"

Ralph nodded.

"They've got money on 'em - right?"

"I suppose so."

George could tell by the blank expression on his brother's face that Ralph still didn't see where he was going. "Reckon they'd have enough on 'em to pay the property taxes?"

A slow smile curled Ralph's lips. "I bet they would."

"Let's rob us a train!" George took his brother by the shoulders, his heart accelerating with excitement.

"You think we could?"

"Of course we could!" George released Ralph to use his fingers for calculation. "First we'll need to take the fuses out of the train lights so they can't signal for help."

"Do you know how to do that?"

"Sure. I spent a little time around that train when I was working at the mine."

"We'll need guns," Ralph noted.

"Right, and we should probably cut the telephone and telegraph lines so we can get away without anyone callin' the law."

A grin split Ralph's face as he warmed to the plan.

"We'll have to lay low afterwards," George continued, "but I can sneak the money to Lulu to pay the taxes." Meeting Ralph's gaze, he knew at once to give his brother reason to risk his own neck. "What you gonna do with your half of the haul?"

Ralph mulled over the idea.

"What do you say?" George patted his brother's shoulder.

"Count me in."

Chapter 9: When the Train Comes

Durham Coalmine, Lookout Mountain, Georgia
Saturday, March 18, 1922

Joe stood outside the mine, keeping an eye on things. Ever since he'd busted up that still, he'd had an uneasy feeling. Several ex-convicts worked the mines, men who spent a fair share of their off time nursing jugs of corn liquor. They were none too happy. No one had come right out and said anything, but Joe felt it in his bones. Thankfully, he had many friends at the mine as well, people who would have his back if anyone got out of line.

"Sheriff Morton." Joe felt a hand on his arm and looked over his shoulder at Dave Williams. "You have a telephone call over at the office."

Joe's eyes narrowed. The only calls he received were from the Walker County Sheriff's office. He wondered what the trouble was. Joe walked alongside Mr. Williams toward the mine office.

"Have you turned in your report about the still to Sheriff Harmon yet?" Dave asked.

"Not yet. Haven't had a chance to get down into Lafayette. Besides, I'm hoping to figure out whose it was and tie up all the loose ends before submitting the report."

"Any luck with that?" the mine manager asked.

Joe shook his head. "I checked the land deeds, but they're a dead end. The cave was on mine property."

"Hmm." Williams opened the office door and waited for Joe to enter before he turned away.

Joe took the receiver propped on top of the wall phone. "Deputy Sheriff Morton here."

"Papa, it's me, Mary Ann." His daughter's voice quivered.

"Mary Ann? What's wrong?"

"It's Christeen. She fell out of the big oak tree, and I'm afraid she's broken her arm."

"Is it bleeding? Did it break the skin?" Joe raked a hand through his gray hair as he thought about his little granddaughter with the blonde curls.

"No, nothing like that. But she can't bend it and it's swollen at the elbow."

Joe pulled his pocket watch from his vest to check the time. "There's one more train up the mountain. Get her up here to see Doc Rogers."

"That's what I was thinking. I'm at the station now. Would you meet us at the Durham depot, Papa?"

"Of course. I'll see you soon."

"Thank you, Papa."

~*~

Mary Ann breathed a sigh of relief to know her father would be there when she got off the train. Her mind went back to childhood when she'd fallen out of a tree like Christeen had. She'd busted open her knee but hadn't broken anything. Her father had carried her to the house with calming words and set her on her mother's lap. Then he carefully cleaned the wound and bandaged it. With a hand to her cheek, he promised she'd be "good as new" in a week or so. Mary Ann smiled. Her papa had always had a way of making her feel everything would turn out all right.

She knelt to look Christeen in the eyes. "Honey, we're going to ride the train to the mines to see Grandpa. Won't that be fun?"

The little girl's eyes lighted. She'd cried quite a bit after the accident, but with her arm in the makeshift sling her mother had crafted from sewing scraps, she didn't seem to hurt as much now.

Mary Ann stood, took the child's uninjured hand, and led her toward the boarding area. The Durham Coal and Iron Company ran a train from the mines to Chickamauga and back at least twice daily. The company used ovens on Chickamauga's north side to transform coal into coke for iron and steel foundries in Chattanooga.

While they hauled about a dozen carloads of coal down the mountain each trip, the last two cars were reserved for passengers. Fortunately, the train also stopped in Hinkle, which had made it easier for Mary Ann to take her little girl the five miles to the doctor.

Mary Ann and Christeen waited on a bench for the train to arrive. She'd already purchased the tickets, so she encouraged Christeen to rest her head on her lap and take a little nap. She was grateful that her sister, Josephine, had kept the other two children. Like the father after whom she was named, Josephine was always good about things.

Soon a crowd formed, ready to board. Mary Ann patted her daughter's back. "Christeen, honey, wake up. The train's here." Christeen lifted her head. "It's the choo choo, honey. You wanna ride the choo choo?"

"Uh huh." The four-year-old rubbed her eyes and struggled to her feet.

Mary Ann found a spot in the first car and encouraged Christeen to sit by the window to enjoy the view.

It didn't take long to board. The conductor blew his whistle and the train lurched forward. Christeen smiled at her mother, excited to be going for a ride.

They hadn't traveled far when a ruckus began at the back of the car.

"Come on, you know you want it," one man coaxed another in a slurred voice.

"No, you put that away," the other replied.

Mary Ann turned to look at the two men. The one in the seat was Mr. Peterman, but she didn't know the younger man who stood over him with a bottle of whiskey in hand.

He shoved it in Mr. Peterman's face. "Take a sip. It's good stuff," the ruffian insisted.

"I don't drink." Mr. Peterman pushed the bottle away.

To Mary Ann's horror, the man with the bottle pulled a blue steel pistol from his jacket. He shoved it into Mr. Peterman's belly. "I said, take a drink," he growled.

Mary Ann gathered Christeen in her arms and lowered them both behind the seatback.

"Put that thing away," Mr. Peterman ordered.

Mary Ann peeked around the back. There was a second young man who didn't look more than sixteen. He stood silently by while his older companion continued to shove his pistol into Mr. Peterman's stomach.

Mary Ann's heart pounded. She held her breath and hunched down further, shielding Christeen with her body.

The conductor, Mr. McCurdy, stepped into the car from the caboose. "What are you boys up to?"

"Just having a friendly conversation," the younger boy answered, putting a hand on his companion's shoulder.

"You two come along with me," the conductor ordered.

"Maybe you didn't understand me," the younger man said as he eased a pistol from inside his coat. "I said we're just havin' us a friendly conversation."

"Doesn't appear too friendly to me," the conductor observed, rubbing his hand over his mustache.

"It won't be too friendly when I put a bullet through your skull," the younger one snapped.

"Now settle down, boys. I ain't trying to start nothing here," the conductor soothed. "I've got a nice soft seat back here you boys might like."

Mary Ann lifted her head to look. To her amazement, the conductor finally coaxed the two drunks into the rear car. She breathed a sigh of relief. When she felt it was safe, she sat up and looked back at Mr. Peterman. He pulled a handkerchief from his pocket and patted it to his pale, perspiring brow. Mary Ann's hands trembled the rest of the way to Durham.

When they pulled into the train station, Mary Ann looked out the window to see her father standing at the corner of the depot landing. What a relief! Between her worries over Christeen's arm and the armed men on the train, she felt as tense as a clothesline pulled so taut it was ready to snap. She craved the comfort only Papa could give.

Mary Ann and Christeen stepped off the train and hurried to Joe. Mary Ann hugged her father. He returned the embrace and then looked into her eyes., "Are you all right?"

"I am now."

Her father bent to take a look at Christeen's arm. "It does look mighty swollen. I told Doc Monroe you'd be coming in. He said he could take her in about an hour."

"That's good," Mary Ann sighed.

"What were you doin' up in that tree, little 'un?" Joe patted his granddaughter's head.

Christeen's blue eyes met her Grandpa's. "Just playin.'" She shrugged. "I slipped."

"You've gotta be more careful."

From the corner of her eye Mary Ann saw the two boys from the train approach. Instinctively, she put her arms around Christeen from behind. Her heart accelerated with each step the men took in their direction. Surely, she consoled herself, they wouldn't dare bother her or Christeen with a deputy sheriff right there. To her horror, it was soon evident the men intended to talk to her father.

"These fellas are trouble, Papa," she whispered as she pulled Christeen back. The older boy extended his hand toward her Papa and asked, "Is this Mr. Morton?"

"Yes," Joe replied. "Who are you?"

"You have a warrant for us, have you?" the man said.

He reeked of alcohol—so much so that Mary Ann held her breath.

Joe shook his head. "No, boys, I have no warrant for you."

"You're a damned old liar," the younger one growled. He was behind Joe now.

Mary Ann felt sick. The men were drunk and clearly irrational. She saw from the bewildered look on her father's face that he didn't know them. A feeling of dread swept over her, and Mary Ann backed farther away, pulling Christeen into the commissary. "Stay right here," she instructed. "Don't move."

"Damn you!" the older boy cried. "Serve it if you think you can." He hadn't released Joe's hand; now he was crushing it.

"You boys run along," Joe said calmly. "I have no warrant." Mary Ann prayed they'd follow her father's instruction, but in the next instant the man hit Joe in the face.

Joe put up his hands to ward off the blows, but the young man hit him again. When Joe pushed him back, hard, the ruffian lost his balance and fell into a shallow ditch. The younger boy drew his pistol.

"Papa!" Mary Ann screamed, look out! He's got a gun!"

A man somewhere echoed that the boys had guns and urged the deputy to arrest them.

There was no time for Joe to react. The first bullet slammed into his chin.

Mary Ann's heart seemed to stop as a terrified scream tore from her throat.

Her papa shook his head, dazed. Blood poured down his neck as he at last fumbled at his hip for his pistol.

The man in the ditch rose and came toward Joe as the younger boy continued to shoot.

Mary Ann gasped, her hands covering her mouth as she watched her father finally return fire. One shot pinged against the metal of the train, another dug into the dirt. Mary Ann knew then how severely wounded Joe was. Normally her father could shoot a tick off a dog's back.

"I'm not scared of you!" Unflinching, the boy reloaded and fired again.

Mary Ann fell back into the commissary in shock. The flurry of gunfire outside sounded to her like a packet of firecrackers set off on the Fourth of July.

Everything slowed as Mary Ann continued to gaze through the open doorway. Her father staggered around in a futile attempt to defend himself. As they scurried for cover, men yelled for help and women screamed. One woman fainted.

The younger boy ran to the corner, still firing back at Joe. At last the shooting stopped and Mary Ann ran to her father. Tears poured down her cheeks as she held him in her arms; then, with a strange man's help, she got him into the depot commissary.

"Is that hot enough for ya, or do ya want some more just like it?" one of the villains yelled from outside. Mary Ann looked back, fearful they would fire again, but they turned, walked across the railroad track, and ran off.

Feeling numb, Mary Ann helped to lay her father on a bench inside the depot. "Oh, Papa, they've killed you!" she cried, pulling his head onto her lap. Blood was everywhere. With trembling hands she held her handkerchief to his neck wounds and her palm to his chin, trying futilely to staunch the profuse bleeding.

"Oh, Papa! Please be all right," she begged, her eyes burning with tears. "Oh, please, heaven, help us!" she prayed.

Joe's eyes met hers for an instant before wilting closed. "They've got me."

As her father's chest rose and fell with each blood-congested breath, Mary Ann became aware of the people standing around, watching helplessly. When a man offered his handkerchief, she pressed it listlessly to Joe's chin.

"Oh, Papa! Papa!" Mary Ann moaned. Within minutes, Deputy Sheriff Joseph W. Morton—Mary Ann's papa, protector, confidant, and loyal friend—lay dead in her arms.

She would never be the same.

Chapter 10: On the Run

"We better split up," George Baker told his younger brother. "You go that way, I'll go this."

"I'll catch up with ya at the hideout." Ralph slapped George on the back and raised a triumphant fist with gun still in hand. "At least we got old man Morton!" Ralph shoved the pistol inside his coat, handed a second one to George, and sprinted into the woods.

George ran across the road. He could still hear men shouting and women screaming. His heart raced and his mind told him to run, but his legs wouldn't cooperate. Too much corn liquor made it hard to think. Had Ralph just killed a deputy sheriff?

He shoved the gun into his jacket pocket. He'd reached for a weapon himself when the deputy pushed him down, but had only come up with a bottle of whiskey. Then he remembered: upset by the botched train robbery, Ralph had taken the gun from him as they got off the train. He could still see his brother's angry expression. He removed the almost-empty bottle from inside his coat and stared at it. How stupid! He'd ruined everything. Again. In frustration, he threw the bottle as far as he could and staggered down the road away from the depot.

George's whiskey-soaked brain struggled to piece together what had happened after that. Travis had told them Morton had a warrant because of the still. When they got off the train, it was clear to them both the deputy was there to serve it. What George couldn't figure out was why Morton wouldn't admit it. Had the old man played dumb because he was too chicken to take them both on at once?

Stumbling over his own feet seemed to jar loose yet another question: How did Morton know they were on the train? They'd cut the telephone and telegraph lines. No way could he have been tipped off that they'd be on that train. And what about the woman and little girl who were with him?

George shook his head violently to clear it. What did it matter anyway? True, if he'd been sober it probably wouldn't have come to gunfire, but he couldn't do anything about that now. The deed was done and all he could do now was focus on getting out of here.

Behind him, the men's voices grew louder. Any small voice of remorse was drowned out in the angry din. *Run!* was now the only word that echoed in his mind.

George fled as fast as wobbly legs could carry him, but the shouts grew nearer with each step. He glanced over his shoulder and saw the mob. The white eyes and teeth in the coalminers' blackened, contorted faces made them look like a pack of hunger-crazed panthers after a kill. His imagination scarcely needed liquor to convince him they meant to tear into his flesh.

Panic electrified his body. George plunged off the road, hoping to lose them in the forest. After running for several minutes, he hid behind a bush and pulled out the gun to check for bullets. There were none.

"Thanks Ralph!" he muttered and tossed the gun in a ravine behind him. He resumed his flight through the woods until he tripped over a protruding root. George swore as he fell face first into the underbrush, dazed. When he regained his senses, it sounded as if a thousand boots trampled around him. Before he could push himself up, fingers clawed his back and arms. A couple of men yanked him upright then pushed him down again, this time on his back. George landed hard and his shoulders ached.

He looked up into eyes that seemed to glow and his heart accelerated with terror he'd never before experienced. When one of the coalminers slammed his fist into George's face it was as if an iron anvil had knocked him senseless. George rolled to his side and vomited on the man's boot.

"Get up, you sorry, good for nothin' killer." The man with the soiled boots lifted him by the arms.

At least a dozen men circled him, clutching, grabbing, pushing, and hitting wherever they could. George put his arms over his face and head in a useless attempt to protect himself from their blows.

"You killed Joe Morton and we're gonna kill you!" The man who spoke punched George in the ribs.

He doubled over gasping for air and collapsed onto his knees. They again pulled him to his feet.

"Please, no, don't kill me!" George begged when he could get enough air to speak.

The mob forced his hands behind his back and bound his wrists with cord. When George saw another miner fashioning a noose, horror stabbed through his heart.

"Hangin's really too good for ya," the man said as if he were a farmer about to slaughter a pig. He spat a wad of chewing tobacco in the grass, and continued to work the knot.

"There's a good hanging tree!" another man cried.

Several mobsters turned toward a tree across the road. Two men grabbed George's shoulders and dragged him toward the tree. One of them took his gun and the others pushed his back.

George fell to his knees. "Please, no! I didn't mean to hurt nobody! Honest, we didn't do it on purpose." Though it was the truth, he might have said anything to keep them from stringing him up with that rope. He knew they'd do it. The year before, some of these locals had lynched a black man for supposedly raping a white woman. Only after he was dead did they discover the man was innocent. What George had done was far worse.

If only he'd never touched that bottle before boarding the train, George thought. If he'd been sober he'd never have agreed to Ralph's idea. Or was it Ralph's idea? George wondered. Maybe it was his. He couldn't remember. Ever since they'd found the still smashed, everything had been a blur of anger, fear, hate, revenge—and corn liquor. Too much liquor. He'd been so sloshed he'd bumbled the train robbery.

The men ignored George's pleas for mercy and threw the rope over the limb. George's heart hammered against his chest, liquor only exacerbating his fears. The panthers really were determined to rip him to shreds and dangle his carcass from a tree.

Just when he was ready to abandon hope, a shot sliced the air. George was sure that someone had fired a bullet into his chest, but there was no pain, only the steadily-hammering panic.

The men who held him turned in unison toward David Williams, the coalmine manager. The man stood like a thunderbolt of reason over a sea of madness, his still-smoking gun pointed skyward.

"Settle down, boys," he ordered. "This man's got to be brought to justice."

"We can dish out justice right here!" a miner retorted.

"No, this is for the law to handle, boys. You don't want this on your heads." Williams lowered his weapon. "You don't want the law comin' after you. He killed a lawman. Let the law handle it."

The man who held George by the collar asked, "What do you propose we do with him, then?"

"I'll take him to Esquire Gladden. He'll see that he's handed over to the sheriff."

"What if they let him off?" another man bellowed. "They're killin' lawmen left and right these days and ain't nobody's been hanged for it."

"This one's different," Williams explained. "There's plenty of witnesses. He'll get his just reward for killin' poor old Joe." When the men seemed to see reason he continued. "Jed, you come with me. We'll take him to Gladden. The rest of you go on home."

"What about the other fella?" someone yelled.

"Yeah, let's go find him!" another exclaimed.

George watched the pack of panthers lope on after their next victim. He hoped Ralph had got away.

Chapter 11: Breaking the News

Sherman pulled the truck up in front of his grandparents' house and tapped the horn in greeting. Then he hopped out and sprinted up the steps. Rapping on the open front door, he hollered inside, "Grandma, you here?" When he saw the familiar small head with gray hair pulled back in a bun he smiled.

Grandma Josie looked up from her knitting. "Why, Sherman! What are you doin' here?" She started to rise from the sofa, but he stepped inside and motioned for her to remain seated.

Sherman hugged his grandmother and kissed her cheek. "Papa sent me to fetch some tools and such that wouldn't fit on the truck the other day."

"I sure hope ya kin stay a spell."

"Papa told me to stay the night and go home tomorrow after church."

"That's wonderful! I'm just tickled pink to see ya!"

"I'm glad to be here." Sherman looked around. "Grandpa out workin'?"

"Yeah, he had some things to do at the office. He'll be runnin' a little late today. Poor Christeen fell out of a tree and Mary Ann had to take her up the mountain on the train to see the doctor. So he'll have to wait a spell and bring 'em home."

Sherman sat down next to his grandmother. "Is she gonna be all right?"

"Well, I think the poor little thing's broken her arm, bless her heart, but she should be all right after the doctor sees to her." Josie's eyebrows furrowed, "Do you hear a truck a-comin'?"

Sherman went to the door. "It's Uncle Howard's truck. He sure is flyin'." Clouds of dust billowed behind Howard's truck as it jostled and bounced its way up the dirt road. "Wonder what the hurry is."

Grandma Josie grabbed her cane. She eased to her feet and joined Sherman at the door. He opened it and they both stepped out on the front porch just as Howard screeched to a halt. The truck sputtered, backfired, then died. Howard shoved open the door and jogged toward them.

"Where's the fire, Howard?" Josie asked.

Howard stood before his mother without even acknowledging Sherman. He put shaking hands on her shoulders. "Mama, let's go inside and sit down."

"Sit down? What fer?" Josie searched her son's eyes. "What's wrong, Howard?"

Sherman's stomach turned. Something was terribly wrong; he saw it in Uncle Howard's eyes. Whatever it was, his grandmother should sit down to hear it, so he helped Howard guide her into the house. The three of them gathered around the kitchen table.

Howard took one swipe at the moisture glistening in tracks down his coal-stained face. He shook his head.

Josie clutched her son's sleeve. "Is Christeen hurt worse than we thought?"

"No, no. Christeen's gonna be fine," Howard said. "She and Mary Ann are at the doctor's now."

Josie sighed in relief.

Sherman's heart drummed in his chest, and he wished Howard would spit out what he'd come to say.

"Mama, I just...there's no way...to say this other than to..." Howard's words trailed off.

"Say it!" Sherman ordered.

Howard's eyes flickered in his nephew's direction. "What are you doin' here, Sherman?" he asked, noticing him at last.

"Never mind. What's wrong? If it's not Christeen—"

"Tell us what's gotcha so worked up, Howard," Josie interrupted.

Howard took Josie's hands in his. "It's Papa. He's...he's been shot...he died in Mary Ann's arms."

"What?" Josie's thin lips trembled. A moment later, her glistening eyes met Sherman's.

Sherman shook his head. "You're kiddin'. This is some kind of sick joke you're playin'."

"No. Papa went to meet Mary Ann and Christeen at the station and two drunks came up to him and started a fight. One thing led to another and they shot him...right there in front of Mary Ann and Christeen."

Sherman rose, shoved back his chair, and paced to the door. There he stopped, helplessly staring out over his grandparents' property while Howard related the details. How could this be true? He'd been so close to his grandfather. He was his mentor, his role model. Sherman wanted to be just like Grandpa Joe, and now he was gone, stolen from him.

"They've caught one of 'em already," Howard concluded, "and there's a manhunt for the other. I ran home to tell you, Ma, but I gotta go help." Howard rose.

"I'm goin' with ya," Sherman managed around a lump in the throat that threatened to strangle him.

Josie shoved back her chair. She leaned the heels of her hands on the table and pushed herself to her feet.

"Sherman, you're stayin' here with me," she ordered.

Howard looked from Sherman to his mother and back. "Ma's right. We can't be leavin' her alone right now."

"I can't sit here and do nothin'," Sherman protested. His heart pounded and he felt as if every cell in his body trembled. He pushed open the door and started toward his truck.

Before he'd taken three steps, Howard grabbed his arm and spun him around.

"Sherman, I said stay here with your grandmother." His steel-blue eyes reinforced the insistence of his words.

"But—"

"Stay here," Howard repeated.

"If you think I'm not man enough to help—"

"This has nothin' to do with bein' man enough." Howard leaned close and lowered his voice. "Mama needs you. If there's anybody on this mountain who can help her through this, it's you."

"Me? Why me?" Sherman glared at his uncle. How could he, a seventeen-year-old boy, help an old woman through the death of her husband? His eyes darted to Grandma Josie. She leaned against the doorway, her handkerchief drawn to her face. She was trying to be brave, but traitorous tears streamed down her cheeks and sporadic sobs jolted her frail body. Sherman would much rather fight the men who'd done this than witness his grandmother's grief. What could he say? He'd never been a talker and this didn't seem like the time to start.

Howard took him by the shoulders and forced him to meet his eye. "Papa'll never be dead as long as you're alive. For Mama's sake, stay here, stay safe, and sit with her."

"I don't know what to do," Sherman murmured. "I don't know what to say."

"You don't need to say anything. It ain't about that." Howard turned him around and shoved him back toward the house. He lifted his voice so Josie could hear, "I've gotta go now, Mama. I promise ya, we'll get the men who did this."

Howard stomped toward his truck, started the engine, and left.

Sherman wrapped his arms around his grandmother, and she collapsed in his embrace.

Chapter 12: Hiding from the Law

Ralph Baker doubled back toward the mining community. Many of the houses were deserted with the women clustered together and the men out looking for him and George. He paused at the edge of the forest, looked this way and that, and ran toward one of the larger houses. He peered in the window and decided no one was there.

Still cautious, Ralph inched his way around the building until he came to the back door. Taking the knob in hand, he eased the door open, freezing when it creaked. Long moments passed, but he didn't hear anything to indicate a presence, so he slipped inside and closed the door behind him.

Tiptoeing through the house, he spotted steps leading up to the attic. Pausing after each step to avoid making the boards creak, Ralph climbed the stairs and entered the small, cluttered room. He smiled at a large chest that had been stacked with boxes. That would give him somewhere to hide. Through a tiny window he saw the sun begin to set. He eased toward the glass, stood to the side, and looked out. In the distance was the train depot. All was quiet there now. He went to the corner and curled himself behind the chest.

He'd stay the night here, he decided, and slip out the next morning after the people who lived there left.

Ralph's thoughts raced. He hoped George had also managed to get away. How had they gotten themselves in this mess to start with? Sure, they'd wanted to retaliate against old Morton as soon as they heard what he'd done, but now that the liquor and rage had worn off some, Ralph realized it wasn't too bright to have shot the deputy out in the open that way.

He turned fitfully, trying to better fit his lanky frame into the narrow space. Then again, he thought, there Morton was, ready to serve that warrant. It had been him or them, now or never. They'd teach him once and for all not to mess with their business.

Ralph grimaced at the memory. Never had he been so furious! There Morton stood, smug and confident while he and George still reeled from having their still busted up and income taken away. It must have been fate, he told himself, George flubbing the train robbery because he was drunk but then stepping off the train to find Morton on the depot landing. They'd done what any men would have.

No matter how often he told himself he'd done the right thing defending his brother and their livelihood, it didn't seem so clear-cut anymore, cowering in a dirty corner, fearing discovery. He cursed. If George hadn't botched the train robbery...Ralph shook his head. Even that was his fault. He'd encouraged George to drink in order to be tough. The problem was George had either had too much or that last bottle had gone bad.

Ralph patted his pockets and pulled out his gun. He'd unloaded it into the lawman. Fortunately, he had extra bullets in his pocket. As he reloaded the weapon, he again hoped that George had regained his wits enough to get off the road and hide.

~*~

Dave Williams made sure Jed had a secure hold on George Baker, then knocked on Esquire Gladden's door.

After a few moments, Gladden answered. "What have we here?" Gladden's eyes widened as he looked at George's bloodied nose and black eye.

"This is one of the fellows who shot Deputy Morton over at the depot," Dave explained.

"Shot Mr. Morton?" Esquire Gladden's eyes grew larger. "Is Joe all right?"

"I'm afraid they've killed him." Dave felt moisture well in his eyes. It was just now catching up to him that his old friend was dead.

Morton had worked at the mines for as long as Dave had been there. One always knew where he stood with Joe. He saw the world in absolutes—black and white, good and evil—and could quote the Good Book to prove where those lines were drawn.

"Why would you go and kill poor old Mr. Morton?" Gladden studied George as if he were no better than a sack of manure dumped on his doorstep.

"He had it comin' to him," George grumbled.

It took all the reserve Dave could muster to keep from blacking George's other eye. "You better get in there with Esquire Gladden before you get what you've got comin' to *you*."

Dave shoved George inside the office and Jed followed, keeping a hand around George's upper arm. Gladden put a wooden chair by the stove. He went to his desk and pulled out a set of handcuffs. Dave and Jed shoved George onto the chair. Gladden fastened one end of the cuffs to the prisoner's already-bound wrist and the other to the stove.

Dave wished the stove was lit. Maybe it would sear some of the meanness out of the devil, but he shook off the thought as quickly as it came. He wouldn't lose his head. The law could handle George Baker. He'd murdered a lawman and surely the law would show no mercy to the killer of one of its own.

"So what happened, exactly?" Gladden asked Dave.

"There were two of them," Dave began. "Joe was at the depot meeting his daughter and granddaughter when the two Baker boys came up and picked a fight. Shot him right there in front of the woman and little girl. Cold-blooded murder."

"No provocation at all?" Gladden asked.

"None in the least."

"No provocation?" George spit on the floor. "There was plenty o' provocation."

"What did Joe Morton ever do to you?" Dave growled, his fists tightening.

"He destroyed our property, that's what he done! Demolished what belonged to us." George's eyes flamed. "Then he showed up to arrest us for what he done!"

"What did he destroy?" Gladden looked at George, but the man neither met his eye nor replied.

Dave suddenly understood. "It was *your* still he busted up the other day, wasn't it? You two've been runnin' moonshine and Joe busted up your still!"

George scowled at the floor.

"I should've figured that out sooner," Dave said. "You reek of the stuff." His hand clenched into a fist. "You two got mad at Joe for bustin' your still, got hopped up on corn liquor, and set out to kill him!" He was just about to slam the fist into George's midsection when Gladden cleared his throat.

"We didn't set out to kill nobody," George argued. "He was there with a warrant and he was just too chicken to serve it. Besides, he fired first. Ralph was just tryin' to keep him from killin' me. And I didn't shoot nobody."

"Boy, a word to the wise from someone who knows the law." Gladden paused, waiting for George to look up. "I think you'd better keep your lip buttoned 'cause everything you say is digging you a deeper grave."

"Let's lock him up," Dave said. "I need to help hunt for the other one."

Gladden unlocked the cuffs, then accompanied Jed and Dave as they dragged George down the street to the jail.

A tall, blond man leaned against the side of the building. Dave paused a few steps from the door, trying to remember the face. At last he realized it was Earnest Hollingsworth, a man who had worked at the mines before marrying and moving to Kentucky.

"Earnie, what're you doin' here?" Dave asked.

"How do, Dave?" The man tipped his hat. "George, Jed. Squire Gladden, I need to talk with you and Dave."

Dave scowled. "You can see we've got our hands full."

"This is important," Earnie insisted. "I saw what happened."

"You did?" Gladden approached Earnie.

"Yeah, and Terry's been tellin' it all wrong."

Dave knew the "Terry" Earnie referred to was Harvey Terry, the depot agent.

"How's that?" Gladden asked as Dave opened the door and maneuvered George into the jail.

"George didn't shoot nobody," Earnie insisted. "It was Ralph who shot Mr. Morton. Terry's goin' around town tellin' everybody that they were both shooting, but Terry wasn't close enough to see. He'd ducked inside the depot."

"You can tell us all about it after we get George inside where it's safe," Dave said. "I only just kept a mob from stringin' him up all ready."

Jed and Dave ushered George back toward a cell. "Tell 'em how it was, Earnie!" George yelled. "Tell 'em how Morton drew his gun and Ralph thought he was gonna kill me! It was self-defense. You tell 'em!"

Dave locked George in the cell. Jed stayed behind to act as guard. When Dave returned to Joe's office, he found Gladden sitting at Joe's desk with Earnie seated across from him.

Gladden motioned for Dave to join them. "I told him to hold off until you could hear what he has to say."

Dave pulled over a chair and sat down facing Earnie. Overall, he trusted the man. He'd been a hard worker—a bit full of himself—but a good Christian just the same. He'd never drunk or swore like most of the other miners he'd worked with over the years. Then again, Earnie knew the Baker boys well and might therefore see things differently from other witnesses.

"First, tell us why you're in town," Dave prompted. "I thought you and Flossie moved to Kentucky."

"The mine I'm working at in Kentucky is on strike, so Flossie and I thought we'd make the most of it and bring our little boy home to get to know his grandparents."

Gladden nodded. "So what took you to the depot this morning?" he asked.

Earnie crossed a leg over his knee. "Every day we've been here I've been meeting the train to buy a paper and check the mail, hoping to get word that the miners are going back to work. Today I bought a magazine from a boy and took a seat on a railing next to the railroad track."

Dave knew the one he meant.

"I was waiting for the train," Earnie continued. "It stopped a few feet before reaching me and backed up on the Y. A few minutes later, the conductor came to the crossing and started to yell for Morton. He was with Mr. Terry then."

Gladden jotted down what Earnie had said and then nodded for him to continue.

"I stopped reading to listen. McCurdy said, 'Arrest these two boys.' Everyone stopped walking but the two Baker boys. Again the conductor said, 'Arrest these two boys—they have a gun.' I saw no pistol," Earnie added. "Then George went straight to the sheriff and said, 'Let's see you arrest me,' to which the sheriff asked, 'What for?'"

As Gladden scribbled notes, Dave considered the miner's words carefully.

"Again the conductor said, 'Arrest them, they have a gun.' About then George slapped at the sheriff but missed and went sprawling to the ground. Again the conductor yelled, 'They have a gun.' Morton pulled his pistol from his right pocket and pointed it at George lying in the road."

This was a different version than Dave had been told previously. He leaned forward as Earnie continued.

"At this point the conductor yelled, 'The other boy has the pistol.' Morton then pointed his pistol at Ralph, and within a split second they both fired. I don't know who fired first, but Morton was shooting with one hand and each time he shot he raised the pistol and fired as his hand went down. Ralph's first two shots were with one hand but he gripped the pistol with both hands for the other four."

Gladden held up a hand to ask Earnie to pause while he wrote feverishly. When he'd caught up he looked at Earnie. "Do you know how many shots were fired?

"Both emptied their pistols," Earnie replied. "Morton fired five rounds and Ralph six, and both finished at the same time."

It didn't add up to Dave. "And you stood there through all the shooting?"

Earnie nodded. "The engine had reached the back of the coal cars when the shooting started. Because of the cars passing by, I had to stay put. Otherwise I would've got out of there like everybody else."

Earnie was happy to add his own interpretation of events. "Had McCurdy met the deputy and told him about the boys instead of yelling his head off and attracting everyone's attention, and if Morton hadn't pulled his pistol and pointed at George there in the dirt, it might have been different."

"Hmm...maybe." Gladden rubbed his chin but kept writing.

Earnie grew more insistent. "By law Ralph had every right to protect his brother, even to kill if he had to."

Gladden shook his head. "You're wrong on that score. Never is one justified to shoot a lawman just because he draws his weapon. Ralph should have raised his hands and surrendered, not shot Joe to death."

"That's right," Dave added, relieved at Gladden's response. "It's that kind of disrespect for the law that makes things so wild around here. Why, just last year the Walker county sheriff was shot and killed. This has got to stop."

Earnie frowned and Gladden drew the conversation back to the present. "From what you're saying, Tim McCurdy yelled that Ralph had a gun and George pushed Joe around."

Earnie nodded.

"Then Joe had every right to retrieve his weapon," Gladden explained. "And that doesn't mean Ralph should've shot him full of lead."

"Obviously Ralph shot first," Dave interjected. "If Joe had got off a shot, one of those boys would have a bullet in him. Joe didn't miss."

Earnie rose, indignant. "All I know is George didn't do any shooting. That I did see. You just make sure the law gets my statement. I'll be happy to stand witness."

Gladden rose and extended his hand. "Thanks for coming in, Mr. Hollingsworth."

After Earnie left, Dave looked at Gladden. "What do you think?"

Gladden shrugged. "We'll have to give his statement to the sheriff and see what happens. I'd say the defense attorney will be happy to have his testimony."

Dave shook his head. "They won't use him."

"Why not?"

"Because he's a Mason."

Gladden grimaced. "Ah, that's a shame."

It was common for folks in that part of the country to mistrust anything a Mason had to say. Masons were viewed as secretive and untrustworthy. George had better hope that someone else could confirm his innocence.

Chapter 13: The Tortoise and the Hare

"Sherman, can you tell me a story?" Christeen leaned her sleepy head against her older cousin's chest.

"Mmm…hmm." Sherman pressed the heel of his hand to one eye and rubbed. With the other he looked over to where his aunts and grandmother still sat in the parlor. Aunt Josephine and Grandma had their arms around Mary Ann. They'd been trying to console her ever since the doctor had driven her and Christeen home.

Mary Ann's other two children had fallen asleep on the sofa, but Christeen was still awake on his lap.

"I think I might be able to sleep if you'd tell me a story," the little girl said with a yawn.

Sherman wondered what nightmares the child would have when she did manage to sleep. There was no telling what effects the day's events would have. Sherman hugged Christeen a little tighter and sifted his fingers through her blonde curls.

He cleared his throat. "Grandpa always liked to tell me this one when I was little. He said it made him think of my Pa. They call him 'Plodding Will'."

Christeen nestled closer.

Sherman's voice had broken at the mention of his grandfather. He cleared his throat. "Once upon a time, a tortoise and a hare decided to have a footrace."

Christeen sighed with pleasure. "I like this story."

"The tortoise was slow and plodding and rarely got anywhere on time. The hare could run like the wind. Everyone in town laughed at the tortoise when he decided to race the hare. They all said there was no way he could win. But the tortoise was confident he had a chance."

Sherman shifted the child's weight a little and continued, "They decided to start at the old oak tree and run around the countryside until they reached the foot of the mountain. Then they'd come back to the finish line at the oak tree. When the pistol fired and the race started, the hare took off in a flash while the tortoise plodded along. When the tortoise was still just only a few feet from the starting line, the hare was long gone and out of sight."

Christeen smiled.

"It was a long race," Sherman continued, "and so around lunchtime the hare decided to stop on the side of the road at the foot of the mountain. He nibbled lettuce leaves. Then, he found some carrots. He ate and ate until he'd eaten so much he got very sleepy." Sherman yawned for effect, and it made him realize just how tired he was. "He checked his watch and decided he had plenty of time. 'That dawdling tortoise is not even close yet,' he said. So the hare settled under a weeping willow tree and fell asleep."

Christeen's eyes were still open.

"He slept for hours—so long he didn't notice when the tortoise passed and headed for the old oak tree. When the hare finally woke up, it was dusk. He looked frantically at his watch and then took off in a sprint. As he approached the finish line he saw the tortoise already there, a big blue ribbon tied around his neck and all the townsfolk patting his shell.

"The hare hung his head as the words of the crowd rang in his ears, 'Slow and steady wins the race.'"

Sherman listened to Christeen's soft breathing; she'd fallen asleep at last.

"'Slow and steady wins the race'," he repeated in a whisper.

Sherman looked over at his grandmother. With tears beading along the wrinkles of her face, she looked old and frail. For the first time she actually seemed crippled.

Sherman felt an instant, visceral desire to destroy something. He looked at the china on the coffee table and envisioned slamming it against the wall. He wanted to take his Grandpa's empty chair and throw it through the window, so that he could hear the glass crash and watch it splinter into a thousand pieces. He clenched his fists and the muscles in his arms tightened, yearning for the satisfaction of violent movement.

Realizing he still held Christeen in his arms, Sherman forced himself to relax. He eased Christine onto the sofa and stood.

"I need a breath of fresh air," he muttered and stomped to the door. Outside, he headed for the woodpile. Grandpa's ax was nearby, so Sherman grabbed it and reached for a log. He set it on its end atop a stump and lifted the ax. With all his might, he slammed it into the log.

The air cracked with the noise as Sherman chopped again and again. The log split in pieces, which he picked up and slung aside on the grass. He leaned over for another piece of hard wood and set it atop the stump. Log after log he split, flinging them into a disorganized but steadily growing pile.

Sherman chopped wood until his biceps burned and his back ached. Perspiration dampened his hair and dripped from his sideburns, leaving trails along his red cheeks.

He raked a sleeve across his eyes. "Why?" he asked himself. "Why?" he inquired of the heavens. The stars winked at him through the trees, silent and mocking.

He reached down with both hands, lifting a wedge of wood in each.

"Why?" he growled through clenched teeth and threw one of the logs at the old woodshed. It pounded against the structure, and ricocheted to the ground.

"Why?" Sherman repeated, slamming another against the building. Over and over he picked up logs, threw them, and repeated the same unanswerable question

No matter how many times he assaulted it, the woodshed had no reply.

Sherman inhaled a ragged breath and stared up at glowing orange eyes in the tree. The only wisdom the owl could offer was a solitary hoot, as lost and mournful as Sherman felt himself. He continued to stare heavenward, hoping for an answer, for some kind of understanding.

If God was there at all, He apparently wasn't speaking to Sherman.

Chapter 14: In the Hands of Justice

Esquire Gladden sat behind Joe's desk, reading the file Joe had put together on the Baker boys' still. He lifted his head when he heard voices outside.

"You hear that?" Jed called from his post outside George's cell.

Gladden got up and crossed to the window. Peering out, he saw a crowd gathered. They held carbide lamps, most of their faces still black from a day's work in the mine.

"Bring 'im out. We're ready to serve justice!" a voice called.

Jed stepped into the office and his eyes met Gladden's.

"Watch the prisoner. I'm gonna go try to talk some sense into them," Gladden instructed. He eased the door open just enough to slip out and then shut it behind him.

"You boys run on home." Gladden waved his hands as if shooing off pesky critters. "We've got matters under control here."

"Now, squire, you know that boy's gotta hang for what he done to Mr. Morton." The ringleader stomped up on the sidewalk so his steely eyes could meet Gladden's. "Bring him on out and we'll take care of everything."

"I'm sorry, boys, but I'm holding Baker here until Sheriff Harmon can come get him." Gladden tried to appear calm, but perspiration had started to bead on his brow.

"We don't need the sheriff," the thug insisted. "People saw what that fella done to Mr. Morton. This is cut and dried; that man's gotta die." The ringleader tried to push past, but Esquire Gladden put out a staying hand.

"Lynch 'im!" cried another man.

"Yeah, hang him from the old willow!" shouted another.

Gladden reached inside his vest and pulled out a pistol. "Now, boys, I don't want to have to use this, but I will if I have to. It's my job to see justice done, so you get yourselves on home."

A man stepped forward, intending to enter the jail, but Esquire Gladden pointed his gun at the man's chest. "Don't make me use this. I don't want to hurt anybody while protecting this scoundrel, but I'll do it to make sure the law's observed."

"Come on." The leader put out a hand to block the man who had started to enter. He pushed him back. "Let's go. It ain't worth gettin' ourselves shot over."

The leader turned and put out his arms, pushing the others back. "Let's go see if they caught the other one yet." They all took off down the road toward a cluster of lights in the distance.

Esquire Gladden stepped back inside and shut the door. He leaned his back against it, inhaling and exhaling to quell his anxiety. After a minute or two, he peered out the window to double-check that the men had indeed left. Noting that all was clear, he went into the jail where Jed stood guard.

"Jed, we've gotta get this fella out of here before they string him up," Gladden said.

"I thought Sheriff Harmon was coming for him in the morning."

"He's not safe 'til morning. Those men had murder in their eyes and I don't think I can hold 'em off with my little pistol next time."

"I'll get him ready," Jed agreed.

Esquire Gladden went outside and around the building where he'd parked his Model T. He looked around, hoping no one would hear him start the engine. He gave it one crank, then two, then three before the engine rumbled to a purr. He slid behind the wheel, pulling the car up to the front of the jail. He left it running while he went inside to help Jed get George.

They put the prisoner in the middle of the seat and Jed scrunched in next to him. Jed kept his gun pointed at George while Gladden got behind the wheel and started down the road.

They'd barely started down the mountain before George again pled his case to Gladden. "Earnie told you what really happened, didn't he? You know I'm innocent now, don't ya?"

Gladden didn't respond.

"He told you I didn't shoot that deputy, didn't he?" George continued, flexing his fingers with his wrists tied together.

"I'm not at liberty to discuss any of that with you." Esquire Gladden kept his voice bland.

"That deputy drew his gun and started shooting," George insisted. "You think my brother should've stood there and let him kill us?"

"Save your story for your defense attorney." Gladden leaned forward, keeping a close eye on the road.

"That deputy sheriff brought all this on himself," George repeated.

"Settle down and be quiet," Jed interjected. "Can't you see Squire Gladden's trying to watch the road?"

George wiggled in the seat. "Can't you go any faster? That mob's liable to catch up to us at the rate you're dawdling."

"I wish I could, but there are too many ruts," Gladden said. "We're liable to end up with a flat or slide off the road. Then we would really be in a pickle."

In spite of the esquire's caution, halfway down the mountain the car hit a bump, bounced a few yards, and then wobbled to a stop.

"Blast it!" Gladden exclaimed, pounding his fist on the steering wheel. "We've got a flat."

George cursed.

"Watch him close," Gladden muttered as he opened the door. He got out and slammed it shut.

From the trunk, he retrieved a lamp and a jack. The jack clanked down as Gladden lit the lamp and set it on the ground by the back tire. He carried the spare around, let it drop, and rolled up his sleeves. Just as he'd finished mounting the spare, a truck pulled up. Men poured out of the back and the cab.

Gladden grabbed the tire iron and spun around. He pulled out his pistol and pressed his back to the driver side door, prepared to fend them off with the tire iron in one hand and gun in the other. Jed pointed his rifle out the passenger side window. Within seconds an angry mob surrounded them.

"Give us your prisoner!" a burly man yelled.

The others growled and paced around the car like blue tick hounds that had treed a possum.

"We're taking this prisoner to Sheriff Harmon." Esquire Gladden cocked his pistol and pointed it at the big man in front of him.

The men ignored the weapons and drew closer. Spotting Jed's brother Bill in the crowd, Gladden turned toward the car. "Jed, get your brother to settle these fellas down."

"Bill!" Jed called out and his brother stepped to the passenger window. "Get these men to back off. We've gotta get this prisoner to the sheriff."

"What're you protectin' this murderer for?" Bill retorted. "He deserves to hang."

"And he will. He'll hang and the law'll do it. He killed a deputy sheriff, for Pete's sake. He'll swing and the law'll see to it," Jed responded.

They seemed to be listening to Jed, so Gladden went along with Jed's line of reasoning, "That's right, fellas. There's plenty of witnesses to what this boy did and the law will see he's hanged proper. If you do it yourselves, the Sheriff's liable to drag you in, and you'll be the ones standing trial. And I know none of you want that."

It took some time, but eventually the men listened to Jed and Esquire Gladden. Jed cranked the car engine and he and Gladden got back into the car.

George sat there inhaling and exhaling heavy breaths. Gladden glanced down at George's wrists, where bloody welts had formed. He'd evidently wrestled so much with his handcuffs that he'd worn his wrists raw.

Gladden patted George on the leg. "Calm down, they won't be back."

But the only reply George gave was a horrified expression in his eyes.

Soon they were on their way again. It would be another hour before they pulled into the county jail and delivered George Baker to Sheriff Harmon for safekeeping.

~*~

Dave Williams, the mine manager, joined the posse in search of Ralph Baker. He knew he had to stay with the hunt, not only for the sake of the Morton family, but also because he knew that whoever found Ralph would probably want to hang him too. Dave considered it his duty to see that law and order ruled. After all, it was the Durham Coal and Mining Company's deputy sheriff who had been murdered. Dave and the others had been searching through the mountain forests for hours. With the darkness it became less likely they'd find Ralph.

Dave's thoughts were interrupted by a shout. The group of men took off running toward the shanties. Dave grabbed his rifle and followed the parade of lights until he came to where they had congregated around one of the homes.

"What's going on?" Dave asked one man as he drew closer.

"Mr. Gray found one of them murderers up in his attic," the man said.

Dave worked his way past the group into the cabin. Once inside he saw Ralph, his hands bound behind his back. He had chains fastened to his ankles. Someone shoved him, and he toppled to the ground, falling flat on his face. The men rolled him over and one man kicked him in the stomach.

"You yella-bellied varmint! Kill poor old Joe and then hide in an attic like a scared rat!" The man kicked him again and Ralph doubled over, drawing himself into a fetal position.

Dave tried to get closer to break up the attack, but there were too many people crowding him out. Two men jerked Ralph to his feet and one placed a chain around his neck. He dragged Ralph aside from the others. "Whoever thinks we oughta hang him, step on over here."

The men didn't even think twice. They stomped to the other side of the cabin, where the man stood holding Ralph like a dog on a leash. Only Dave remained on the opposite side of the cabin.

"You boys don't want to do this. Leave it to the law to handle. They'll set things right," Dave reasoned.

"You just don't wanna get your hands dirty, Williams!" a man barked.

"Hey now, don't go besmirchin' Mr. Williams! He's a good man." Another man stepped away from the group to join Dave.

"Believe me, fellas. I'd like to see this boy pay as much or more than any of ya. Joe Morton was a good friend. But the law is the law, and it'll take care of this fella. We don't want to go lowerin' ourselves to his level, do we?"

Several of the miners who knew Dave well, stepped away from the mob and joined him. The two groups stared at each other for a few silent moments until Dave ventured forward and removed the chain from Ralph's neck.

"Let's get this boy to the sheriff. Harmon will see justice is served." Dave took Ralph by the arm and headed back toward the mine with the others close behind him.

Chapter 15: Sitting Up with the Dead

The longer Sherman watched his aunt Mary Ann, the more his stomach twisted into knots thinking about what she had witnessed. He wanted to get up and leave, to be a part of the group bringing the murderers to justice. But one look at his grieving grandmother, and he remembered his uncles' words. It seemed his presence had comforted her somewhat. He hadn't needed any special words. Just being there for her and hugging her had seemed to help her cope.

Mary Ann, on the other hand, didn't seem to be coping as well. She couldn't stop wringing her hands. "Why? Why didn't I watch Christeen better? If I hadn't let her get hurt, Papa wouldn't have come to the station. He wouldn't have been there when those men got off the train."

"It's not your fault." Josephine put her arms around her sister. "None of this is your fault. You've got to stop blaming yourself." Sherman could sympathize with Mary Ann. He would have been blaming himself if he'd been in her shoes. Yet, he certainly didn't blame her for any of it - none of them did.

"It's a nightmare," Mary Ann muttered. "It keeps playing over and over again in my head." She leaned her elbows on her knees and rubbed her temples.

Sherman pulled over a chair and sat facing his grandfather's body, which a neighboring couple had cleaned and brought home a few hours earlier. Now, Grandpa lay on a board atop a layer of ice in the parlor with a veil draped over his corpse. The ice dripped onto the wood floor.

Josephine carried a steaming pot of tea to the coffee table and poured a cup for her mother. She poured one for Mary Ann and another for Sherman. When his aunt handed him the cup she put a gentle hand on his shoulder. Her simple gesture of comfort made his eyes ache with withheld emotion. Sherman clutched the cup tighter, letting it warm his hands.

"Are you sure you won't have a little tea, Gordon?" Josephine offered Mary Ann's husband.

"No, thanks. I'd best be gettin' the little ones on home." Gordon knelt by his wife and put a hand on her hip. "If you wanna stay here with your mother and sister, I'll take the children home."

Mary Ann's gaze shifted from her tea to her husband's face. "Hmmm?"

"I think it might be best if you stayed with your Mama and sister tonight," he said. "No tellin' when your brother's will be back from the search. I can take the children on home so they can get some sleep."

She glanced toward the body. As disconcerting as the custom of sitting up with the dead could be, in some strange way it seemed to give Mary Ann the same comfort it did Sherman. It was as if Grandpa Joe was still with them, sleeping. Sherman half expected him to sit up, push back the veil, and tell them all to stop crying.

Mary Ann's attention did not leave the body, but she answered Gordon with a slight nod. Her gaze shifted to her sleeping children and then toward the window behind them. There was only blackness outside—a dark void broken only by chirping crickets and bullfrog moans. "When did the darkness come?" she muttered. "Have I cried the light away?" She stared blankly out the window. "You reckon the sun will ever shine again?"

Sherman watched Gordon put a hand to Mary Ann's cheek, searching her eyes, and ask if she was going to be all right. Something about the gesture made Sherman think of Edna. He could picture himself being there for her should she ever be suffering. He wanted to protect her, to keep her safe, to make everything right in her world.

Mary Ann didn't reply to her husband. Instead, she put her arms around his neck and held tight. Sherman wished Edna were here with him now, that he could hold her and feel the comfort of her embrace. It would ease his suffering and help dull the pain that stabbed at his heart.

Gordon brushed a strand of dark hair from his wife's eyes and caressed her face. "If you wanna go home, I'll take you. You just tell me what you want to do."

She seemed to be struggling to make up her mind. She glanced at her father's body and then toward her mother and sister. Sherman knew she'd stay. She'd cling to every moment with her father before he disappeared into the obscurity of the grave. They all would.

"I better stay," she whispered and kissed Gordon's cheek. "Thank you for understanding."

Gordon rose to his feet, hugged Josie and Josephine, then crossed to the couch. He lifted Evie in his arms. Mary Ann joined him and gave the little girl a kiss on the cheek. He carried the child to the wagon. Sherman lifted Christeen and carried her while Gordon went back for his namesake. Mary Ann kissed each child's sleeping brow before they were carried outside. She stood at the door, leaning on the frame.

After covering the children with a blanket, Gordon joined Mary Ann at the door and kissed her. He held her for a moment. "I'll come back for you some time tomorrow mornin'. Sleep late. You need it."

Sherman returned to his seat by the body, but Mary Ann remained in the doorway, looking out into the night.

"Someone's comin'," she said a few minutes later.

Sherman turned and saw a pair of headlights jostling up the road. The truck parked beside the house, and Sherman's Uncles Howard and Thea stepped out. Their faces were grimy and their hands black from working in the mines. They slammed the truck doors and trudged toward the house.

Howard hugged Mary Ann as Thea embraced his other sister. At last they stepped past her and fell to their knees before their mother.

Grandma Josie, who sat in a chair near the coffee table, gathered her big sons in her frail arms and buried her head against them.

After several tearful moments, Josie broke the silence. "Did you get a telegram to Will?"

Howard lifted his face. "We couldn't. The telephone and telegraph lines are down. "

"That's odd," Josephine noted. "The weather's been beautiful."

"It is odd. Mr. Terry said they were working just fine before the murder. But by the time Papa was shot and Terry tried to get help, both the telephone and the telegraph lines were down."

Josie's brow furrowed. "Somebody's gotta get word to Will and Nancy!"

Before Sherman could offer to drive back, Thea put a hand on his mother's shoulder. "Don't worry, Mama. One of the deputies said he'd see they get told."

Howard stood and crossed to the washbasin, where he cleaned his hands and forearms. Thea rose, but remained beside their mother.

"So, did you catch them?" Sherman asked.

"They caught the older one straight away—before Howard and I were even out of the mine," Thea related.

"They took him to the jail in Lafayette," Howard said, glancing over his shoulder as he worked his hands and forearms into a soapy lather.

"What about the other one?" Sherman pressed.

"Got him, too." Thea shoved his dirty hands into his pockets, then walked across the room and stood over his father's body.

"Were you there when they found him?" Josephine asked.

"No. They found him in one of the miner's shanties. We reached the group when Mr. Williams was taking him back to the jail. He was pretty beat up."

"Beat up?" Josie asked.

"They tried to hang him—tried to hang the other one too—but Mr. Williams stopped 'em." Howard dried his slender face with a towel and approached his brother. He put his hand to Thea's back as they both stared down at their father's body.

"I wish they'd done it," Thea grumbled. "Just string 'em up and get it over with." He stepped away from Howard for his turn at the washbasin.

"Theophilus!" Josie scolded. "Your papa wouldn't hear of such a thing!"

Thea didn't reply, just poured more water from a bucket into the washbasin.

"I wish they'd done it too." Howard's voice was cold, matter-of-fact as his hazel eyes studied his father's covered form. He turned toward Josie. "We know they killed Papa right there in front of Mary Ann and Christeen. I say hang 'em and get it over with."

Sherman couldn't have agreed more. Why prolong the suffering?

"You two know better than that." Josie looked first at Howard and then at Thea. "Your Papa was a man of the law, and he'd want to see the law take its proper course."

"That may be, Mama, but the sooner those two are brought to justice, the sooner I might be able to forget...what happened." Mary Ann clenched her hands, opening and closing her fingers. "The sooner I might be able to forget his blood covering my hands, and his last words ringing in my ears."

The room fell silent until without warning. Thea pounded his fist on the wall. "I'm with Mary Ann. Justice can't be served fast enough to suit me!"

Every one of them agreed. Even Grandma Josie.

Chapter 16: Establishing Law and Order

Tom Tarvin sat across from Sheriff Harmon in the main office of the Walker County Jail. Harmon rubbed his bearded chin as he filled out paperwork at his desk. Tom tried to read a newspaper, but found himself glancing repeatedly at the clock on the wall. It was ten minutes before midnight—two minutes since the last time he'd looked. Time crawled as he pondered the Baker boys, sleeping it off in a cell deep within the jailhouse.

"What would possess two boys to shoot a deputy sheriff in broad daylight?" Tom wondered aloud.

Harmon didn't lift his head, just peered over his spectacles at Tom. "Obviously, the corn liquor they'd been guzzling wasn't conducive to clear thinking."

"Do you think their still was the one Joe found the other day?"

"Appears so." Harmon continued to peruse Joe's report. "Evidently they keep a stash at home or in another cave. They'd guzzled plenty this afternoon before meeting up with Joe at the depot."

"They had to've been drunk to their gills," Tom replied, "killing poor old Joe with his daughter and granddaughter watching!" He shook his head. It made him sick to think of Joe dying the way he did; he couldn't bear to imagine his family's suffering, especially his daughter and grandchild! Joe Morton had been a good, God-fearing man. He'd had a calmness about him that settled most miscreants. Tom suspected the outcome might have been different if he hadn't been caught so off guard. "If only he'd realized who the Baker boys were, Joe might be alive right now."

"Could be." Sheriff Harmon pulled off his glasses and rubbed the bridge of his nose. "The problem was these boys don't look like your typical troublemakers. If Joe had taken them for moonshiners he'd have been more careful."

Tom nodded. In his experience, moonshiners weren't known to value human life. Most would gun down a man as quick as they'd shoot a pesky gopher. But these boys didn't seem that type.

Tom leaned forward, his elbows on his knees and his head in his hands. He was bone tired and there was plenty of night left. Most men in town were just a few hot words away from forming another lynch mob. Tom and Sheriff Harmon would have to take turns keeping watch.

He closed his eyes for several moments and then opened them. Tom noticed a folder on the desk with Earnest Hollingsworth's name handwritten in the corner. "What's this?" he asked the sheriff.

"Hmmm?" Sheriff Harmon lifted his gaze to where Tom pointed. "One of the things Gladden gave me when he dropped off George Baker."

"Have you read it?"

"Not yet. Still looking over Joe's notes." Harmon flipped a page.

Tom lifted the folder as Sheriff Harmon returned to his reading. He read Esquire Gladden's handwritten dictation of Hollingsworth's account. When he reached the end where Hollingsworth insisted George didn't shoot, Tom raised an eyebrow. The last line made him frown. Gladden identified Hollingsworth as a Mason and noted that, therefore, he might not be usable as a witness.

Tom cleared his throat and the sheriff looked up again.

"What's the matter?"

"You should read this." Tom handed over the folder and watched the sheriff read. Harmon's face remained somber and unreadable. When he finally looked up, Tom asked, "So what do you think?"

"Don't know. We'll have to compare it to other witnesses' testimony and see how it fits."

"Do you think Gladden's right? Will Hollingsworth being a Mason disqualify his testimony?"

"It won't disqualify it, but the defense might be afraid to use it." Sheriff Harmon tapped his pencil on the stack of papers in front of him. "We'll turn it over to the court. They can take it from there."

Before Tom could respond, the sound of a crowd outside removed any thought he might have had. His eyes met Sheriff Harmon's in alarm.

"Sounds like we've got company." Harmon groaned and rose to his feet and reached for the rifle he'd propped in the corner.

Tom checked his pistol, making sure the chamber was loaded. They'd established a plan in case the mob came. It was Tom's job to distract them while Sheriff Harmon and the jail guard slipped out the back with the prisoners.

The voices grew louder and fists pounded on the locked jailhouse door. Harmon nodded at Tom and headed for the cells.

"Hold your horses!" Tom called as if he'd been caught asleep. He went to the window and looked out. There were at least thirty of them. Tom swallowed hard. Glancing over his shoulder he saw Sheriff Harmon and Deputy Acknow take the prisoners from their cells and cuff their hands behind their backs.

There was a door few people knew about that led from the jail to the municipal building next door. Tom knew they'd slip through that and out the next building. From there they'd walk a couple blocks to a waiting car and take the prisoners to Rome for safekeeping. Tom needed to buy them enough time to get to that car.

He yelled out the window. "You fellas go on home. We're takin' care of things."

"We ain't goin' nowhere 'til you bring those two murderers out!"

"Now, now. Settle down," Tom soothed as if talking to children.

"Not until those two are as dead as Joe!"

"The law'll take care of these men. Don't you worry about that." Tom put his hand to the door and felt a jar from the men's pushing. He eased toward the window again and peered out. Four men had walked away. Tom hoped the rest would follow their lead. But after a few minutes the men returned, carrying a tree trunk with the limbs stripped off. They lined up and grabbed on, intent on beating down the double doors to the jailhouse. Rather than let them destroy the building, Tom gripped his pistol, opened the door, and slipped out, closing it firmly behind him.

"You men need to settle down," he said. "We'll see that these boys are brought to justice."

"We'll see to it ourselves!" a man called.

"Those boys gotta hang!" another yelled.

"Hand 'em over and we'll see justice is done tonight!" ordered a man at the rear.

Tom stared from one angry face to another. "Don't you boys respect the law? A lawman's been killed. We, of all people, want to see justice done."

"Then do it tonight!"

"Enough of this!" another yelled and pushed Tom out of the way. In an instant the door flew open and a stream of men poured into the jail. They made their way back to the cells.

"Where are they?" a man yelled. "Where're you hiding 'em?"

Tom stood in the doorway, watching the mob turn over chairs and slam their fists into the cinderblock walls.

One man grabbed Tom by the collar. "Where are they?"

"Gone." Tom slipped his pistol back into its holster, trying to assume a calmness he did not feel.

"I oughta..." The man doubled up his fist.

Tom raised one open hand. "If you hurt me, what makes you any better than those boys that killed Joe?" His eyes locked on the other man's until he released Tom's collar.

"Come on, boys!" the man called, waving the others toward the door. "Let's get outta here."

When the last mobster had left the building, Tom shut and bolted the doors. Ruefully, he raked his hands through his hair and returned to his desk. As bad as that had been, it wasn't the worst he had to face. In the morning he'd be the one to tell Will Morton and his family about Joe. As much as he dreaded the task, he knew it would be better coming from him than from a telegram or unknown officer from Mowbray.

Chapter 17: Laid to Rest

Tuesday, March 21, 1922
Payne's Chapel Methodist Church Cemetery, Walker County, Georgia

Sherman looked across the open grave and saw the moisture brimming in his father's eyes. He tightened his grip on the handle of the oak casket and helped the other Morton men lower it into place.

The minister tugged on his starched collar and cleared his throat. The pages of his Bible rustled as he fumbled for the right passage.

Will put a hand on Sherman's shoulder and guided him toward Nancy and the children. Staring at the ground, Sherman stepped around the casket. For an instant he glanced up to observe tears streaming down his aunts' cheeks.

He lowered his head and studied his boots. A knot tightened in Sherman's throat. It was too much. His heart hammered and anger rose inside him like a candy thermometer stuck in boiling divinity. Sherman gritted his teeth and leaned closer to his father's ear. "Them Bakers better hang for this. That's all I gotta say."

His father tightened his arm around Sherman's shoulder and whispered. "Justice'll take its course. All in God's good time... We have to be patient."

Sherman rolled his eyes. Patient. "Plodding Will" and his lectures on patience. That was his father's philosophy about everything—trudge along, take your time, and trust things will work out in the end. It was the way Will Morton lived, the way he worked, and the way he carried himself. He wouldn't even drive a car; instead, he was content to lumber along with his slowpoke wagon and mules.

"Never in a hurry, are ya, Pa?" Sherman grumbled.

Nancy Morton shot her son a warning glance and nudged her elbow into his side. The minister droned on.

Sherman made little attempt to comprehend the words, which were like annoying bees buzzing in his ears. He glanced at his father. Pa might be content with a tortoise's pace, but Sherman wasn't. Sherman wanted justice when it counted most, now while the pain was fresh. *An eye for an eye and a tooth for a tooth.* Isn't that what they always read from the Bible?

The minister concluded his remarks and asked everyone to join in song. While the others sang, Sherman stood mute, his arms across his chest and his eyes on the closed casket.

Where was Grandpa Joe? In heaven? Or was he here with them now—unseen but watching the mournful scene? Was he happy, or did he miss his family as much as they missed him?

Sherman heard a sob and looked up to see Mary Ann with her handkerchief to her face and her head buried against her husband's shoulder.

As the voices increased in volume, Sherman's gaze shifted to his grandmother. He watched Grandma Josie close her eyes and sway a little. There she was, paralyzed and alone, deprived of her lifelong companion.

Vermin, that's what those Baker boys were. Vermin no better than rats in a cellar begging to be picked off with a rifle. Sherman's stomach twisted in knots. He shoved his clenched fists deep into his pockets and silently vowed never to forget what the Bakers had done. No matter what, he'd do whatever it took to see them pay for killing Grandpa Joe.

~*~

Josie Morton stood at her husband's graveside surrounded by her family and friends. All around her, voices rose in song, but Josie's throat was constricted and her chest ached. She closed her eyes.

Oft I sing for my friends
When death's cold hand I see
When I reach my journey's end
Who will sing one song for me?

Had he been ill, she could have tended him, could have prayed for him, could have exercised her faith in his behalf. Had he been sick, she would have prepared for the inevitable, but the doctor had just given Joe a clean bill of health. Healthy as a horse, the doctor had called him—said he'd live forever.

I wonder (I wonder) who
Will sing (will sing) for me
When I'm called to cross that silent sea
Who will sing for me?

Josie had always expected to go first—especially after her stroke. Joe had stayed by her bedside then, his hands clasped in prayer for her. He had never left her side through the entire ordeal until he was positive she would be all right. Yet here she stood, listening to the voices of her loved ones singing farewell to their father, farewell to their grandfather.

When friends shall gather round
And look down on me
Will they turn and walk away
Or will they sing one song for me?

She opened her eyes to see her husband's faithful friends—Tom Tarvin, Sheriff Lam Harmon, and Dave Williams—their voices lifted in song. Her vision blurred. Each one had visited her, said they would check in on her and make sure she had the things she needed. Thea stood on one side of her and Howard on the other. Granville stood behind her, with his hands on her shoulders. They would see to her needs. She held no fears for her temporal well-being. Joseph had given her strong sons who would see to that.

So I'll sing 'til the end
Contented I will be
Assured that some friends
Will sing one song for me

It was her heart that had splintered. She hurt for Mary Ann—so listless and tearful. She worried about her grandchildren—especially little Christeen, who had witnessed the murder.

She looked across the grave at Sherman. Never had there been a boy as fond of his grandfather; never had there been a young man so like his grandfather as Sherman. Yet, he stood dry-eyed and scowling. He looked as if he were preparing to fight an enemy. Tears swelled in Josie's eyes anew as her heart broke for those who had lost so much without warning.

The song concluded and a prayer was said. Howard reached down, grasped a clod of earth, and handed it to his mother. She stood with her arm extended over the open grave. For several moments she waited, unable to release the dirt—as if doing so meant she must release the man she loved.

Howard put an arm around his mother. "He'll always be with us, Mama," he whispered in her ear. She put her handkerchief to her heart and opened her palm, letting the dirt slip between her fingers onto the oak casket.

She turned into Howard's arms and he held his mother, letting her cry on his shoulder. Her other children gathered around her, taking her into their embrace.

At length, her sons helped her to Howard's Model T. She sat on the passenger side and just as Howard was about to shut the door for her, Dave Williams approached with a box in his hand.

"Mrs. Morton." He bent over, looking into the car where Josie sat. He held out the box. "This was in Joe's office, Ma'am. I believe it's yours."

With trembling hands, she took the package and placed it on her lap. "Thank you, Mr. Williams." Josie extended her gloved hand.

Mr. Williams gave it a gentle squeeze. "I'm so sorry for your loss, Ma'am." His misty eyes met hers. When she nodded he released her hand and Howard shut the door.

While Howard cranked the engine, Josie opened the box. Inside was a beautiful blue hat with a folded note on top.

Happy Birthday, my love.
May it be as blissful as you've
made my life all these years.
Your loving husband,
Joe

She hadn't thought about her birthday yesterday. It had passed in a blur of visits from family and friends, of funeral preparations and mourning. A sob caught in Josie's throat and she dabbed the handkerchief to her eyes. She had forgotten her birthday. Her children had forgotten, but Joe had not. Even from the grave, he'd reached out and confirmed the truth of Howard's words—indeed, Joe would always be with her.

Chapter 18: The Gauntlet

New York City, New York
Monday, April 2, 1922

Gregory Ables entered the corner café on 43rd Street with the current edition of the *New York Times* tucked under his arm. He scanned the dimly lit establishment, looking for the man responsible for his present humiliation. Gregory peered from one round table to the next until he spotted his nemesis in a dark corner, celebrating his latest victory over a steak dinner.

Gregory's eyes narrowed upon Rupert Merewether. Conceit seemed to drip from the man's slicked-back hair. Gregory straightened his suit and marched toward Rupert. He slapped the front page of the *Times* down on the table and put this thumb on the headline: *Jury Finds Trixie Pendleton Innocent of Murder Charges*

"Glad to see you're keeping up with the news." Rupert cocked an eyebrow, but didn't bother to look up. "You're a day late and a dollar short again, aren't you?" Rupert took a bite of his steak.

"How does it feel to set the guilty free?" Gregory eyed his competitor.

With his white shirtsleeves rolled up, Rupert continued to saw on the steak. "Oh, come now." He swallowed and pointed his knife toward the chair across from him. "Have a seat. I'll buy you a steak and we'll discuss the concept of reasonable doubt."

"I'm not hungry," Gregory growled. He glanced left and noticed a young couple staring at them from a neighboring table.

Gregory didn't like making a scene. He sat down and the chair screeched as he pulled it closer to the table. His brown eyes examined the man who had once been his friend. Leaning in, he watched Rupert take a drink. He appeared completely oblivious to the damage he'd done. Was it some kind of act or was his sense of justice that deficient? "What's happened to you, Merewether?" he finally said.

Rupert looked up from his meal, his green eyes taking on a devilish glint. "I've become successful, while you, my friend, have never grasped the power at your fingertips." Rupert wiggled his fingers as if he were plunking the keys of his typewriter.

Gregory shook his head. "We came from the same mailroom, the same reporting floor, yet I've remained dedicated to reporting the truth, while you've taken on some kind of warped quest to twist it beyond recognition."

"Truth!" Rupert spat as if the word were as bitter as lye. "Truth is what we make it." Rupert motioned from Gregory to himself. "We decide. It's our role as the press. Unfortunately, you took that job at the *New York World*. Outside my guiding tutelage you've lost your way." Rupert shook his head in pity.

Gregory held his clenched fist on his knee, willing it to stay put. "And that's the irony of it—Adolph Ochs and his crusade for fair and accurate reporting—no editorials, only the facts." Gregory shook his head. "Ironic isn't it, that you, the king of fact-twisting, are his little pet."

"I'm nobody's pet," Rupert retorted, and then his expression lightened. "And who said I'm not reporting the facts?" He leaned back and drummed his fingertips on the table. "You report what you see, and I report what I see. Facts are in the eye of the beholder. Haven't you learned that yet? How many times have you interviewed five witnesses only to receive five different stories? Each of them swears they're telling the truth—and they *are* from their own perspectives."

Gregory shook his head in disgust. "You know good and well Trixie Pendleton murdered her lover. Yet, you deliberately twisted the facts and made her out to be a poor, pathetic victim so she'd get off scot-free. Why? So you could display the 'power' of your almighty pen? To sell papers for Ochs? To ensure a byline?"

"Whoa now, Greg." Rupert put up his palm to stay Gregory's onslaught of accusations. "All I did was bring certain facts to the forefront—facts the jury felt created reasonable doubt."

"Facts," Gregory scoffed. "Facts twisted to sway public opinion in the direction you wanted it to go!"

"Well, now, that's your opinion, Gregory, isn't it? That's the way *you* see it." Rupert frowned and then the glint returned to his green eyes. "You're just jealous your articles don't have the punch to sell papers."

Gregory's fist clenched anew. "You really think you have this town wrapped around your little finger, don't you?"

Rupert shrugged and pointed to the headline. "I believe we've established that fact, haven't we?"

Gregory shook his head. "You're despicable, you know that? You with your D.A. secretary girlfriend and police detectives who slip you information for a price. It's not your pen that's powerful, it's your connections!"

"A good reporter knows how to make friends. It's part of the job. But it's my ability to sway emotions, to tug at the public heartstrings, that sells papers. It's a gift." Rupert took a bite of his steak and stared at Gregory as if he were still a naïve mailroom boy.

"If we dropped you in the middle of another part of the country, another town where you didn't have connections, you'd never wield the power you do here. You couldn't get the guilty off in another town. You couldn't send the innocent to the gallows like you've done here. New York is the only place on earth you could manipulate people, coerce information, and twist facts for your own sick pleasure."

"Sick pleasure?" Rupert snorted. "You really should save some of this melodrama for your column." He tapped his forefinger to his chin and his eyes lit up. "All right, then, I'll prove it to you." He reached for his briefcase and pulled out a newspaper. He thumbed through it and opened it to middle page. "Here, take a look at this."

Gregory read the article in the *Chattanooga Times,* one of Adolph Ochs' other projects. It was an article about a Georgia deputy sheriff murdered by two young men who had narrowly escaped lynching.

Rupert gave Gregory time to read and when he lifted his gaze, Rupert cleared his throat.

"What about that case? Do you think I could sway the outcome? Do you think I could ride into Georgia and convince the town to free those boys?"

"Not likely," Gregory scoffed.

"Are you willing to put your money where your mouth is?" Rupert reached in his back pocket, opened his wallet, and placed a crisp one hundred dollar bill on the table. "I'll wager you a hundred dollars I can turn the outcome of this case."

"That's easy money." Gregory smiled.

"For me, but I'd bet coming up with a hundred dollars on your paltry salary won't be so easy."

"You're not going to win. You can't do it when you don't have your finger in every pie," Gregory retorted.

"I'll bet you I can keep at least one or both of those boys from hanging."

Gregory's smile widened. This was his chance to nail Rupert for the fraud he was. "All right, I'll take you up on that wager. But you have to prove it was something you wrote that turned the tide."

"Fair enough." The two men shook on the deal. Rupert added, "Pay attention, Gregory, because you're about to learn the power of the press."

Gregory released Rupert's hand and rose. "Enjoy steak while you can. Pretty soon you're going to be eating crow."

"Now that was good, Gregory. You really should use something like that in your column. Maybe you'd get a bigger byline and could afford to pay off this wager when you lose."

Gregory turned his back, and left with Rupert's laughter still ringing in his ears. "That's right, Rupert, laugh," he muttered. "But you don't know Georgia. That laugh will be your last."

~*~

Durham, Walker County, Georgia
Friday, April 13, 1922

Rupert Merewether stepped off the train at the Durham station and approached the commissary. Catching his reflection in the window, he set his suitcase down on the sidewalk. He removed his derby and let it rest atop the luggage. Turning his head this way and that, the reporter combed back his black hair, then replaced his hat. He straightened his tie and buttoned his jacket before lifting his suitcase once more. Upon entering the commissary, a man greeted him with a nod and a wave.

"Anything I can do for you, sir?" the man asked.

Rupert retrieved a card from his vest pocket and handed it to the man. He allowed the man ample time to absorb what was written on the card and then cleared his throat. "I'm doing a piece on the Baker case. I'd like to interview anyone who may have seen what happened."

The man straightened his lapel. "Why, I was right here when it happened. I saw the whole thing."

"You did?" Rupert removed his hat and set it on the counter. He put down his suitcase and retrieved a small pad and pencil from his inside jacket pocket. "May I ask you a few questions?"

"You most certainly can." The man nodded eagerly. "Will this be in the *New York Times*?"

"Yes, my article will appear in the *Times*." Rupert watched the man spruce himself up as if he were a peacock strutting his feathers. *Did he think his picture would be included?* Rupert smiled and asked his name.

"Harvey Terry. I'm the depot agent here. Had quite a scuffle with those two boys the day they came in on the train."

"Is that so?"

"Yes sir." Terry leaned his hands on the counter. "They pulled a gun on Mr. Peterman, who travels through these parts quite regularly. And then they threatened Mr. Tim McCurdy, the conductor, when he tried to stop 'em. Then, once they got here and Mr. McCurdy hollered for me to help him with those two, the older one threatened me as well.

"I see." Rupert nodded and jotted down Terry's story.

"The older one, George, started it. The younger one, Ralph, kind of egged him on, though."

"What happened exactly?" Rupert asked.

"George picked the fight with Joe, then Ralph shot him. George finished him off after he was down."

"He did?" Rupert's eyebrow rose. "George shot Morton after he was on the ground?"

"He sure did." Mr. Terry gave his head a dramatic bob. "Everybody saw it."

"Could you show me exactly where it happened?" Rupert pointed his pencil toward the door.

Terry stepped from behind the counter and motioned for Merewether to follow him. "It was just right over here." He walked out of the commissary toward the corner of the depot and pointed. "Right here. See, you can still see the blood stains."

Rupert noted the rusty-brown splotches and jotted down some notes. "Who else saw it happen?"

"Mary Ann Phillips, the victim's daughter. And then there was Mr. McCurdy, the train conductor and..." Terry scratched his head. "Well, Mary Ann and Mr. McCurdy are your best witnesses besides me."

"Anyone else?" Rupert prodded. "You looked like you were about to say someone else."

Terry shook his head negatively. "There's just that Hollingsworth boy, but he had his nose in a magazine and didn't see things the way they really happened."

"He didn't?" Rupert could feel the excitement growing within him. This is what he needed—someone who told the story differently than the others.

"No, he keeps sayin' only Ralph shot," Terry explained.

Pay dirt. Rupert had hit pay dirt. He squelched his inner excitement and asked as calmly as he could, "What's his first name?"

"Earnie—, Earnie Hollingsworth. He's just in town visiting his parents." Terry's hand slapped the air as if it were all a waste of time. "And, like I say, he had his nose in that magazine and wasn't paying close attention. I wouldn't fool with him."

"All right," Rupert nodded, pretending he had no intention of interviewing Hollingsworth. "Where can I find McCurdy and Mrs. Phillips?"

"McCurdy's right over yonder." Terry pointed toward a conductor standing near the outside train. "And Mary Ann Phillips lives in Hinkle."

Rupert spent the better part of the day interviewing people and tracking down Earnest Hollingsworth. Sure enough, the young man had a completely different story to tell. According to Earnie, George had no gun and didn't fire a shot.

As Rupert walked down the road from the Hollingsworth farm, he jotted down Earnie's final words: *Deputy Morton shot at George first. Ralph only shot to keep Deputy Morton from killing his brother.*

Rupert marveled at the way stories came together. He knew from experience that each witness to an event filtered it through his or her own perspective. His job was to find the most sensational one, wrap it up in heart-stirring words, and convey it as the truth.

Chapter 19: Grieving in One's Own Way

Mowbray Mountain, Daisy, Tennessee
Friday, April 14, 1922

Sherman jabbed his pick into the earth again and again. "'Rejoice O ye nations, with his people for he will avenge the blood of his servants, and will render vengeance to his adversaries and be merciful unto his land, and to his people.'" Sherman repeated the verse from Deuteronomy 32:43 over and over, committing it to memory. With renewed strength he struck the earth, dislodging more coal.

"Slow down a mite, will ya, Sherman?" His partner Chester Owens patted Sherman's shoulder.

Sherman lurched away and shrugged off Chester's hand. "Speed it up," he demanded instead.

"What's your all-fired hurry?" Chester grumbled and leaned on his shovel. Sherman could tell where he was staring because the lamp affixed to Chester's hat spotlighted the pile of coal Sherman had made. It was Chester's job to shovel it into the conveyance box, but he took his sweet time with the task.

Sherman didn't miss a beat with the stroke of his pick. "We get paid by the tonnage, Chester. You know that as well as I do."

Chester shrugged. "So?"

Sherman's head jerked toward Chester. "What do you mean 'So?' The faster we get this job done, the more money we make."

"I don't see your point." Chester stooped a little to keep his head from hitting the cavern ceiling and leaned on his shovel handle.

What an imbecile! Sherman glared at Chester, then raked more coal into the ever-growing pile.

"The way I see it," Chester continued. "This coal ain't goin' nowhere, so if we take our time and bring out a decent average of tonnage per day, we keep our spot, and we keep it longer. If we dig it out at the bat out o' hell pace you've set, we're gonna end up injurin' ourselves or work ourselves out of a job."

"There ain't much chance o' you injurin' yourself, not unless you fall asleep leanin' on that handle and bump your noggin on a rock."

"Watch your mouth, boy."

"I wouldn't have to say anything if you'd just quit your yakking and get that coal loaded," Sherman barked and drove his pick into the coal.

Chester pounded his finger on Sherman's shoulder. "You better watch your mouth, boy. I've been workin' at this mine since you were runnin' around in short pants. I think I know best about pacin' myself."

Sherman slung his pick to the earth and swatted Chester's hand from his shoulder. "Leave me alone and do your job."

In the next instant, Chester released his shovel and punched Sherman in the face. Sherman staggered a little and then tore into Chester. He slammed one fist into the man's nose and the other into his stomach. "I said get to work, you lazy slug."

Chester doubled over coughing and blood poured from his nose. Lights danced on the cavern walls as workmen came running. Sherman stood over Chester, prepared to hit him again if necessary. Within seconds two men had grabbed his arms and held him fast.

"What's goin' on here?" the foreman demanded.

"All he does is yak—doesn't lift a finger, just yak, yak, yak." Sherman kicked a chunk of coal toward Chester.

The foreman put a hand on Chester's back. "Sit down. Let's see how bad you're hurt."

Chester complied, and the foreman pulled out a handkerchief and held it to Chester's bloody nose.

"What's goin' on here, Chester?" the foreman asked.

"This stupid boy is reckless and I was just tryin' to talk some sense into him before he gets us both killed. That's when he just hauled off and punched me." Chester looked up at Sherman.

Sherman clenched his fists and struggled to get free of the hands that held him . "You're not only lazy, but you're a liar to boot!" Sherman directed his next words to the foreman. "Just look at the coal I've dug while he's been leanin' on his shovel, grumblin' about how we need to slow down and make the job last longer."

The foreman faced Sherman. "All right, settle down, boy. We'll split you two up tomorrow. For now, you go clean yourself up, Chester. And Sherman, go home."

"I can't go home," Sherman countered. "I just dug all this coal and if it's not loaded, I don't get paid."

"You should've thought about that before you started pickin' fights," the foreman countered.

Sherman pointed at Chester. "I didn't pick a fight—he did!"

"I said, go home, Sherman," the foreman repeated.

"I ain't goin' until this coal is loaded. I don't care if I have to do it myself!" Sherman tossed aside his pick and reached for a shovel. Without waiting for permission, he set to work putting the coal on the conveyer.

"Suit yourself, but whatever you load, the pay gets split with Chester." The foreman walked past him without another word.

Sherman balled up his fist and turned toward his boss. To his surprise he found himself face-to-face with his father. Someone must have told him. The disappointment on his father's face was enough to make Sherman abandon his desire for revenge. He whipped around and jabbed his shovel into the coal and scooped it up on the conveyer.

Without a word, Will joined him in the task. They worked in silence for ten minutes. All the curiosity seekers dispersed and the foreman left to supervise other teams.

"What's gotten into you, boy?" Will finally asked.

"I guess I just got sick and tired of bein' the only one carrying his weight," Sherman answered and tossed a shovel full of coal.

"You know better than to pick fights with your elders," Will said. "Your mama and I've taught ya better than that."

Sherman rolled his eyes. "This is different. If he's gonna be my minin' partner and split the money then he's gotta carry his weight. It ain't fair otherwise."

"Life ain't fair, Sherman. You oughta know that by now."

"It'll be fair if I make it fair."

"You can't make everything fair. It just don't work that way." Will's eyes were sympathetic, but his voice insistent. "I know you're tryin' to drown yourself in work, tryin' to forget what happened to Grandpa, but you've gotta do things in moderation."

Sherman paused and looked at his father. "Moderation, eh?"

"Yeah, moderation and balance." Will nodded.

"I suppose you're right." Sherman tossed a shovel of coal on the conveyer. "What point is there in workin' so hard when life could end at any moment?" Sherman held out his blackened hand, extending his fingers. "Why work toward the impossible when it could all slip through my fingers like sand?"

Will looked taken aback. He shook his head, his eyes holding sympathy for his son's pain. "Now that's not moderation, Sherman. That's just defeat talking. Quittin' ain't the answer, either."

"Good, cause I can't quit. I'd go crazy if I had to quit. Working helps. It takes my mind off things." But Sherman was lying. With nearly every stab of his pick, he vented what seemed to be a never-ending reservoir of pent up anger.

~*~

Sherman stomped into the shanty and tossed his work gloves on the table. His father followed on his heels.

Nancy looked up from her sewing then rushed to her son. Putting a gentle hand to his bruised cheek, she asked, "What happened?"

"Sherman picked a fight with Chester Owens at the end of the shift." Will sighed and tossed his own gloves on the floor by the door.

"He's as lazy as a snake, always sloughing off," Sherman grumbled.

"Sherman, what's gotten into you?" Nancy looked into her son's eyes then went to retrieve a wet rag. She hurried back to him, washing his face.

"He's turned into a regular hothead," Will told his wife. After a few moments, he seemed to regret his words and put a hand on Sherman's shoulder. Sherman jerked away from him, but there was nowhere to go in the shoebox they called a home. His three sisters were huddled in the bedroom playing paper dolls, and his brother lay across the bed that he and Sherman shared.

"This place ain't big enough for a kitten, much less seven people!" Sherman barked, raking his black hand through his hair. "I hate this place."

"Now, Sherman, you know we discussed this. It's only for a little while," Nancy soothed and stepped closer to clean his face again.

Sherman stood still, letting her examine his bruise. "Ouch!" he exclaimed when she cleaned the small cut below his eye. Stepping away from her he stomped toward the washtub. "I can do it myself." Sherman splashed water on his face. He took the lye soap, worked it into a sudsy lather and rubbed it to his cheeks. It stung even worse than what his mother had done.

He swore and splashed more water to his face, rinsing it over the washtub. Before he could remove the lather from his face, he felt his father take hold of his shoulder and spin him around.

Will pointed a finger at him. "None of that in this house, boy, or you'll be washin' your mouth out with that soap!"

Sherman glared at his father.

"Apologize to your Mama," his father ordered.

Sherman released a slow exhale, "Sorry." He sidestepped his father and his boots clomped across the wood floor toward the door.

Will started to go after him, but Nancy put a hand on her husband's shoulder, "Just let him get some air. He's worked solid ever since Grandpa Joe's funeral. He just needs some time to grieve."

His mother's words caused a single tear to form in Sherman's eye. It was the first tear he'd shed, even if it was only an angry one. He swiped it away with his fist and kept marching. His strides long and furious, he made his way to the lake.

"Morton!" he heard someone call from the trees.

Sherman turned toward the voice. It was Earl Farmer, Chester's friend.

Earl started toward him. "I hear you were causin' trouble for Chester today."

Sherman put up his hand. "It's over Earl. I don't want any trouble with you."

"Ah, but you started trouble with me when you started trouble with Chester."

Sherman turned to walk away. "It's all took care of. Chester'll have another partner tomorrow, and he won't have to put up with me anymore."

Earl caught up with Sherman, grabbed his arm and spun him around. "You better watch yourself, Morton, or you'll be sharin' your grandpappy's fate."

Sherman didn't think. He just flew at the man, shoving him to the ground. It didn't matter that Earl was at least thirty pounds heavier than Sherman. He sat on the man's chest and pounded his fist into his face. First his left, then his right, then his left again.

Earl put his hands over his face, shielding himself from Sherman's frenzied blows. But Sherman didn't relent. It was as if a dam of pent-up frustration couldn't be contained any longer and had burst.

At the height of his furious retaliation, Sherman felt something slam against the back of his head and knock him over on his side. He pressed his hand to the spot. The colors of the trees and lake turned gray, then fuzzy, then black.

Chapter 20: Avenge Mine Enemies

When Sherman regained consciousnesses, he tried to figure out where he was and how he'd come to be lying face-down in the grass. He struggled to sit up and pressed his hand to the large knot on the back of his head. It ached and felt tender to the touch.

His head swam and he sat there in the grass, looking around to see if Earl and whoever had hit him were still around.

There was a group of girls picnicking by the lake about five hundred yards away. Their giggles carried on the wind and mingled with the hoots and hollers of the boys swimming in the lake. Happy people. What would it feel like to be happy?

There was no sign of Earl. "Probably left me for dead," Sherman mumbled. He looked at his watch. He'd been unconscious for at least twenty minutes. He sat there with his head in his hands for nearly thirty more, giving himself time to recuperate a little before staggering to his feet.

He thought about going home, but decided he wasn't ready to face his parents again. Before long, Sherman found himself at the blue hole. He stripped off his clothes and dived into the water. He dunked his head beneath the surface over and over, letting it wash over him as if somehow it could cleanse away the confusion and frustration that lingered on his soul like the coal dust clung to his clothes.

At length, he got out of the water and stepped into his pants. He sat down on a rock and put on his socks and boots. Sherman picked up his shirt, and tied the sleeves around his waist. He'd wait until he dried off a little more before replacing it. Besides it was hot, and the shirt was filthy. He wished he'd thought to bring a change of clothes. Then again, Earl and whoever attacked him probably would've stolen them out of meanness.

"I bet it was Chester," he said to himself, realization dawning that wherever Earl went Chester usually followed.

"'Arise, O Lord, in thine anger, lift up thyself because of the rage of mine enemies: and awake for me to the judgment that thou hast commanded.'" He quoted the passage from Psalm 7:6 that he'd memorized. He'd been consoling himself—arming himself, really—with Bible verses that spoke of God's vengeance and wrath upon the wicked. It made him feel good to know God would see justice served on the likes of the Bakers and now Earl and Chester. He rubbed his head and prayed that God would avenge him of his enemies. He felt very David-like—feeling persecuted and hated without cause, telling himself that his only desire was to do his work and be left alone.

When Sherman came back to the path where he could either turn right to ascend the mountain or turn left to descend it, he didn't think about the choice. He turned left and made his way toward the spring. He knelt by the water's edge and scooped up the cool liquid in his hands. He guzzled one handful after another and flopped down, sitting on the creek bank.

His mind went back to another day at this spring, and he wondered how a month could change everything. No, one afternoon had changed everything. Those demon Bakers had murdered his grandfather, and Sherman would not rest until they were cold in their graves.

As he looked down at the babbling creek, his thoughts wandered to the first time he'd come to this place and met Edna. How he wished he could turn back time! He remembered her long hair and her tall, slender figure.

Then he thought of her family. They were different from his. Edna had mentioned in passing that she and her family attended church at Daisy Methodist. He too was a Methodist, but how could her family justify drinking and dancing with gypsies when he'd been taught those things were sinful? How did the Springfields justify their behavior? It didn't make sense. His family was a lot more serious-minded. Was it the carefree, fun-loving nature of the Springfields that made them lax in spiritual matters? Yet, it was her carefree and fun-loving nature that made Edna so attractive.

Sherman would have been back to visit her weeks ago, but then everything changed with his grandfather's murder. It had dominated his thoughts. Still, she'd lingered on his mind; but he felt somehow he must deal with the murder before he could allow himself the pleasure of Edna's company.

Sherman leaned his elbows on his knees and his head in his hands. "I don't know what to do, Lord," he prayed. "I've never felt so alone in all my life. Nobody understands. Not even my parents. How could they just forget what those men did to Grandpa? They've left me alone to plead for justice. Am I the only one who hears Grandpa's blood crying from the grave? The only one who will plead for vengeance on his behalf? Please, Lord, please hear my plea. Only then will Grandpa and I find peace."

Sherman concluded his prayer and sat pondering. At length he heard leaves rustle. He lifted his head and looked up to see Edna staring at him. He hopped to his feet.

"Hello," she said.

"Hello."

She was even more beautiful than he remembered. No words came.

Edna gestured toward the spring. "I just came for water," she said as she stepped past him and put one of her buckets into the spring.

"Here, let me help you," he offered.

"That's all right, I've got it."

"It—it's been a while," Sherman ventured.

"Yes," came her cool reply. "It has."

When she'd filled her first bucket, he took it from her and held it, letting her fill the second one. When she'd finished, he reached out to take that one as well.

"I really don't need help, Mr. Morton." She put out her hand for the container he held.

Instead of relinquishing it he took the other one from her and set the buckets on the ground. Stepping toward her, he said, "I've missed you."

"Have you?" She lifted a doubtful eyebrow.

Something about her aloof demeanor made Sherman bold. He stepped closer and lifted his hands to her cheeks.

Edna trembled for a moment then she stiffened. "Where have you been?"

"Working." Sherman's thumb caressed her lips.

He could feel her weaken at his touch, but she still seemed determined to shield herself from his advances. "Working for a solid month?"

He nodded.

She looked at his bruised cheek. "What happened to your face?"

"Just got into a little tussle at work." His hands slipped to her neck, caressing the softness of her skin.

Edna closed her eyes and leaned into his touch, but after a moment she opened her eyes again. Her expression grew resolute. "It's been a month. I thought you said you'd—"

"My grandfather died," he blurted out before she could remind him of the promise he'd broken to come back and visit weeks earlier.

"Oh!" her eyes widened with surprise and compassion. "I'm so sor—"

Before she could finish the word, Sherman's lips covered hers. He couldn't bear to hear that word again—especially not from her pretty mouth. His hands slipped behind Edna's head, sifting his fingers through her soft locks. He kissed her long and hard, his frustration and confusion pouring from him.

At first, Edna seemed tentative. Her hands went to his chest as if she might push him away. But she didn't. Her palms against his skin made him forget everything. He forgot about his grandpa, forgot about the things he wanted to do to the Baker boys, forgot about the fog he'd carried with him for the last few weeks. His anger started to melt away, replaced with an emotion he had never before experienced. She matched his fervor with her own, slipping her hands around his neck. Breathless, she took his face in her hands, eased her head back, and searched his eyes.

His kisses fell to her neck. She tasted every bit as sweet as she looked. Sherman put his hands to her waist and pulled her tighter. Her hands still on his face, Edna directed his mouth back to her own.

They kissed as if they were the only two people in the world until suddenly Edna seemed to come to her senses. She stepped back from Sherman and put her palms to her pink cheeks. She stared at him, her breathing as labored as his.

"I'm sorry." Sherman shook his head and raked a hand through his dark hair. "I shouldn't have... I don't know what's gotten into me lately." Sherman thought about the anger that constantly simmered beneath the surface of his soul, about the fight with Chester Owens, and about how he had almost lost control with Edna.

"It's all right." She stepped closer.

"I'm really sor—" he started to say, but Edna pressed her finger to his lips.

"Please don't say you're sorry." She gave him a soft kiss and then reached down for her water buckets.

"Here." Sherman took them from her. "I'll walk you home."

She strolled alongside him in silence until they reached the foot of the mountain.

"Do you want to talk about what happened?" she asked when they stepped onto the road on which she lived.

His eyebrows narrowed a little and his heartbeat accelerated. "You mean about what just happened between us?"

"No." She shook her head with a blush. "I mean about your grandfather. Do you want to talk about what happened to him?"

"Maybe later." In a way, he did want to talk with her about what happened. He had the feeling he might be able to talk with her in a way that he couldn't with his family. It might help to talk with someone who wasn't experiencing the same pain he felt. But they were too close to her house now; there were too many siblings to eavesdrop.

They walked to the door, and she invited him inside.

"I'd better not; I'm a mess." He gave Edna the buckets, then untied his shirt from around his waste and put it on.

"You sure?" she asked. "Nobody here will mind."

"Maybe we could go for a walk?" he suggested and held the door open for her.

"All right," she nodded. "I'll be right back."

When Edna went inside, Sherman turned and looked out over the Springfield farm. He saw Edna's father and brothers tilling the fields while the girls planted beans in the furrowed rows. He ducked back under the eave, hoping the shadows would shield him from their view. He liked Edna's little sisters, but he but didn't feel up to conversing with anybody besides the young woman he'd sparked with at the spring.

Sherman smiled at the thought of it. He should probably be ashamed of his behavior, but he frankly wasn't. Moreover, if he had it to do over, he'd do it again. Remembering the sensation of her hands against his chest, he looked down and finished buttoning his shirt.

Edna stepped out on the porch carrying two glasses of lemonade. She handed him one and he thanked her. They stood there sipping their lemonade and enjoying the light breeze. When they'd finished their drink and set the glasses on the porch, Sherman extended his hand.

Edna's hand slipped into his and he felt as if it belonged there. He looked at her and smiled. Having her by his side was the most comforting feeling he'd had in weeks. They strolled in the opposite direction of her family, Edna waiting patiently for him to speak first.

"He was murdered," Sherman began. Edna listened attentively as Sherman related the story of his grandfather's death and the capture of his murderers.

"I just can't believe he's gone," Sherman concluded. He kicked a small rock at his feet.

She squeezed his hand. "You must have been close, working together the way you did."

"We were. He taught me so much." He stopped in the middle of the field and faced her. "The thing is... I can't remember him. I close my eyes and try to remember his face. I try to remember the things we did together, and it's like those memories have been erased." Sherman closed his eyes and with a break in his voice admitted what he'd not verbalized to anyone. "What kind of person forgets his own grandfather?"

He felt Edna's hand on his cheek and opened his eyes to see her green eyes misted in compassion. "You'll remember." Her voice was soft and sincere. "When it matters most, you'll remember."

Sherman put his arms around Edna and pulled her into his embrace. She nestled her head against his shoulder and held him tight. It felt good to have her in his arms. It gave him courage to speak of the other thing that had been weighing on his mind.

"The trial's next Thursday," he said when he released her at last.

"Are you going?"

Sherman shrugged. "I might… I just don't know if I can sit in the same room with those men and not wring their necks. I'm so mad I can hardly see straight."

"I think you should go," she said.

"Why's that?"

"It might help if you watch them come to justice—might help you move on and let go."

Sherman took her hands in his. He started to say he didn't think he'd ever be able to let it go until the Bakers hanged from the rafters of the Walker County Jail. Instead he simply said, "Maybe you're right."

"Oh, I'm always right." She gave him a teasing wink.

"I'll have to remember that."

"Yes, please do."

When she laughed softly, Sherman smiled for the first time in weeks.

He looked toward the sun lowering in the sky. He hadn't brought his rifle and dared not climb the mountain after dark without it. As much as he hated to leave, he knew he must.

"It's getting dark. You need to get home," she said before he could.

They turned and strolled back to the house. He accompanied her to the door, and Edna leaned her back against the doorframe, looking into his eyes. Sherman put his palm to her cheek. "I have to work late tomorrow and extra hours next week if I intend to go to the trial on Thursday, but I promise I'll come back and see you next Friday or Saturday."

She gave him an understanding nod.

"I'll miss you." He stepped closer to her, taking her face in his hands.

"You, too," she said just before his lips lowered to hers. This time he kissed her the way he should've kissed her the first time—not the kiss of a tortured soul, but the affection of a man falling in love with a woman.

Chapter 21: Building a Case

Walker County Courthouse, Lafayette, Walker County, Georgia
Thursday, April 20, 1922

Rupert took a seat on the long oak bench toward the middle of the stuffy courtroom. He wanted to be where he could see reactions from the family and the defendants. The wooden planks creaked beneath the weight of the crowd, who milled around talking and looking for places to sit. The large windows on either side of the judge's bench were open, but that did little to relieve the heat.

Rupert pulled out his notepad and pencil. Today was about reconnaissance. A less experienced reporter would have tried to launch a media campaign to save the Bakers before the trial ever began. There simply wasn't enough time to do it justice. Rupert's lips curled into a smug smile. If he was going to win the wager with Gregory, things needed to go south for the Bakers today. He needed this case to look like the big bad state of Georgia against two pitiful boys. And from everything he'd heard about town, Rupert wouldn't be disappointed.

He adjusted his derby on his knee and loosened his tie. He'd be glad when he had his research done and he could get out of this tropical climate and back to New York.

He studied the defense attorneys, Stephen Chambers and Everett Glenn, as they conferred with one another. Young Ralph Baker nervously adjusted his tie. At the opposing table sat the representatives for the state, Solicitor Ed Taylor and Attorney James E. Rosser. Rosser glared at him. Rupert had spent all of three minutes with the prosecuting attorney, but already Rosser hated him. Then again, that's what Rupert wanted. Hate he could twist; indifference was useless to him.

After the usual opening preliminaries and statements, it was time for Rosser to call one of his pivotal witnesses. "The state calls Mrs. Mary Ann Phillips."

Rupert watched Mary Ann rise from her seat. The floor creaked with each step she took toward the witness box. She placed her trembling hand on the Bible and swore to tell the truth, the whole truth, and nothing but the truth. Her brothers and family leaned over in their seats, resting their elbows on their legs as if they could somehow lend support to the woman by leaning toward her.

The prosecution had already established motive. The Baker boys were moonshiners and Joseph Morton had destroyed their still.

Mary Ann patted the beads of perspiration from her pale brow with her handkerchief. She was nervous, that was for sure. Then again, everyone in the courtroom was perspiring from the moist heat. Large fans spun overhead in the ornate recessed ceiling, but they did little to alleviate the stickiness or the odor.

Mr. Rosser rose to his feet and approached Mary Ann. He folded his handkerchief into a neat square and ran it along his brow. "State your full name for the court, please." He straightened the lapels on his black suit.

"Mary Ann Morton Craig Phillips," she answered with a quiver to her voice.

"And what is your relationship to the victim, Deputy Sheriff Joseph Morton?" the District Attorney asked, putting a hand in his pants pocket.

"I'm his daughter." Mary Ann glanced toward Ralph Baker and then down at her hands in her lap. Rupert had to strain to hear her because the acoustics were so bad in the courtroom. He glanced at Ralph Baker. The defendant didn't seem any more interested in looking at Mary Ann Phillips than she did at him. George Baker, who sat near his brother, also looked down at his lap.

"Mrs. Phillips, where were you on the afternoon of March 18, 1922—the afternoon your father died."

"I... I was at the Durham Depot, in Walker County," Mary Ann answered.

"Mrs. Phillips," the judge interjected, "I'm sorry, but we need to ask you to speak a little louder so the jury can hear you clearly."

Mary Ann looked like a scared rabbit. "Yes, yes sir." Again she glanced at the Baker brothers then down again.

"And why were you at the Durham Depot?" Mr. Rosser continued.

"I'd ridden the train up with my daughter to have the doctor look at her arm. I got off the train and Papa... my father met us there." Mary Ann laced her fingers together and rested them on her lap.

"How old is your daughter?"

"She's four years old."

The District Attorney paced in front of Mary Ann. "So you got off the train and met your father at the depot. Then what happened?"

"Father and I were talking near the corner of the depot at Durham when Ralph and George Baker came up to us. George shook hands with my father and asked, 'Is this Mr. Morton?'"

"And what did your father say?"

Mary Ann's hands fumbled nervously with each other. "He said, 'Yes,' and asked who they were."

"And did George Baker tell him who he was?" Mr. Rosser asked.

"No." She shook her head.

"Did George or Ralph Baker say anything in response?"

"Yes, sir. George Baker said, 'You have a warrant for us, have you?' And then he said..." Mary Ann paused and, with hesitation, continued quoting George. "'Damn you, serve it if you think you can.'"

She stopped her account and stared at George with an expression of loathing and fear in her dark eyes. George stared at his shoes.

The prosecutor gestured for her to continue. "Then what happened? Please tell us exactly what happened in your own words."

"He still had Papa by the hand, and hit him in the face. Papa pushed him off. Then Ralph Baker was standing with a gun behind Papa. He drew it and shot my father. Papa shook his head. When George Baker straightened up, he came out with his gun, and they were both firing at Papa at the same time." Mary Ann closed her eyes and swallowed hard before continuing. "After Papa was shot, he reached for his gun, pulled it out, and fired at them."

Rupert cocked an eyebrow and continued to jot down Mary Ann's testimony as fast as he could. He watched her eyes. He'd learned to read people over the years, and he'd wager the woman was telling the truth. She really believed what she was saying. That was the odd thing about perspectives—each person tells a different story, yet each of them is telling the truth as they perceive it. It was Rupert's job to select the perspective that best suited his needs.

Mary Ann began to choke up, and Mr. Rosser waited for her to dab a handkerchief to her eyes. "What happened next?" he prompted.

Mary Ann seemed to rein in her emotions and then continued, "After Ralph Baker got to the corner, he turned around and shot back at Papa." Tears trickled down Mary Ann's cheeks. "I grabbed Papa in my arms and helped him into the depot. I set him down and tended to him the best I could. But..." Mary Ann closed her eyes and sniffed back tears. "It was no use. Within a couple minutes he was gone."

Mr. Rosser paused, letting Mary Ann pull herself back together. Finally he said, "Did your father say anything to you? Anything to offer an explanation for his relationship to the defendants?"

Mary Ann shook her head. "When I ran to him, I said, 'Oh, Papa, they have killed you,' and he said, 'They've got me.' That's all he ever spoke." Mary Ann wiped her eyes again.

The District Attorney rested his hand on the stand. "When did you first see the Baker boys with a weapon?"

Mary Ann cleared her throat. "I first saw the pistol on the train. And when George shook hands with my father, I stepped back and saw Ralph behind him with it in his hand." Mary Ann's voice broke. "When Papa pushed George back, just as Ralph got back far enough out of the way, Ralph shot Papa."

"I know this is difficult, Mrs. Phillips, but if I might ask you a few more questions..." Mr. Rosser patted Mary Ann's hand where it gripped the stand in front of her.

Mary Ann nodded.

"Where did the bullets strike your father?"

Mary Ann swallowed and closed her eyes. "The first shot struck him in the chin in front." She opened her eyes and put her hand to her own chin.

"Did your father have his gun drawn at the time?" the District Attorney interjected.

"No, not at that time."

"Where were his hands?" the prosecutor asked.

"They were near his pockets. Papa didn't get his pistol until after Ralph had shot him."

"How many wounds did you see?" The District Attorney directed Mary Ann back to his original question.

"He had three wounds. I saw them all—one in the chin and two in the neck." She pointed to her own chin and neck as she spoke. "He died from these wounds about two minutes after they were inflicted."

"Mrs. Phillips, you said your father had a weapon. Please clarify for the court where he kept that weapon," the District Attorney instructed.

"He had his pistol in a scabbard down on his hip there." Mary Ann put her hand on her hip.

"How many shots did each person fire—your father, George and Ralph?" asked the prosecutor.

"I don't know how many shots my father fired. George was shooting, too. My father was shooting at both Ralph and George."

"Who fired first?" asked the District Attorney.

"My impression is Ralph was the one who shot first," Mary Ann said.

"And where was each man standing there on the corner of the depot?"

Mary Ann thought for a moment. "George and Ralph were about two steps apart. They were stepping around during the firing, and my father was stepping also, all moving about. Ralph didn't seem to be dodging. He had his gun this way." Mary Ann held her hand up, as if she were pointing a pistol at the prosecutor.

"Did Ralph Baker say anything during this time?" The District Attorney folded his arms across his chest.

"He said..." She paused before continuing, "'Damn you, I am not scared of you.'"

"Did Ralph say this before or after shots were fired?"

"He had already shot Papa, and Papa had the pistol and was shooting at him at the time."

"Thank you, Mrs. Phillips, that will be all." The District Attorney tapped his palm to the stand and returned to his seat.

The people in the courtroom rustled in their seats, whispering softly to one another. The defender, Stephen Chambers, conferred with his associate, Everett Glenn, for a few moments. Rupert took this opportunity to observe the reactions of each of the players in the courtroom. The Morton men leaned forward in their seats, nodding their encouragement to their sister. Father Baker leaned his head in his hands while his wife gripped a handkerchief, opening and closing her chubby fingers around it—as if she could squeeze hope from the cloth by doing so.

Rupert's attention shifted toward the defendant. Ralph Baker fidgeted with his tie, then bit his fingernail and spit to the side. Ralph's lawyer gave him a slight shake of the head, and Ralph slipped his hands under his legs. Evidently, Stephen Chambers had coached the boy on not looking nervous. He hadn't coached him well enough.

Mr. Chambers approached Mary Ann. After greeting her, he asked his first question. "So... when Ralph and George Baker approached your father initially and George struck your father, were Ralph and George moving at the time?"

"I don't think Ralph moved right then. My father pushed George back, and George fell down to his knees."

"Had a shot been fired up to the time George fell down?" the defense attorney inquired.

"No. No shot had been fired up to that time. George had risen before my father shot. Ralph fired after my father pushed George down."

"And were you on the sidewalk or on the road when the Bakers approached you? Where were you standing exactly?" Mr. Chambers asked.

"My father and I were standing right at the road. There was a little ditch between us and the road. When George hit my father, Papa pushed him back with his hand. Then George staggered into the ditch and fell to his knees on account of the ditch. When he got up, he had the gun."

"So your father pushed George back before a shot was ever fired? Is that correct?"

"Yes sir."

"That was quite a flurry of bullets. How did you keep from being shot?"

"I took my daughter into the commissary," she said.

"At what point did you take her into the commissary, Mrs. Phillips?" Mr. Chambers asked.

"Uh, I'm not sure... it happened so fast."

"I understand... it must be almost a blur for you now," he said sympathetically.

Mary Ann nodded and blew her nose into a handkerchief.

"Can you at least remember whether you stepped into the commissary before or after the shots fired?"

Mary Ann looked as if she were straining to remember. "I started backing away with my daughter when they first started talking to Papa. I had to get Christeen to safety. So by the time I saw the defendant with the weapon, I was nearly to the commissary door, I believe."

"And how far would you say the commissary door is from where the shooting took place?"

Mary Ann shrugged. "About three or four yards, I'd guess."

Mr. Chambers turned his back to Mary Ann, walked toward the jury and looked at them as if Mary Ann's answer held significance. "How old was your father, Mrs. Phillips?"

"He was sixty-six years old," Mary Ann replied, her eyes narrowing as she watched the back of the attorney's head.

He spun back around facing her. "How large was your father relative to George and Ralph Baker?"

"My father was larger than George. George is smaller than the defendant Ralph. Ralph is two or three inches taller than George I'd guess."

"Thank you, Mrs. Phillips. The defense has no further questions." The defense attorney returned to his seat.

That's the best you've got? Rupert thought with scorn. He shook his head. *These boys don't stand a chance.*

"The witness may step down," the judge instructed. Mary Ann went back to sit with her family. Rupert watched one of Mary Ann's brothers put an arm around her shoulder.

The judge called a ten-minute recess, and Rupert rose to his feet. He watched the Mortons stand. They stepped away from the wooden benches, leaving Deputy Morton's widow with one of her daughters sitting by themselves. The others gathered in a circle toward the front of the courtroom.

Rupert went straight for them. They were a lanky lot, tall and thin with high foreheads.

Rupert cleared his throat and extended his hand. "Good afternoon. I'm Mr. Rupert Mereweather with the *New York Times*." None of them offered their hands in return. They stared at him without a word. Rupert's attention shifted to Mary Ann and he addressed her. "I was wondering if I might have a word with you for a moment."

Her brothers closed around her like sheepdogs protecting a lamb from a predator.

"What do you wanna talk to her about?" the oldest one asked, putting his arm around his sister.

"I'd like to know how you feel, Mrs. Phillips, knowing your testimony could send a child to the gallows." Rupert's gaze held Mary Ann's. Her face grew ashen.

As if on cue, the men stepped in front of their sister, forming a barrier between her and Rupert.

Every last one of them looked as if they would like to tear off his head and spit in the hole. It was just the reaction Rupert hoped for. The youngest one came forward and took Rupert by the collar.

"Sherman... Now, son, remember where you are." Will Morton put a hand on Sherman's shoulder.

"Yes, Sherman, remember where you are." Rupert repeated with mock gentility. Sherman responded by pulling on Rupert's collar until he had to stand on his tiptoes to keep from choking.

Sherman gritted his teeth and his face drew within inches of Rupert's. "If that fella goes to the gallows, it won't be my Aunt Mary Ann who sent him there. It'll be his own actions that brought him to it."

Rupert did not flinch. He knew the boy wouldn't kill him in the courtroom, and he wanted a scene—something to cause a stir and make the Mortons appear out for blood. "So you've already sentenced the boy yourself? I suppose you were among the mob that tried to lynch him without trial?"

Sherman ignored the last remark and addressed the first. "It'll be God who sentences Ralph Baker... justice for an innocent man's blood on his hands." Sherman released Rupert's collar and then straightened it for him. "You can print that in your paper."

In unison, the Mortons turned their backs on Rupert. Encompassing their sister in a protective crowd, they ushered her back to her seat.

Chapter 22: A Speedy Trial

"So, Sheriff Harmon." The District Attorney faced the jury. "It is your testimony that the bullets found in Joseph Morton's body were of two different calibers."

"Yes, sir," Sheriff Harmon nodded.

"Would you agree the presence of two different types of bullets indicates two separate weapons?"

"Yes, sir, that would be a logical conclusion."

Rupert watched George Baker's expression. George stared down at his twiddling thumbs.

James Rosser cleared his throat. "Sheriff, when you took in the prisoners, what did you find on their persons?"

"The usual items you might find—a wallet, a set of keys, pocket knife, tobacco..."

"What about pistols?" James Rosser asked.

"Ralph Baker had a pistol on him. George did not."

Mr. Rosser held up a pistol, "Is this the pistol that was found on Ralph Baker."

"Yes, sir, it is," the Sheriff nodded.

"The state would like to submit this pistol as Exhibit B." The judge nodded and Rosser continued. "Did you find anything unusual on George Baker?"

The Sheriff replied. "I found a set of fuses."

George closed his eyes and rubbed the back of his neck.

Mr. Rosser returned to his desk and held up the fuses. "Are these the fuses you found on George Baker?"

"Yes, sir."

"The state would like to submit these fuses as Exhibit C. We'll call another witness to explain their use." Mr. Rosser set the fuses on a table and thanked Sheriff Harmon for his testimony.

Stephen Chambers rose to his feet, straightened his suit, and approached the sheriff for cross-examination. "Sheriff Harmon, is it possible one person fired two weapons, thus causing both types of bullets to be found in the victim's body?"

George looked up and his eyes riveted on the lawman.

"It's possible." Sheriff Harmon shrugged. "Unlikely, but possible."

George smiled and released a heavy breath. Ralph, on the other hand, closed his eyes and grew rather pale.

"Thank you. No further questions." Chambers returned to his seat.

Mr. James Rosser stood up. "The state calls Mr. Franklin Peterman."

Rupert listened as Mr. Peterman testified he was a passenger on the train with George and Ralph Baker on their way to Durham. George had a pistol, and tried to force him to drink whisky by sticking the weapon against Peterman's stomach. Ralph was present, but made no effort to stop George from poking the gun at Mr. Peterman.

After Mr. Peterman stepped down, the state called Mr. Timothy McCurdy, the train conductor. Rupert remembered interviewing the man and thought his account rather useless to the state—especially when it came to the shooting itself.

Mr. Rosser went to the exhibit table and lifted the set of fuses. "Mr. McCurdy do you recognize these fuses?"

"Yes sir."

Mr. Rosser looked at the jury as he spoke. "In your expert opinion as a train conductor, what do these fuses belong to?"

"They belong to the train that goes from Chickamauga to Durham and back," the conductor replied.

"And what exactly do they control?"

Rupert watched George fidget again. Evidently, he didn't like the subject of the fuses.

"They control the signals and lights on the train. If the engineer needs to signal ahead for help—if there's a problem or something—they can use those lights to do it."

"And will those signals work without the fuses."

"No, sir, they will not." Mr. McCurdy shook his head.

"So, if for instance, the train were being robbed, would these signals be used?" Mr. Rosser held them up for the jury to see.

"Yes, sir, we have a specific signal we use for such situations of distress."

"And did the engineer attempt to use them on the day of the murder?" Mr. Rosser continued to face the jury.

"Yes, sir, but the signals wouldn't work," Mr. McCurdy answered.

"And why not?"

The conductor pointed to the fuses in James Rosser's hand. "Because those fuses were in George Baker's pocket instead of where they were supposed to be."

The people in the courtroom broke into a low murmur and the judge rapped his gavel on the bench.

"Thank you Mr. McCurdy. No further questions." James Rosser sauntered back to his chair.

Mr. Chambers stood and tapped his pencil on his hand. "Mr. McCurdy, did you see either of the Bakers with a gun?"

"Yes, sir, I saw Ralph with a pistol when he was about 125 yards from Joe. He had it sorter under his coat."

"Did you see the defendant approach Deputy Morton?" Mr. Chambers asked.

"I don't know. The first I noticed was his brother either slapped at Mr. Morton or hit at him. I saw the shot. I saw Ralph and Mr. Morton shooting."

"Did you see the very first shot? Do you know who shot first?" Mr. Chambers asked for clarification.

"I did not see the first shot, nor know who shot first."

"What was the first thing you saw?" Chambers inquired.

Mr. McCurdy ran his hand along his mustache in a downward motion. "The first I noticed was George either slapping at Mr. Morton or hitting at him. I saw Ralph and Mr. Morton shooting."

"And where was George while Ralph and Mr. Morton were shooting at each other?" the defense attorney asked.

"George's back was to me. I seen him all the time, but could not tell what he was doing. Ralph was shooting at Mr. Morton and Mr. Morton had his pistol out when I first saw them. Mr. Morton was shooting both at Ralph and at George, going from one to the other, that way." Mr. McCurdy pointed his finger to his left then right as if he were mimicking Joe with his pistol. "I can't say whether he shot first after I looked or not."

"What made you look in their direction?"

"I was attracted by the sound of the shot, and Mr. Morton had his pistol sorter this way." Mr. McCurdy held his hand out as if he were holding a weapon aimed at the floor.

"Do you know how many shots were fired?" Stephen Chambers asked.

"I don't know exactly; it was done in quick succession, as fast as you could bat your eye." Mr. McCurdy snapped his fingers several times. "Sounded like a bag o' fire crackers lit and popped off one right after another."

"So, Mr. McCurdy, is it your testimony that while you did not see the first shot fired, you saw the remaining shots from your position on the train?"

"Yes, sir." Mr. McCurdy nodded.

"And in all of that shooting, you only saw Mr. Morton and Ralph firing weapons, but did not see George fire a shot?"

"Yes, sir, that's correct," Mr. McCurdy replied.

"Thank you, sir. No further questions." Mr. Chambers took his seat.

Ralph gnawed on his fingernail and Rupert wondered that the boy had anything left to bite. Rupert couldn't say he blamed the poor kid for being unwilling to sit on his hands. His attorney seemed to be presenting a better case for his brother than for him.

"The state calls Mr. Harvey Terry." Mr. Rosser's voice echoed through the chamber.

Mr. Harvey Terry, who worked for the Durham Mine and Coal Company, offered his familiar account of the afternoon's events. "I was about 30 yards from where the men were when the shooting began. I saw it begin. Ralph shot first at Mr. Morton, who had just shoved George out of the way. At the time Ralph began shooting I did not see Mr. Morton's pistol."

Mr. Terry bent over, reaching down toward his thigh. "He leaned over like this, and came up and pulled it and began shooting aimlessly." Mr. Terry pointed in various directions as if he were shooting a gun randomly.

"So how did it start, exactly?" the prosecutor asked.

"As the boys walked toward Mr. Morton, I saw George walk up to him and stand for a moment and then begin knocking at Mr. Morton, or slapping at him. Mr. Morton was kinder wardin' off the licks, and he kept that up for some little bit. Mr. Morton kept shoving him out of the way, and my attention was called to Ralph because I knew he had a gun. When I looked at him he was standing with his gun behind him like that." Mr. Terry demonstrated how Ralph held his gun behind Joe's back.

"Directly, Mr. Morton shoved George out of the way, and it seemed he dropped on one knee and got up and got back further. Ralph leaned over like that and shot Mr. Morton." Mr. Terry acted as if he were reaching around someone and shooting at their face. "And then Mr. Morton went down like this." Mr. Terry bent over as if he were reaching for a gun on his thigh. "And then Mr. Morton came up and began shooting. Ralph fired very rapidly several times."

"When did you first see Ralph had a gun?" Mr. Rosser asked.

"I first saw Ralph's pistol when the boys got off the caboose. He had it under his jumper-jacket, in his hand, with the barrel protruding under the coat. I watched him as he went toward Mr. Morton. He did not have the pistol in his hand then. He put his gun in his pocket after he had the trouble with Mr. McCurdy and myself."

"I see." the prosecutor rubbed his chin. "So did you call for help?"

"Immediately after this shooting I made an effort to communicate over my telegraph wires to Chickamauga. They were grounded, making it impossible for me to send a message. I'd used them not an hour earlier. They were all right at the time, but not when we needed 'em to call for help."

"And where is the telephone located?"

"The telephone wires are in the commissary, in the Durham Coal and Iron Company's store or office. It was also out of commission when I tried to use it to call for help. The weather was all right. No storm or anything like that."

"Thank you, Mr. Terry." The district attorney sat down and allowed the defense to cross examine.

"Mr. Terry," Mr. Chambers began, "is it true that you saw Ralph fire his weapon after Mr. Morton pushed his brother in the ditch?"

"Yes, sir." Mr. Terry nodded.

"But did you ever see George fire?" Mr. Chambers asked.

"Well, uh, I couldn't really see him too clearly from where I was standing." Mr. Terry looked down at his hands.

Rupert noted how Terry was not as willing to talk about George shooting now that he was under oath. When he thought he'd get press coverage, he acted like he knew a lot more. Typical.

"Thank you. No further questions." Mr. Chambers returned to his seat.

When the judge told the state to call its next witness, Mr. Rosser rose to his feet. "Your honor, the state rests."

The people in the courtroom rumbled, and the judge pounded his gavel on the desk a couple times. "Come to order, the court will come to order."

The noise ceased and the judge instructed the defense attorney to call his first witness.

"The defense calls Mr. Ralph Baker."

Again, a flurry of chatter erupted, louder than the previous time. The judge struck his gavel to the desk four times and the bailiff called the courtroom to order.

The noise died down and Ralph Baker rose to his feet. He wore a navy suit, and appeared a respectable young man with his neatly cropped hair and youthful face—but Rupert knew it was standard practice to clean up a defendant before his day in court.

Ralph placed his hand on the Bible and promised to tell the truth, the whole truth and nothing but the truth. The defense attorney approached the witness box. "Mr. Baker, please tell the jury in your own words what happened on the afternoon of Saturday, March 18th, at the Durham depot."

Ralph sat up straight, a confident expression on his face as he addressed the twelve men. "Well, gentlemen of the jury, I started up to visit my sister, and George and his wife started up to visit his wife's people. George got a hold of this whisky and got crazy on it, and I took it away from him and also the pistol. I thought I could control myself better than George could, and control him also. Him and Mr. Morton got into it some way; he was in front of me going on, and Mr. Morton and him got into it, and Mr. Morton shoved him down backwards and shot at him, got his pistol from his right side and shot at him."

In response, the courtroom erupted again. Some people rose to their feet, shouting that Ralph was a liar and shaking their angry fists in the air. The ruckus didn't subside until the judge threatened to clear the courtroom if there was another outburst. When the courtroom finally fell silent, the defense attorney addressed his client, "Continue with your account, Mr. Baker. Please tell the gentlemen of the jury why you fired your weapon."

"Well, like I said, Mr. Morton got his pistol from his right side and shot at George, and the reason I shot—I shot to protect my brother's life. I didn't have anything against Mr. Morton. I'm so sorry it happened."

"Is there anything else you wish to add?" his attorney asked.

Ralph shrugged, "That's all I recollect just now."

After Mr. Chambers returned to his seat, Mr. Rosser stood and approached the witness.

"Mr. Baker, is it true you and your brother intended to rob the train?"

"No, sir," Ralph shook his head and rubbed his neck.

"Why did your brother have the fuses to the train in his pocket when he was taken into custody?"

"I don't know," Ralph shrugged.

"Isn't it true you intended to rob the train but your brother became so inebriated that he ruined your plans?"

Ralph put his finger in his collar and stretched it. "No sir."

"Mr. Baker did you board the train to Durham with the intent to retaliate against Mr. Morton for destroying your moonshine still?"

Ralph gave his head a vigorous shake. "No, we didn't even know he'd be there."

What was the attorney thinking, putting this boy on the stand? Rupert watched the jury to discern their reactions to the brash move. Several of them stared at the boy with cocked eyebrows. A few others were shaking their heads negatively. Putting him on the stand was foolish and only proved that his attorney had put together a shoddy case.

"No more questions." James Rosser shook his head as if he pitied the boy and returned to his seat.

"Mr. Chambers, please call your next witness," the judge said.

Mr. Chambers halfway stood. "No more witnesses, your honor. The defense rests." As he plopped back down, the jurors looked at each other as if they expected something more.

The judge pounded his gavel. "We'll take a fifteen-minute recess, followed by closing arguments.

Chapter 23: The Verdict

Attorney Stephen Chambers began his remarks in an impassioned plea. "Gentlemen of the jury, this is a case that calls for mercy, not malice. The sad story you have heard told today is a series of unfortunate events that led to the accidental death of a respected citizen of our community." Mr. Chambers slowly paced from one side of the jury to the other, meeting the eyes of each juror as he spoke.

"It was a sunny afternoon on March eighteenth when two young men, Ralph and George Baker set out on the train to visit family members atop Lookout Mountain. They held no malice in their hearts, no objectives for crime, only a visit to see loved ones. George, who admittedly has a weakness for liquor, carried with him a bottle of whiskey. With the rash of contaminated liquor we've seen on the mountain, it's highly probable that the whiskey was what made him act irrationally."

Mr. Chambers gestured toward George. "Even now, he cannot clearly remember his actions on the date in question. As witness testimony indicates, George and Ralph Baker made no attempt to rob the train. George simply tried to share a drink with a traveling salesman. The fact that Mr. Peterman did not want the drink does not make George and Ralph train robbers or murderers."

"Upon leaving the train and encountering Mr. Morton, there seems to be a case of mistaken identity. In his irrational state induced by poisoned liquor, George Baker hallucinated that Deputy Morton held a warrant for his arrest. Unable to process Mr. Morton's rebuttal, he slapped at Mr. Morton, who retaliated by pushing George away.

Because Mr. Morton was a larger man, he easily shoved George down in the ditch, where he lost his balance and fell."

"When George pulled himself out of the ditch, Mr. Morton evidently thought George had a gun, but he did not. Ralph knew his brother had no weapon because he had already taken George's gun from him on the train. You will notice that the only eyewitness the state provided that claimed George had a gun after disembarking the train was the victim's daughter, Mary Ann Phillips, who by her own admittance was so distraught that even now the memory of the event is somewhat blurred. Could it be that from her inconvenient vantage point inside the commissary that she only thought George had a gun?"

Rupert watched the Mortons lean over and whisper in each other's ears and shake their heads.

"When Ralph saw the Deputy firing at his unarmed brother, he shot Mr. Morton in his defense. Of course, Mr. Morton retaliated by firing at Ralph and a series of shots ensued, at which time Mr. Morton sustained his fatal wounds. The reason there were two calibers of bullets in Mr. Morton's body was because in the chaos that ensued, Ralph used bullets from both guns—his and the one he had taken from George on the train." Mr. Chambers stepped back and faced the jury.

"There is no doubt that Mr. Morton was a credit to his office, but his death was an accident." Stephen Chambers shook his head as he continued, "A strange twist of fate caused by an unfortunate series of events and the foibles of youth." He pounded his fist on his palm. "It is your duty, gentlemen of the jury, to have mercy on this boy, Ralph Baker, whose only crime was in trying to protect his brother's life."

Mr. Chambers put a dramatic hand to his own chest. "Had it been my brother who was being fired upon, I'd venture to say I, too, would have done everything in my power to preserve his life." His eyes scanned the jury. "And I think if you are honest with yourselves, you know you would do the very same thing yourselves."

Mr. Chambers looked each juror in the eye and returned to his seat.

James Rosser rose to his feet and approached the jury. "Gentlemen of the jury, the defense has tried to convince you that Deputy Sheriff Joseph Morton's death was rooted in a misunderstanding and the foibles of youth—that Ralph Baker simply misunderstood that he couldn't gun down an officer of the law in broad daylight in a public place. While, as Mr. Chambers puts it, Joseph Morton was 'a respected citizen of our community,' he was much more than that. He was an officer of the law—a deputy sheriff no less— —on duty at the Durham Depot. It doesn't matter who fired first or who thought who had a weapon; Joseph Morton was an officer of the law and was therefore owed respect as a legal representative of this county.

"By his own admission, Ralph Baker repeatedly shot and murdered Deputy Sheriff Joseph Morton. Several eyewitnesses have confirmed that he asked him whether he 'had enough' or 'wanted some more.'" James Rosser shook his index finger. "This blatant disrespect for the law must cease and it must cease today."

"As you know, over the last eighteen months several of our law officers in this county, including a sheriff, have been murdered in a savage manner. If we allow this chronic disrespect for the law to continue, none of us will be safe in our beds or on the streets. It must be stopped, and you can stop it today by returning a guilty verdict."

"The burden of proof is upon the state to illustrate beyond reasonable doubt that the defendant has committed murder. In the preceding hours you have heard testimony from several credible witnesses: Sheriff Lam Harmon; Mr. Harvey Terry, who runs the commissary in Durham; and Mr. Timothy McCurdy, a well-respected train conductor. You've also listened to eyewitness testimony from the victim's daughter."

Mr. Rosser paced to the other side of the jury. "You have seen exhibits A - the knife taken from George Baker. This same knife the state contends was used to cut the telephone and telegraph wires so that word could not be relayed regarding their attempt to rob the train. You have seen Exhibit C, the fuses found on George Baker's person when he was captured. These fuses, the conductor testified, were used to signal for help in case of an emergency such as a train robbery."

"You've heard testimony from Mr. Peterman that George Baker held him at gunpoint aboard the train to Durham. In his inebriated state, George Baker botched the train robbery, at which point Mr. McCurdy escorted George and Ralph Baker to the back of the train, where they were held until they could disembark at Durham."

Mr. Rosser walked toward the other end of the jury. "You've heard Mrs. Mary Ann Phillips, the daughter of the victim, relate her account. You've listened to her describe the horrific moments when Ralph and George Baker gunned down her father right before her eyes while her small child was forced to watch. You've listened to her explain how her father died in her arms some two minutes later. You've heard at least three witnesses testify that Ralph Baker asked Mr. Morton if it was hot enough for him yet and whether he would like some more."

"The state has presented beyond reasonable doubt that Ralph Baker, with the assistance of his brother George, not only attempted to rob the train to Durham, but also gunned down an officer of the law, Deputy Sheriff Joseph Morton, in cold blood."

Mr. Rosser tapped his clenched fist on the railing that separated him from the jury, "Gentlemen of the jury, it is your duty, your sacred duty, to see that the guilty are punished for their crimes against an innocent officer of the law."

Rupert watched the Mortons nod their heads in agreement with James Rosser's remarks. In contrast, tears streamed down Mrs. Baker's cheeks. She blew her nose into her wrinkled handkerchief. Her husband, who had his arm around her shoulder, pulled her toward him and kissed her forehead.

~*~

Within an hour of the closing arguments, the jurors returned to the courtroom. Rupert wiped his brow with his handkerchief and made his way back to his seat along with the others. The bailiff brought the court to order. Mrs. Baker held her handkerchief to her face. Her eyes were closed and her hands clasped in prayer. Her mouth moved as if she were praying for a merciful verdict. Ralph's father sat beside her with his arm around her shoulder.

The appointed jurist rose to his feet, addressing the judge, "The jury finds the defendant, Ralph Baker, guilty of murdering Deputy Sheriff Joseph Morton. We recommend the death penalty in this case."

The people in the courtroom broke into applause. Deputy Morton's family embraced each other.

"The court will come to order." The judge rapped his gavel on the bench. "Order in the court," he repeated with another stroke of the gavel. "Ralph Baker is sentenced to death by hanging one year hence for the willful murder of Deputy Sheriff Joseph Morton of Walker County."

"No!" Mrs. Baker's voice shrieked above the uproar. "Please, Lord, not my boy!" she cried. "He's just a child!" she sobbed against her husband's chest. Ralph reached for his parents, who stood behind him. They gathered him in their arms one last time before the officers escorted him away. George Baker stood with his head bowed and tears streaming down his face. His parents embraced him and his mother cried out in grief.

Three hours—jury selection to verdict in three hours! Rupert marveled to himself as he followed the crowd into the stairwell.

Later that day, Rupert watched George receive a similar verdict. The South certainly believed in speedy justice or injustice—depending upon one's point of view.

Chapter 24: Wolves in Sheep's Clothing

Floyd County Jail, Rome, Georgia
Friday, April 21, 1922

Rupert Merewether looked at the sign on the Floyd County jail. He buttoned his suit jacket and opened the door. Once inside, he stepped toward the front desk and waited for the young officer who sat there to notice him. He was too busy searching through a stack of papers to lift his eyes.

After several moments, he ran a hand through his tousled blonde hair and looked up at Rupert. "How may I help you, sir?"

Rupert produced a card from his vest pocket and handed it to the young man. "I am Rupert Merewether. I'm here to interview the Baker boys."

The officer took Rupert's card and stared at it for several moments. "I'll have to see if this is all right with the sheriff." He pointed to three chairs by the entrance. "Have a seat over yonder and I'll see what he says."

Rupert removed his hat and stepped toward the chairs, but did not take a seat. Instead, he stood with impeccable posture, examining the framed newspaper clippings and various certificates hanging on the walls.

After a few moments, the officer returned. He extended Rupert's card toward him. "Sheriff says to bring you on back. You can have fifteen minutes with 'em."

Rupert put the card inside his suit pocket and followed him through a door and down a corridor. The officer fumbled with a ring of keys, unlocked a metal gate and motioned for Rupert to follow him. He walked past several cells where various prisoners were incarcerated.

On his way, the officer grabbed a chair. He scraped it across the wooden floor and plopped it in front of a cell containing the Baker boys. The officer pointed to the chair, "You have fifteen minutes."

"What do you want?" George lay on his cot staring up at the ceiling and rubbed the heels of his hands to his eyes. Ralph stood up and approached the bars, taking Rupert's extended card.

"I'm here to make sure the nation hears your side of the story," Rupert responded.

"He's from the *New York Times*, George!" Ralph whispered, and held the card for George to see.

Slowly, George sat up and reached toward his brother's extended hand. He took the card and, after a momentary examination, his attention turned to Rupert. George's eyes roved over the reporter's suit until his gaze rested on Rupert's face.

"How do we know you're not here to make us look bad?" George countered.

"Son, there's no way to make you boys look any worse than you already do." Rupert's slender fingers encircled one of the bars. "But if you'll let me tell your story, we might be able to get you out of here."

"How could you get us out of here when our lawyers couldn't?" Ralph demanded.

"Because your lawyers are small town—small town with small minds. You need someone who thinks big, big enough to get the entire nation clamoring for your release."

"And you can do that?" George appeared doubtful, but he rose to his feet and stood opposite Rupert.

"I've done it before and there's no reason I can't do it again," Rupert replied.

"Awful sure of yourself, aren't ya?" George observed.

"Simply stating facts." Rupert checked his watch. "If you want my help, we better get started. The clock is ticking."

"What do you need to know?" George asked.

Rupert sat down on the chair and motioned toward George's cot. "Sit down and tell me what happened."

Ralph looked at George. Rupert suspected the lad was debating on whether to relate the lawyer's coached answers or the truth.

"You may as well tell me the truth, boys. Your lawyers have already failed you," Rupert pulled a pad of paper and pencil from his pocket.

"I honestly don't remember much," George shrugged. "I was poisoned on bad liquor."

"George wasn't himself," Ralph interjected. "He picked a fight with Morton and the old man pushed him back. George fell into the ditch. It looked to me like Morton was pulling out his gun and pointing it at George. I was afraid Morton was going to kill him. I had to shoot or George would be dead right now."

"George, did you shoot?" Rupert asked.

"No, I don't remember shootin' anybody." George shook his head. "I reached for my gun to protect myself, but it wasn't there—just my bottle of whiskey. Maybe that's what that woman saw—" George scratched his head as if he were figuring something out for the first time, "—the neck of the bottle or something."

"I'd taken his gun away from him 'cause he kept pointin' it at people on the train," Ralph explained.

"So, how come there were two calibers of bullets in Morton's body?" Rupert asked.

Ralph shrugged. "I used both guns, I guess."

Rupert continued to write on his notepad. "How old were you when this happened, Ralph? I've heard different ages,"

"Fourteen," Ralph answered.

"My, that's incredibly young. I wonder why your lawyers didn't bring that out in the trial?" Rupert crossed one leg over the other.

"Legal age in Georgia's fourteen," George answered for his younger brother.

"Well, that's too young to hang a boy," Rupert observed and his lips curled into a smile. "This is good. We can work with this." He tapped his pencil on his notepad, excited to have another angle to pursue. "Now tell me, is there anyone in your family who isn't quite right?" Rupert tapped his index finger against his temple.

"You mean crazy?" George's eyebrows rose as if he were offended.

Rupert put up a staying hand. "Don't get upset with me now. I'm trying to see what sympathy we can raise. Do you have a crazy aunt or uncle maybe? Someone who wasn't quite right in the head?" Rupert prodded.

"Papa's great aunt Lucy was a bit of a loon." George stroked the bristle on his chin.

"What exactly did she do?" Rupert scooted his chair forward.

"She used to swear people were peekin' in her house at night. And then there was that time after she had a baby that she went off to the creek and tried to drown herself. She was lucky her husband tracked her down and pulled her out of the water." George put his hands on his knees.

Rupert smiled. "Great, this is good." He wrote down, *Insanity runs on Baker side of the family.* "Now what about you two? I know you boys are perfectly sane, but have you had any health problems in your life? Any illnesses or accidents or such?"

"I broke my toe last summer," Ralph offered.

Rupert kept a straight face in spite of his desire to scoff at the stupidity of Ralph's answer. "Anything else?" he prompted.

"I broke my arm when I was fourteen." George patted his left arm.

Rupert shook his head, "Any head injuries or fevers or—"

"Oh!" George exclaimed. "I had meningitis when I was young."

"Any lasting effects from that?" Rupert asked.

"Just a touch of nerve trouble." George rubbed his elbow.

Rupert snapped his finger, "Perfect, that'll work!" He wrote down, *George Baker is of unsound mentality, both by reason of nerve trouble brought on by meningitis, and by inheritance.*

Rupert rose to his feet and flipped his notebook closed and shook it triumphantly. "This'll do it."

"Don't you want to ask us more questions about what happened?" George rose to his feet.

"No, I believe I've got exactly what we need." Rupert put the notebook inside his vest and patted it. He extended his hand to George. "Cheer up, boys. I'll have you out of here." Rupert gave George's hand a firm shake.

George reached through the bars with his other hand and put it on Rupert's shoulder. His steadfast gaze met the reporter's. "Whatever happens, promise us if one of us lives, the other lives. Or if one of us dies, the other dies."

"We want to share the same fate," Ralph added, placing a hand on his brother's shoulder.

"I'll be heading back to New York to stir up some sympathy for both of you," Rupert replied.

"How will sympathy in New York help us here?" George's eyebrows furrowed.

"Oh, trust me. It's going to help. It may take a little time, but it will work." Rupert shook Ralph's hand and added, "It always does."

Chapter 25: Facing Facts

Daisy, Tennessee
Friday, April 21, 1922

Edna tossed a two of spades on the discard pile and rearranged the cards in her hand.

"So what're you all gussied up for tonight, Edna?" Frank asked from across the kitchen table. He slouched in the straight-back chair, lying more on his back than sitting on his rear end.

Edna simply shrugged.

"You're not expectin' that Morton fella to show up tonight, are ya?" Hab stretched his long legs out beside her. He tossed down a card and retrieved one from the pile.

"He said he'd come to call either today or tomorrow," Maude answered for her daughter.

"I hope he don't leave ya hangin' high and dry again," Thad Springfield chimed in. "You moped around here nigh onto a month the last time that fella didn't keep his word."

Edna looked up from her cards. Her father thumbed through his hand with a somber expression. No man was ever good enough for Thad Springfield's daughters. And yet he gave her no options in life other than to marry. "He'll come this time," she insisted. She felt it was true, but a small corner of her mind wasn't swept clean of doubt.

"His grandfather was murdered, ya know." Maude's voice was distorted from the snuff stuffed under her lip. "Makes sense he'd be occupied with other things."

"Murdered, eh?" Thad took his turn and placed a six of hearts on the discard pile. "So was he that deputy sheriff I read about in the *Times*? They just had the trial, didn't they?"

"That's him." Edna stacked her cards together and placed them face down on the table while her mother took her turn. "Killed by moonshiners," Edna added as Frank took a swig from his flask. He looked at her over the top of it and paused with it to his lips. He shrugged, gave Edna an impish grin and replaced the cork. She frowned as he set it on the table in front of him. That was one thing Sherman Morton had going for him. At least she knew he wouldn't disappear for days on end in a drinking binge. He was a moral, upstanding young man. Edna had decided long ago that even though she loved the men in her family, she wouldn't be marrying anyone like them. She wanted something different for her and her children.

"Maybe we should keep the liquor put up when Mr. Morton comes to call," Maude suggested. "It might be a sore spot."

"I don't see why we need to put on airs just 'cause this Morton fella comes to call on Edna." Frank sat up a little, but still slouched.

Maude's eyes gave Frank a stern warning. "We're not puttin' on airs. We're simply displayin' common courtesy." She spit her snuff into the spittoon beside her and spoke more clearly without it under her lip. "You don't drink liquor in front of a man whose grandfather was murdered by moonshiners."

Thad gave his son a nod, and Frank picked up his flask and slipped it into his shirt pocket.

Edna heard the screen door slam and soon Thadda came skipping into the kitchen. She opened a lower cabinet door and started rummaging through it.

"Seems to me if this Morton fella really had his eye on Edna, he wouldn't have waited a month to come see her—no matter what happened to his grandfather." Frank tossed a card on the table.

Edna could feel the moisture stinging her eyes. She lifted her cards and studied them, trying to force Frank's biting words from her mind.

"Oh, he likes her," Thadda insisted with her head inside the cabinet.

"What do you know?" Frank waved his hand as if Thadda couldn't know anything at her age. He knocked Edna's arm, indicating she should take her turn.

Edna was so flustered by everyone's comments that she threw down a card she meant to keep.

"I know plenty," Thadda retorted as she set some of the contents of the cabinet on the floor beside her. "I saw him kissin' her good-bye last week."

"Ooooh!" Hab teased, nudging Edna's arm as he retrieved a card from the deck. "Edna's gettin' some sugar!"

"Ah, probably one of those little peach kisses." Frank's lips drew into a tight pucker as he accentuated the word *peach*. "That's probably all that stiff fella could muster."

"Or was it a plum?" Hab nudged Edna again. "Maybe he ventured a plum?" Edna's face felt like it had baked in the sun all afternoon.

"Oh, it was clearly an alfalfa!" Thadda exaggerated the "l" sounds in the word. "Lots of alfalfas."

"Ooooo, Edna, we didn't think ya had it in ya!" Frank teased, but a yelp immediately followed his remark. He winced and grumbled at his mother, "Ma! Why'd ya go and kick me?" He rubbed his calf.

"Leave your sister alone. Can't you see you're embarrassing her?" Maude waved her hand toward Edna.

Embarrassing her? How about *humiliating* her! Edna felt like crawling under the table. It would be a miracle if Sherman Morton ever wanted to marry into her crass family.

"Sparkin's all well and good, but remember, Edna." Thad waved a card at his daughter and set it on the pile. "A man won't buy the cow if he's gettin' the milk for free."

Edna's eyes widened. What did her father think she'd been doing? Didn't he know her any better than that?

"You might want to rethink your use of the word *man*, Daddy," Frank snickered. "That boy ain't old enough to be buyin' no cows." Hab snickered. Frank yelped again. Maude glared at Frank as he rubbed his shin. She retrieved a card and set another one down.

"How old is he anyway?" Thad asked, looking from Edna to the other members of the family. Edna did not respond and everyone else shrugged.

"He's about Frank's age," Edna answered finally, nodding toward her brother.

"But you don't know for sure?" Thad prodded.

"The subject hasn't come up." Edna's shoulders rose and fell.

Frank tossed a card down. "That's 'cause she's robbin' the cradle and both of 'em know it." Frank pushed his chair back before his mother could kick him again. He and Hab broke into laughter.

"Thadda, what are you rummagin' for over there?" Maude asked her daughter.

Thadda rose to her feet holding two tin cans. "Just a couple targets," she said and skipped out of the kitchen.

"Targets?" Thad looked at his wife with a puzzled look on his face.

Maude shrugged and Edna took her turn. After Hab tossed down a card, a gunshot jolted everyone's attention.

"Targets!" they exclaimed in unison and everyone jumped up from the table, sending their chairs scratching against the hardwood. They tromped across the floor like a herd of cattle, coming to a stop at the doorway.

There in the front yard was Dot holding Sherman's rifle, aimed at two tin cans propped up on a stump. Sherman stood behind her helping her aim, and Thadda stood a few steps behind them. The rifle fired again and Frank and Hab ambled away, back toward the kitchen. Thad and Maude stepped out on the front porch, and Edna stood just inside the house wondering why Sherman was outside having target practice with her little sisters instead of coming inside to see her first.

~*~

It seemed like forever before they were alone. Thadda and Dot begged relentlessly for more target shooting. Was it possible for a ten-year-old to flirt? Edna despised the foolish sense of jealousy that needled her heart.

"How did the trial go?" she asked as they walked hand-in-hand toward the creek. The evening sky was a blaze of red and purple.

"Went well. They convicted 'em both. Sentenced 'em to hang next April."

"Does that make you feel better?" She studied his somber expression.

"It does, but I'll feel even better when they're cold in their graves." His voice was hard and chilled, and his chin stiffened like granite.

Edna looked away from him, letting a few seconds pass before she asked her next question. "Did your aunt have to testify?"

"She did. She was scared to death, but she held herself together. Her testimony led to a conviction for both Ralph and George." Sherman strolled a few more steps.

"That's good." Edna flicked a mosquito from her skirt. "How are you feeling about things now. Any better at all?" she asked, hoping he'd gained some kind of peace from the trial.

He stopped walking and turned to her. "It just feels like a waste—like Grandpa died for nothing."

"And now those two boys will die for nothing," she remarked.

His face flushed crimson and he growled, "Oh, it won't be for nothing! They deserve to die—today, not a year from now. Grandpa didn't get another breath, so why should they?"

His sudden irritation unsettled Edna, and she fumbled for the words to diffuse his reaction. "I didn't mean they don't deserve their punishment." She put her hand to his chest, trying to calm him down. "I only meant their irrational act ruined their lives—and a lot of other people's too. It's all a waste of human life."

He made no reply, just turned and started walking again. Edna accompanied him, noting the red blotches that gradually started to fade from Sherman's face.

After a few minutes, he reached for her hand again. "I'm sorry. I'm just still upset about it all, I guess."

"I understand." Edna gave his hand a little squeeze.

They strolled in silence for a while until Edna decided to change the subject. "Sorry the girls trapped you outside when you got here. You should've come on in the house. Don't feel like you have to entertain them."

"They said you were playin' cards. I didn't want to disturb you." He stiffened and his cheeks grew red again. What had she done to irritate him this time?

"You wouldn't have been disturbing me," she assured him. "You could have joined us or I could've—"

"I don't play cards," he interjected before she could finish her sentence. His jaw tightened and the dimple in his chin disappeared.

"You don't play cards? You mean like you don't dance?" She stood still. He released her hand and turned to face her. "You don't have to be embarrassed. I can teach you how to dance and..."

"I don't want you to teach me." He blurted, then took a deep breath and exhaled. "I mean, even if I knew, I wouldn't do it." Sherman looked toward the sunset and then back at her. He lowered his voice, "It's sinful."

"Sinful? Dancing?" Edna's eyebrows narrowed. She'd never heard of such a thing. Or was he talking about the cards? "We don't gamble for money, if that's what you're thinking."

He shook his head. "It's still wrong—card playin', dancin', and especially drinkin'."

Edna's jaw slackened and her heart thumped. No wonder he'd acted the way he had with her family. Her mind darted back to the evening at the creek with the gypsies and how he'd been so withdrawn. Then realization dawned. This was more than about her family. It was about her!

"So you're saying I'm sinful?" She pressed her palm to her chest.

"No," he shook his head. "I didn't say that."

"Don't go backpedaling now, Mr. Morton. You just said playing cards and dancing is sinful. I play cards and dance, so that makes me sinful."

Sherman looked down at his hands, and twirled a blade of grass between his thumb and forefinger. "I wasn't sayin' anything about you. I'm sayin' I can't do those things . . . I won't do 'em. I know better, so I have to do what I know." He wouldn't look her in the eyes.

Edna felt indignation swelling in her like the creek rising after a summer thunderstorm. It throbbed in her temples and thundered upon the walls of her chest. "So I'm a dumb ol' girl who don't know no better than to sin." She hoped he realized she never used incorrect grammar, and her use of it now would illustrate her point. How self-righteous could he be? She was a good person. She'd been a good girl her whole life—studied hard, behaved herself, prayed, read her Bible—and here he stood saying she was sinful for dancing and playing cards!

"You're the smartest person I know, Edna. You know I didn't mean that." His blue eyes pled with hers.

"How old are you, Sherman?" she blurted.

He swallowed and his jaw flinched. "Eighteen." His nervous gaze darted to one side and back at her. "I'll be eighteen in October."

Edna swallowed hard. Her eyelids closed momentarily and she continued, "Well, while we're clearing the air, I'm twenty-three."

His eyes widened and she nodded, "Yeah, twenty-three." She paused. "Is that a sin, Sherman? Are your parents going to tell you it's a sin for you to see a woman of twenty-three?" Her breathing grew ragged from the tears threatening beneath the surface. "'Cause if that's a sin, I want to know now so I can avoid further humiliation!"

"No," he shook his head. "It's not a sin."

She waited for him to say something further. He didn't. "They aren't going to like it, are they?" she deduced from the look on his silent face.

"No," he shrugged. "Probably not."

"So where does that leave us? My family and I are sinners, and you and your family are evidently ready for sainthood." She tossed her hand in the air as if he might flutter off toward the heavens at any moment. He winced, but she wasn't finished yet. "I'm practically an old maid, and you're not even eighteen." She hated herself for the blunt cruelty of her words. They were crueler to her than to him, but Edna felt compelled to say what she knew would drive Sherman away.

She genuinely cared for him, but she'd rather rip these feelings from her heart now than have it be worse later.

Tears trickled down her cheeks when he didn't reply. Several moments passed before he muttered, "We're not saints."

"But we come from different worlds."

"We could make it work." His eyes met hers, but he didn't look convinced.

"When you really believe that, you let me know." She swiped the tears from her cheek, turned on her heel, and strode back to the house.

Chapter 26: Enlisting Recruits

Downtown Chattanooga, Tennessee
Friday, April 21, 1922

Rupert sat at a desk in the *Chattanooga Times* office. He leaned back in his chair and stretched his hands high. A smile of satisfaction spread across his face. He'd just completed his article and wired it to the office in New York. His work of art would appear in the *New York Times* the next morning. His editor also promised to wire it to other key newspapers around the nation.

"Let the games begin…" Rupert said to himself. Just then he heard argumentative female voices toward the front desk. He stood up and went to investigate the commotion.

Two ladies were bending the desk clerk's ear, and the bald man didn't look happy about it.

"We wanna speak to a reporter. And we'll not leave until we do," the dark-haired lady insisted.

"All the reporters have gone for the day, ma'am. Y'all will need to come back Monday mornin'," he said as he stacked some papers on his desk, preparing to leave.

"You don't understand. They aim to hang a fourteen-year-old boy and somebody's gotta put a stop to it!" The woman stamped her foot on the wood floor and clutched her purse under her arm. "We watched that atrocious trial yesterday and something simply must be done for the poor family."

Her last sentence caught Rupert's attention and he stepped toward them. "Good evening, ladies. I'm a reporter and I would be most happy to help you."

"Oh, good." the redhead sighed and straightened her blue floral hat.

"We're still closin' up for the day," the clerk interjected. "You'll need to do your business another day if ya aim to do it here."

"It's all right." Rupert said. "There's a little café across the street. We can talk over a cup of coffee."

"Thank you, sir!" The redhead gushed and extended her hand toward Rupert. "I'm Abigail Montgomery and this is my sister, Harriet Lock."

Rupert shook the women's hands. "A pleasure to meet you ladies. I'm Rupert Merewether. I'm actually doing a series of articles on the boys you mentioned. You are speaking of the Bakers, are you not?"

"Oh, yes, those poor Baker boys." Harriet Lock continued to vigorously shake Rupert's hand.

"Wait." Abigail put her gloved hand on Rupert's arm. "Aren't you the man the Mortons were ganging up on at the trial yesterday?"

Rupert nodded. "Unfortunately, they discovered I was a reporter and didn't want to answer my questions." He shook his head. "They're very bitter—very angry, I'm afraid."

"Self-righteous." Harriet lifted her nose in the air.

"Uncompassionate and unforgiving." Abigail said the words as if it were incomprehensible that the Mortons wouldn't forgive a boy's mistake.

The clerk walked past them and opened the front door. With an irritated grimace, he pointed outside. When they ignored him, he cleared his throat to gain their attention. "Closing up now."

"Come along, ladies." Rupert ushered the women outside and escorted them across the street to the café.

Once seated, Harriet and Abigail chattered on about their crusade to raise funds for the Bakers. "We're takin' up a collection for the family. Did you know George's wife is being evicted from her home because she can't afford to keep it with her husband in jail?" Harriet shook her head side-to-side.

"And did you know Ralph is merely a boy of fourteen? Why, who would even consider hangin' a child?" Abigail tapped her clenched fist on the table.

"We came here hopin' the press would say something about our efforts to collect money for the family. We need donations if we are to help Lulu Baker save her home." Harriet explained.

"And it costs the family a lot traveling to Rome and back to visit the boys." Abigail added.

Harriet nodded. "If we could work up enough protest, perhaps we could keep them from hangin' that child!"

Rupert sat there giving sympathetic nods and sipping coffee as they spoke. Finally, Abigail concluded by pleading, "Will you help us, Mr. Merewether?"

"I'd be happy to assist you fine ladies," he said.

"Oh good!" Abigail clapped her hands together.

"The good Lord is smilin' on us!" Harriet put her arm around her sister's shoulder and gave it a squeeze.

Rupert grew animated thinking of the possibilities. "First of all, I'm writing an article that will expose this travesty. I just wired it to the *New York Times* and it will be wired to other major newspapers throughout the country."

"*The New York Times*!" Abigail exclaimed with pleasure.

"Do you think that will help?" Harriet seemed less enthusiastic than her sister.

"Oh, believe me, it will help." Rupert nodded with his usual confident air. "I aim to stir up a national outcry to free the Bakers. Before you know it, the whole nation will be clamoring for their release."

"Really? How will you do that?" Harriet asked.

"This is only the first article. I intend to write many more—all of which will be broadcast over the wires to major newspapers around the country. If you ladies are willing to help, we'll contact every boys' organization in the country and get them to write the governor of

Georgia. When they all write him about the disgrace of hanging a child, he'll have to take notice," Rupert explained.

"Oh, that's a wonderful idea! We'd love to help, wouldn't we, Harriet?" Abigail exclaimed.

"Definitely, we'll do anything to help," Harriet agreed. "We have a whole ladies' organization that's behind us in saving these boys."

"Wonderful, that's wonderful. If you ladies will write the boys organizations and mail them a copy of my article, I'll see that it runs in every major newspaper from New York to California. Before you know it, people everywhere will be writing Governor Hardwick insisting the boys be spared."

"I love it!" Abigail exclaimed. "We could write the Boy Scouts and the Big Brother's Movement, and I'm sure we can go to the library and look up some more..."

"I hope we can do it." Harriet rubbed her chin.

"With your help, we can." Rupert looked into their eyes with his slick sincerity. "You ladies are the angels of mercy sent to save these boys. I have no doubt of it." It always paid to pump people up with the saintliness of their efforts. It worked every time.

Abigail and Harriet looked at each other with an air of pride, and Rupert gloated. He had them wrapped around his little finger. His plan was falling into place.

Chapter 27: Second Thoughts

Daisy, Tennessee
Wednesday, May 31, 1922

"How long you gonna mope around here, pinin' after that fella?" Hab shook his head. Edna rubbed her swollen eyes and plopped in a chair at the kitchen table.

"Leave her be, Hab," Maude scolded. "One day a girl'll break your heart, and you'll be a bigger baby about it than Edna ever thought of being."

"She's been mopin' around here all hang-dog for over a month!" Hab retorted.

"You make it sound like I've been a basket case every day," Edna huffed. "I just have my occasional bad day."

"That's right." Maude patted her daughter's hand. "I think she's handled things very well."

Edna met her mother's eyes with gratitude. Maude had been her confidante since she'd broken things off with Sherman. No one else knew the details. They all assumed Sherman had been the one to end the relationship, that he had learned her age and didn't want an "old maid." Edna would have clarified things, but she didn't have the heart to tell her family Sherman thought they were sinners. She knew if she and Sherman ever did patch things up, it would be better if her brothers weren't aware of Sherman's low opinion of them. Only Maude knew the truth.

After breakfast, Edna's siblings dispersed to go about their chores, working in the fields with their father. Edna would join them soon enough, but she lagged behind to help her mother clean the kitchen.

They stood side-by-side doing dishes, Edna washing and Maude drying. Maude put her arm around her daughter's shoulder. "So what's on your mind?" she prompted.

Edna shook her head, "Oh, I'm just realizing what a fool I've been."

"You're no fool." Maude gave her daughter's shoulder a squeeze.

"Yes, I am. I never should have gotten angry with him over his beliefs. After all, it's a free country. We all have a right to believe what we want about what's right or wrong."

"That's true, I s'pose," Maude mused. "But I'm sure it felt personal."

"It did, but he is right about the drinking. I have no doubt that's wrong. I've seen what it's done to the men in this family and the load it places on the women." Besides Frank, Edna's uncles had their own issues with alcohol. Even her father could spend a weekend intoxicated. It never brought about anything good that she could see.

"I agree with you there," Maude said. "But, I don't really see what's wrong with dancin' or playin' cards."

"Still, is it worth giving up a good man for a dance or a card game? Daddy's made it clear that my only option is marriage. He won't let me work and support myself. So that leaves me needing a man." Edna handed a plate to her mother.

"At least you know Sherman won't be sloshed all weekend or go on two-week binges." Maude pointed at a dirty spot on the dish and handed it back to Edna.

"Exactly." Edna took the plate, shoved it under the water, and scrubbed it vigorously. "Think about it. He works hard, he doesn't drink. He'd be a good provider. He's handsome. I am attracted to him. So what if I have to give up dancing and card playing? I'm not that great at either one." Edna chuckled, and her mother smiled.

"Does seem like a small sacrifice to make." Maude shrugged and took the plate from her daughter.

"The question is how do I let him know how I feel?" Edna picked up another plate and plunged it into the sudsy water.

"Maybe he'll come back around," Maude suggested.

"I don't know..." Edna shook her head and handed the dish to her mother. "It's been over a month. I don't think he's coming back."

"He is young. Maybe he needs a little time to grow up. And when he does, he'll come to his senses and see you're worth fighting for." Maude started to dry the dish with the towel and then noted another dirty spot. She slipped it back into the dishwater for Edna to clean it some more.

Edna offered a weak smile and shook her head. "I'm not convinced I'm worth fighting for."

Maude put her arm around her daughter again. "You are." She gave Edna's shoulder a gentle squeeze. "You are."

~*~

"The Baker boys are appealing their case to the Georgia Supreme Court." Will shook his head and sat down at the supper table with his wife and sons. Nancy had already fed the girls and sent them out to play. Their cramped little table forced them to eat in shifts, so Nancy always fed the girls before Sherman and Will returned from the mine.

"How can they do that?" Sherman asked.

"Ah, they say the jury wasn't properly briefed on the issue of manslaughter." Will tossed the Chattanooga paper on the kitchen table.

"But it wasn't manslaughter." Nancy took the paper and began scanning the article.

"I know, but they're straining to find anything that could call for a mistrial," Will answered.

"I read that people are writing to the governor, asking him not to hang the Bakers." Sherman shook his head in frustration.

Will raked his hand through his hair and sighed, "Yeah, a group of people are taking pity on them, taking up a collection for their family, and trying to get the governor to stay their execution. They say they are boys and that they don't deserve to die."

"And Grandpa did deserve to die?" came Sherman's incredulous retort.

"Odd how everyone was so all-fired eager to hang those boys when it first happened and now they're taking pity on them." Nancy swirled her fork in her mashed potatoes.

"Well, the people who wanted to hang 'em that night were men who knew Papa. These people protesting the hanging didn't know him. All they see are two young boys going to hang, and they don't have the stomach for it," Will explained.

"If they knew Grandpa and what a great man he was, they wouldn't have any pity for those boys," Sherman said. The whole conversation was making him lose his appetite, even though he'd been ravenous when he left work. He pushed his plate back and leaned his elbows on the table, resting his head in his hands.

"Eat somethin', Sherman." Nancy moved his plate toward him. "You're withering away."

"It all makes me sick to my stomach," he grumbled into his hands.

"You need to keep up your energy. You work too hard not to eat properly." Nancy put her hand on Sherman's arm.

"Your Mama's right, Sherman, you need to eat somethin'. Especially before Gordon gobbles it all down." Will tousled Gordon's hair.

"Yeah, I'd be happy to take that off your hands." Gordon reached for Sherman's plate. Nancy gave Gordon's hand a little slap. Gordon chuckled, drew back his hand, and lifted a piece of chicken from his plate.

"You haven't been yourself in months." Will studied Sherman. "Are you still that upset about Grandpa?"

Sherman shrugged. "I've had a lot on my mind."

"Whatever happened with that girl you were seein'?" Gordon asked.

Sherman's eyes narrowed at his brother, issuing him a silencing command.

"What girl?" Nancy looked from Sherman to Gordon.

"Some girl down in the valley Sherman was visitin'." Gordon looked to his mother. "You remember last month when he was getting' all gussied up in his suit."

"I thought you were going to a town social or something," Nancy replied.

"It didn't work out," Sherman grumbled and shoved a spoonful of potatoes into his mouth.

"What happened?" Gordon pressed.

Sherman looked up. All eyes were on him. "I don't wanna talk about it." He picked up his chicken, tearing off a chunk with his teeth. He figured if his mouth was full of food they wouldn't expect him to talk.

"She dumped ya, eh?" Gordon teased.

Sherman glared at him, and Nancy tapped Gordon's arm. "Don't be mean to your brother. If he doesn't want to talk about it, he doesn't have to."

After dinner, the girls washed dishes and Sherman stepped outside for a walk. His father caught up with him after a few minutes.

"You've been doing a good job at work, son," Will said, falling into stride with Sherman.

"Thanks," Sherman nodded.

"Your mother says you're savin' up a nice little nest egg."

"Yeah, tryin' to." Sherman shoved his hands in his pockets.

"Got somethin' in mind for that money?" Will asked.

"Why? Do you and Mama need some of it?" Sherman looked at his father, willing to do his part to help the family.

"No, no, no. That's your money. We agreed when we came out here to Mowbray any money you earn is yours. You're a man now and you need to be able to keep what you earn."

"I could help out with food and such." Sherman reached for his wallet.

"No, don't worry about that. You barely eat enough to keep a bird alive anyway," Will chuckled. Sherman put his hands back in his pockets. "I know you said you didn't want to talk about that girl, and you don't have to, but I was wondering if... if maybe you've been thinkin' you don't have enough money to settle down. 'Cause nobody ever has enough money to settle down. You can't let finances keep you from livin'."

Sherman shook his head, "Money's not the problem. We . . . we're just . . . different."

"It's good to have differences in a marriage," Will suggested. "Keeps things balanced."

Sherman shook his head. "Not our differences."

"What kind of differences?" Will's eyes narrowed as he looked at his son.

"Her family—well, they're different from us." Sherman tried to think of the right words. He still held hopes he and Edna might work things out, and he wanted to be careful what impression he gave his father.

"You don't marry a family," Will chuckled.

Sherman smiled and tipped his head to one side. "True enough."

Will put his hand on Sherman's shoulder. "What happened, son?"

Sherman paused, thinking through his answer. "I said some things that hurt her feelings . . . made her think I didn't think she was good enough for me." Sherman stopped and turned toward his father. His voice grew more animated. "But she's beautiful, Papa. I mean, she looks like an angel. And she's smart and funny. If anything, she's too good for me."

"Then tell her that," Will suggested.

"But I messed things up. She told me to leave."

"She told you to leave?"

Sherman thought back on that evening. "Actually, no. She told me to come back when I really believed we could work out our differences."

"And do you believe you can?" Will asked.

"I think we could, if we really worked at it."

Will slapped his son's shoulder. "Well, I know one fella who's the hardest worker around."

Chapter 28: One More Chance

Daisy, Tennessee
Saturday, June 10, 1922

Sherman thought long and hard about his father's words, but the fact remained he was still only seventeen and Edna was a woman of twenty-three. They needed to take some time to get to know each other, and he needed to save more money.

He sat down on his bed and pulled on his boots, then rose to his feet. As he straightened his tie and smoothed down his hair, he realized if his father had known about their age difference he might not have been so supportive. When his parents found out, they wouldn't be happy. None of this was going to be easy—not persuading Edna to forgive him, and not convincing his parents he should marry a woman five years his senior. Then again, there was no point in discussing it until after he turned eighteen.

As he studied his reflection in a small hand mirror, he determined he would go back and apologize to Edna. He'd work to resolve their differences. He knew he had been far too judgmental. The Springfields were good people. They loved each other, and family was important to them. As night and day as their habits were, that's one thing the Mortons and the Springfields held in common: a love for family. Wasn't that more important than how they chose to entertain themselves? After all, wasn't that what Grandma and Grandpa had taught him? Family was everything.

Sherman slipped on his suit jacket and determined he didn't have to take up dancing or card playing to be with Edna. He'd leave it to her to decide what she wanted to do. She was a genuinely good person. She wanted to do the right thing. Edna would see the light eventually. And even if she didn't, that wouldn't make him stop loving her.

He waved good-bye to his mother, retrieved his rifle and lamp, and set off down the mountain.

When he reached the Springfields', he spotted Edna hoeing the garden. Her arms glistened in the sunlight, and she dabbed her handkerchief to her chest and brow. She went back to her hoeing and tossed a weed outside the garden.

Sherman looked down at the handful of wildflowers he'd gathered on his way down the mountain. He hoped they were enough to entice her to listen to him. She probably hated him. He turned his head and looked back toward the mountain. Maybe he should leave now before he got his heart broken even worse.

Then again, he knew if he turned back now, he'd regret it his whole life. With renewed determination, he strode in her direction. Sherman reached within a few feet of Edna before she even noticed him. She glanced up at him and then back toward the ground. Then, as if suddenly registering his presence, she looked at him once more.

She pulled her handkerchief from the pocket of her dress and dabbed it to her neck. "Sherman," she whispered. He set his rifle and lamp on the ground and stepped closer to her.

He'd expected her to be angry with him, but instead she stood there leaning on her hoe, looking as if she'd seen a ghost. Sherman extended the bouquet of flowers toward her. Slowly she reached out and took them, pulling them to her face and inhaling their fragrance.

"I… I came to apologize," he stumbled. When she didn't respond, he continued, "I said some stupid things to you the last time we were together and I hope, I pray, you'll forgive me."

Edna looked down at the flowers.

"You said for me to come back when I really believed we could make it work." He paused, and waited for her to meet his gaze again. She still appeared stunned to find him standing before her.

"And you need to know somethin' about me, Edna. I'm just about the most determined fella you'll ever meet. So if it's a matter of makin' something work, I'm the man for the job." He thumped his thumb to his chest and smiled, the dimple in his chin deepening. A small smile lifted Edna's lips. "So I guess what I'm tryin' to say is that I hope you'll give me another chance."

Edna dabbed a tear from her eye and nodded. "I think I can do that."

Sherman exhaled a sigh of relief. He glanced around at her furrowed row, pulled off his coat and set it on top of his lamp. When he started rolling up his sleeves, she asked what he intended to do.

"I'll help you finish your gardening so we can go for a walk." He loosened his tie.

"Oh, you don't have to do that. You're all dressed up," she protested, waving a hand at his suit.

"I want to help," he insisted and took the garden tool from her.

"But there's only one hoe, anyway."

"Then have a seat and rest."

"I can't sit here and watch you do my work." She put her hands to her hips. As she continued to protest, her father strode toward them.

"Edna, go on inside and clean up for supper." Thad pointed toward the house.

"But, Daddy..." Edna's eyebrows knit.

"Go on. I'd like to have a word with Mr. Morton here." Thad's face was stern and his overbite seemed more pronounced when he stiffened his jaws the way he did.

Edna put a hand on her father's sleeve. "Daddy, please," she whispered.

Sherman leaned on the hoe and watched the exchange. He never dreamed he'd have to answer to Edna's father today. He knew one day he'd have to face the man when he asked for Edna's hand in marriage, but he thought he'd have more time to prepare.

Sherman's heart hammered as Edna's shoulders slumped and she started back to the house. Thad squared his stance, facing Sherman. "We need to talk, boy."

"Yes, sir." Sherman nodded and set the hoe on the ground. Putting his hands in his pockets, he waited for the tall man to continue.

"You've been draggin' Edna's heart around like a June bug on a string."

Sherman lowered his head, "I'm sorry, sir."

"I wanna know why you're back here." Thad folded his arms across his chest.

"I came to ask Edna to forgive me," Sherman explained, looking up into Thad Springfield's face.

"Has she?"

"Yes, sir," Sherman nodded.

"Well, don't go thinkin' I have," Thad retorted.

Sherman's gaze fell to his boots. "Yes, sir. I'm sorry, sir."

"Sayin' sorry's cheap, Morton. Words are free. Actions. It's actions that prove who you really are."

"Yes, sir." Sherman did not lift his gaze.

"I want to know what your intentions are toward my daughter. I'll not watch her go through this misery again." Thad did not move. He stood there, arms folded, and his eyes fixed on Sherman's face.

Sherman decided to reveal his intentions completely. He may as well get it over with and not have to face Mr. Springfield again later. He looked up and matched the man's stance. Folding his own arms against his chest, he announced, "I intend to marry her."

Thad's eyebrows lifted. "Marry her?" His gaze raked over Sherman from head to toe and back again. "Aren't you a bit young for marriage?"

Sherman didn't flinch. "I'll be eighteen in October. I'm workin' hard, savin' money, and I aim to ask Edna to marry me in the spring." He felt it better to put on a confident façade, even if his insides threatened to dump his last meal on the man's boots.

"The spring, eh?" Thad rubbed the whiskers on his chin. "And how do you propose to take care of my daughter?"

"I'm workin' at the coalmine now, but I'm trying to get on at the railroad like my uncle Gordon."

"The railroad?" Thad studied him, his face never yielding from its stone expression.

"Yes, sir, I'd like to be an engineer." Sherman gave a confident nod.

"And you think you can do that?"

"Yes, sir."

"All right. You listen to me, young man," Thad began, and Sherman really did think he might lose his last meal on Mr. Springfield's work boots. "I'm gonna keep a close eye on you and how you treat my daughter. If I so much as see Edna hang her head in disappointment because you haven't shown up when you said you would or because you've said a cross word to her, that'll be the end of it."

"Yes, sir."

"If you can prove you'll keep her happy, then you can marry her in the spring—that is, *if* she wants you."

"Yes, sir. Thank you, sir." Sherman nodded.

Thad pointed toward the house, "Now go on inside. Maude's got dinner ready."

~*~

"He's comin'." Edna straightened her skirt. "Frank, Hab, put away those cards."

"You're out o' your gourd, Edna. I'm winnin'!" Hab slapped a card down on the sofa. He and Frank faced one another with the deck between them.

"Do as she says," Maude insisted. "Shove 'em in the sofa."

Frank put his cards into the cushions and reached for the draw pile. Hab rolled his eyes. "What is this fella? A preacher?"

Edna looked out the door. Sherman was only a few paces away. "Mama, please."

"Just do it," Maude whispered, taking a threatening step toward Hab.

"Good grief!" Hab shoved his cards into the cushions.

Edna went to the doorway. Sherman propped his rifle outside and set down his lamp. She reached for his suit jacket draped over his arm and set it on the arm of the sofa. Sherman took off his hat, nodded at Maude, and then greeted Hab and Frank. They sat there, twiddling their thumbs with mock angelic faces. Edna couldn't help but shake her head and smile at her brothers' antics. They were anything but angels. At least they were trying for her benefit.

"Boys, y'all wash up and come to dinner now." Maude motioned for Frank and Hab to come along. At that moment Thadda and Dot scurried in through the back door and reached the washbasin before Edna's brothers could rise from their seats. Frank and Hab put their hands behind their heads and leaned back, evidently deciding to wait it out.

Sherman looked down at his palms. "I suppose my hands could use a washin' too."

Edna motioned for him to follow her into the kitchen. Thadda's eyes brightened when he entered the room. "Sherman! Did ya bring your rifle with ya?"

He chuckled. "I sure did."

"Oh, boy!" Dot and Thadda exclaimed in unison.

Sherman winked at Edna. Edna put her hands on each girl's shoulder with a chuckle. "Hey now, you two. He came to see me, ya know."

"Ah, but he brought his rifle!" Thadda pleaded. She stepped back so Sherman could wash his hands.

"What do you say, Sherman? Are you up for a little target practice with us girls?" Edna smiled.

He scrubbed his hands and nodded. "Sounds like fun."

"And I'll try not to shoot the outhouse this time," Edna laughed.

"The outhouse?" Thad questioned as he entered the kitchen, rolling up his sleeves to take his turn cleaning up.

Edna chuckled. "Last time Sherman and the girls set up the tin cans for target shooting, the rifle kicked more than I expected, and I shot through the outhouse. Luckily, there wasn't anyone inside."

"I'll say! Remind me to stay out of the outhouse this evenin'!" Frank added as he entered the kitchen.

Everyone settled around the dinner table. Edna helped her mother carry food to the table, then took a seat next to Sherman.

"We've been followin' the trial in the papers," Thad told Sherman. "We were glad to see those Baker boys' appeal was denied."

Sherman nodded. "We were, too."

"But a lot of folks are still up in arms about it, wantin' them to get off," Maude said.

"I don't understand why people are so against seeing justice served." Thad shook his head and put a slice of bread on his plate. "Two fellas come up and kill a lawman in cold blood, and justice is supposed to turn a blind eye?" Thad buttered his bread.

Sherman's shoulder's stiffened and his teeth clenched. He tightened his fist around his fork, "Papa says it's 'cause they didn't know Grandpa, and they just see two young boys fixin' to die. They don't have the stomach for it."

"Well, if they don't have the stomach for it, they shouldn't watch." Thad gave his head an adamant shake and pointed his butter knife this way and that. "We can't have people runnin' wild shootin' people—especially not lawmen—and gettin' away with it."

Even though the conversation was serious and Sherman's attitude about the subject caustic, Edna couldn't help but be happy—happy her father and Sherman were agreeing on something that was important to Sherman. She took a bite of buttered bread and listened to the men discuss the trial.

"The people who don't want them to hang are collecting money for the Baker family," Sherman said.

"I suppose that's all well and good. After all, they are losing their sons, and the older one will have a widow," Edna said, and then wished she hadn't for fear Sherman would be upset.

He glanced at her and continued, "It was kind o' funny when they went up to the Durham mine to start collectin'. Mr. Williams, the coalmine manager, says, 'Sure, you can collect money for the Baker boys. I know just the fella you can start with. You go over yonder and ask that tall, slim fellow named Howard Morton. I'm sure he'll be happy to toss somethin' in the hat.'"

Thad rubbed his belly, threw back his head and laughed. "Bet that got 'em turnin' on their heels to leave."

Sherman smiled and continued, "Yeah, they got the idea pretty quick that the Durham folks knew Grandpa, and wouldn't be too thrilled about people collectin' for the Bakers."

~*~

After an evening of rifle shooting, Edna and Sherman sat on a blanket under the full moon. Sherman leaned back, resting with his hands behind his head and stared up at the stars.

A gentle breeze brushed his face. "Sure is a nice evenin'," he said.

"It is." Edna pulled her skirt over her knees. "Daddy seems to have taken a shine to you."

"I was kinda surprised by that," Sherman admitted. After the initial confrontation in the field, he hadn't expected Mr. Springfield to soften as fast as he did. He'd seemed quite friendly at the dinner table.

"I think Daddy understands you've had a hard time of things lately," Edna said. "What with your grandfather's murder and the trial and all that mess with the Bakers."

"Yeah, he seemed mighty understandin'." Sherman crossed one long leg over the other.

"How *are* you doing with all that?" She leaned on her hand, sitting there studying his expression.

"What do ya mean?" he asked.

"I mean you were so angry about it all. Is it still eatin' at ya as bad as it was or did attending the trial help?" She looked into his eyes.

He hesitated, thinking about how he should reply to her question. "Do you want to know the truth or do you want me to sugarcoat it?" He watched the moonlight reflect in her green eyes.

"The truth, of course," she reached over and sifted her fingers through his hair. The gesture soothed him even though her question evoked strong emotions.

He closed his eyes and sighed. "I'm still mad. I still feel like my grandpa died for nothin'. And I'd still like to be the one to spring that trap the day those boys hang."

Edna crossed her legs and leaned her hands on her knees. For several silent minutes she looked up at the moon while Sherman's eyes never left her. What was she thinking? Did she think him terrible for wanting to spring the trap on the Bakers? Did she expect him to just forgive and forget what had been done to his grandfather? To his entire family?

Finally, he broke the silence. "Do you think I'm awful?"

She looked down at him. "No, I don't think you're awful."

"Well, you're thinkin' somethin'. I can see it in your eyes. You do realize that everythin' you're thinkin' shows in those green eyes of yours?"

Edna frowned. "I worry about you."

"Worry about me? Why?"

"It's eatin' you up, all this hate and need for revenge. You're better than this."

"Better than this?" he muttered, sitting up.

"I mean..." she rushed on, "It's making you miserable. You've got to let it go."

Sherman stood and walked a few paces away from her. How dare she? What did she know about how he felt? She wasn't the one who'd lost her grandfather. It was easy for her to sit there and talk about letting it go. She hadn't had someone she loved ripped from her life, murdered in cold blood.

Edna came to stand behind him and put her hand on his shoulder. "I'm sorry, Sherman. I know you've been through a lot, but do you think your grandfather would be happy knowing hate is drilling through your heart like a worm in an apple?"

The thought of his grandfather and what he would advise right now lowered the heat on Sherman's boiling anger. He closed his eyes and released a long slow sigh.

She continued, "It's only yourself you're hurtin', not the Bakers."

He turned to face her. "You're right. Grandpa wouldn't want me to dwell on his death." He paused, looking into her eyes, and admitted, "But, Edna, I don't know how to let it go. How in the world am I supposed to just let go of somethin' this big?" He shook his head in frustration. "It's—it's too much to ask." Sherman felt moisture brimming in his eyes, and he was grateful for the darkness. Perhaps under the cover of night, Edna wouldn't see his boyish tears.

Edna slipped her arms around his waist and hugged him. With her head against his shoulder, she offered him a suggestion. "Leave a space for forgiveness, Sherman. You don't have to forgive them tonight or tomorrow. Leave room in your heart for the possibility of forgiveness someday, when you've had time to heal."

Sherman stroked the softness of Edna's hair and tried to imagine a day when he wouldn't think about his grandfather's murder, a day when he wouldn't want revenge—when he'd let it go completely. What would that feel like? Freedom. That's what it would feel like. Freedom and peace.

It wouldn't be tonight, not even tomorrow, but maybe someday…

Chapter 29: Meeting the Parents

Mowbray Mountain, Tennessee
Saturday, September 30, 1922

Edna felt as nervous as a treed raccoon waiting out a pack of yapping hounds. She'd been seeing Sherman for months, but today was the day she'd meet his family for the first time. She looked in the mirror and adjusted her curls again.

"Oh, I give up." She slapped the air. Her hair was never going to look the way she wanted it. She left her room, shut the door, and descended the stairs. Just as Edna headed toward the kitchen, she heard her mother's voice.

"Thad, you're gonna have to call the police again." Maude entered the back door, carrying a basket of eggs into the kitchen.

"Why?" Thad turned the page on his newspaper, not lifting his head.

"We've lost two more chickens." Maude set the basket on the counter and poured some water into a washbasin to clean her hands.

"Must be those gypsies again." Thad lowered his paper to the kitchen table and shook his head. "I just don't understand it. I let 'em glean the fields and this is how they repay me."

"It happens every year, ya know. Every summer they camp down there at the creek, you let 'em glean the fields, and then they repay you by stealin' our chickens. Every year you end up callin' the law to run 'em off." Maude thrust a hand to her hip. "Enough is enough."

"They are an ungrateful lot," Thad admitted. Edna smiled at her parents. As right as her mother was, Edna knew her father wouldn't change. Next year he'd show the gypsies just as much hospitality, only to be taken advantage of once more.

"But they are fun while it lasts," Edna chuckled, stepping into the kitchen and putting her hands on her father's shoulders. She leaned from behind him and kissed his cheek.

"Mornin', sugar," he said as he reached up and patted her arm. Edna stepped around the table and sat down. "Don't you look pretty this mornin'!"

"Doesn't she?" Maude agreed.

The next moment, Edna heard the tromping of footsteps down the stairs as her siblings joined the breakfast table. Maude placed a spread of scrambled eggs, toast, and smoked ham on the table, then sat down to join her family.

"Is today the day you meet Sherman's family?" Dot asked, scooping some scrambled eggs onto her plate.

Edna nodded and took a bite of ham.

"You look right pretty." Dot smiled.

"Why thank you, Dot. You look right pretty yourself." Edna winked at her little sister.

"I wish we could come, too!" Thadda whined.

Edna ignored Thadda's request. She was nervous enough about meeting Sherman's folks without taking her little sisters along too.

"Maybe another time." Maude patted Thadda's hand.

"Are you nervous about meetin' the holy family?" Frank snickered.

Edna rolled her eyes and shook her head. She wasn't about to admit the truth—that she was terrified she might slip up and do something "sinful" in front of the Mortons.

"I'm sure those Mortons have their flaws," Thad interjected. "Ain't nobody perfect but the one they crucified, and if the Mortons are as pious as they let on, they'll know that."

Edna smiled at her father. His comment not only made her feel better, but it was true. What right did the Mortons have to judge her? If only she could remember that later when all eyes would be on her.

"What are y'all gonna do today?" Dot asked.

"It's a picnic for the coalminers," Edna answered.

"That sounds fun!" Dot replied, then ate a bite of ham.

"Oh, can't we go? Pleeeaaase!" Thadda pleaded.

"Now, Thadda, no whinin'. This is a big day for Edna. She doesn't need little ones underfoot," Maude said.

Thadda hung her head, her blonde curls bobbing around her chubby face. Edna almost felt sorry for her. But she really did want to keep herself sharp today. Babysitting Thadda wouldn't help matters.

A few minutes later, Edna heard a honking noise.

"What's that?" Thad's eyebrows lowered.

Thadda shoved her chair back and ran to the door. She started jumping up and down in the doorway. "It's Sherman in a car!"

"Sherman's got a car?" Frank rose to his feet, as did Hab. Everyone else followed, including Edna.

"It's a Model T." Thad leaned his forearm on the doorway and everyone else stepped past him onto the porch. Dot and Thadda scurried toward the car. Within seconds they'd sidestepped Sherman and entered the vehicle. Thadda bounced on the seat behind the wheel and Dot sat next to her, fondling the dashboard.

Sherman sauntered toward the porch and greeted the family.

"Is that your car?" Hab asked after the usual pleasantries.

Sherman nodded and removed his hat. "Just got it this mornin'."

"Wow!" Hab leapt off the porch and moved toward the car. He and Frank circled the vehicle, inspecting it while Thadda and Dot continued to pounce on the seat.

"You're gonna tear it up bouncin' on it like that," Maude called. "And don't be knockin' any gears with it runnin'!"

"I thought you were savin' your money?" Thad's eyebrows narrowed at Sherman. Edna wondered what business it was of her father's how Sherman decided to spend his hard-earned money. She came closer to Sherman, laced her arm through his, and he gave her a peck on the cheek

"I am. Have saved quite a bit." Sherman smiled. "Couldn't resist it. It was a steal of a deal. The fella who owned it took a mining position up in Kentucky and decided not to take it with him."

"It's beautiful." Edna admired the black Model T with its top down.

"Thanks." Sherman smiled at her, and laced his fingers with hers. "I thought we'd go for a little ride before the picnic."

"You do know how to drive, I hope." Thad's face furrowed with caution. Maude elbowed her husband's ribs, and he rubbed his hand to the spot.

"He got down the mountain in one piece, didn't he?" Maude observed.

Edna laughed. "Yeah, Daddy, if he can get down the mountain with it, I'm sure he can get back up it easily enough." She pulled Sherman by the hand toward the car, eager to get going. "Sorry girls, it's my turn." She smiled and motioned for her sisters to vacate the vehicle.

"Aw, can't we go?" Thadda begged, slumping her shoulders.

Sherman looked at Edna with a wink. "One quick drive down the road and back. Will that do?"

The girls eagerly bobbed their heads. Sherman opened the passenger door for Edna. She climbed in and pulled Dot and Thadda toward her so Sherman would have room to get in the driver's side.

"We'll be back in a few minutes." Sherman waved at her parents and backed out of the long driveway, proving he could handle the vehicle.

When they reached the main road, Edna pointed toward the house. "Look at Daddy," Edna giggled. "He can't drive in reverse as well as you did." Sherman smiled, put the car in first gear, and started down the road.

"All right, now girls, let's settle down." Edna put her hand on Thadda's knee to keep her from bouncing on the seat. "You're gonna use up all the spring in the seat."

"Use it up?" Thadda's tone was doubtful. "You talk as if there's only so much to be had," she sneered.

"There is. Didn't you know that?" came Edna's deadpan reply.

"What?" Thadda gave her older sister a shocked stare.

"Every spring can only be sprung so many times. And once you use it up, that's it." Edna nodded as if it were a well-known fact.

Thadda's brows furrowed as she paused in her bouncing to think through what Edna had said. Edna caught Sherman's eye with a wink.

Thadda looked up at Sherman for him to set things straight. "She's tellin' stories, ain't she?"

"Well." Sherman stroked his chin. "The manufacturer says there are only two thousand and forty-seven compressions to those seat springs." He bobbed his head toward the seat.

"Two thousand and forty-seven?" Thadda exclaimed. "Why, that's plenty!" She began bouncing again.

"Now, wait." Edna put her hand to Thadda's leg. "We don't know how many bounces the first owner gave those springs."

"Yeah, what if he had a little sister who bounced on them every day?" Dot joined in with the teasing, but didn't crack so much as a smirk.

"Any minute, you could use up all the spring and that sharp pointy metal could come tearing through the seat and poke you in the fanny!" Edna looked at Thadda with wide alarmed eyes.

Thadda instantly put her hands beneath her bottom, shielding her backside. Her wary eyes went from Edna to Sherman.

Sherman gave her a serious nod, and she rode the rest of the way as still as a china doll. Sherman circled back around to the house, got out of the car, and lifted out the girls.

"You have a good day, now." He waved as they scurried back into the house. Sherman climbed into the car, took one look at Edna, and they both broke into laughter.

"You really had her going," Sherman said as he backed the car out of the drive one more time.

"I wasn't sure you'd play along. I'm glad you did. That was too funny," Edna laughed.

Once they were out on the road, Sherman put his arm around Edna's shoulder and she scrunched over closer to him.

"So you didn't think I'd go along with your meanness?" Sherman grinned.

"Meanness?" Edna shook her head. "You haven't seen meanness until you've played blind man with that little hellion."

"That sweet little girl? What could she do to deserve the title of hellion?" Sherman chuckled.

"Oh, believe you me. She can be meaner than a snake. This was just a little payback for yesterday." Edna's head bobbed.

"What happened?" Sherman prompted, giving her shoulder a squeeze.

"Mama asked us to take some things over to the widow next door after supper last night. On the way back, Thadda says, 'Oh, let's play blind man and I'll be your guide.' She talks us into putting our scarves around our eyes, and she proceeds to lead us home."

"Sounds like a harmless little game," Sherman observed.

"Well, yeah, except for not when Thadda's the guide. I swear, that little monster drug us through every cow patty between Widow Luckman's and our house. By the time we got home, my shoes were ruined."

Sherman snickered. "I guess she did deserve a little payback."

"And she might need a little more!"

~*~

The drive up the mountain was beautiful. The trees had already started to transform into vibrant orange, yellow and red. It was so tranquil Edna almost forgot where she was going and whom she was going to meet. When they reached Montlake, picnickers had gathered around the lake, relaxing on blankets. Sherman parked the car and opened Edna's door for her.

When she stepped out, a cool breeze blew Edna's hair into her eyes and she brushed it back. Sherman took her hand and led her to where his family sat on a picnic blanket. Everyone but Sherman's mother appeared relaxed. Nancy was busy making sure that everyone had food, but she paused in the process to greet them.

"Mama, this is Edna Springfield," Sherman said. "And Edna this is my mama, Nancy Morton. Over there's my father, Will Morton."

Edna smiled at the beautiful woman and shook her hand. Her hair was as dark as night, and her eyes as brown as chestnuts. Edna didn't believe she'd ever seen a woman quite so striking. She glanced at Sherman and wondered where he got his pale blue eyes until she saw his father's. The man rose from the ground, brushed off the back of his pants, and shook Edna's hand.

"We've been looking forward to meetin' ya," Mr. Morton greeted. Edna indicated the same.

Sherman's mother had to crane her neck to look up at Edna. Yet, the expression on Nancy's face as she sized her up made Edna feel small despite her height. She wondered whether Sherman had told his mother about their age difference. It didn't look like he had. Mrs. Morton's words were perfectly kind and hospitable. It was the coldness in her dark eyes that set Edna's nerves on edge.

"Sit down and have a sandwich." Nancy Morton gestured toward an open spot on the ground.

Sherman introduced his little sisters and his brother. Each of them seemed happy to meet her, and their friendly faces set her at ease. Sherman's family seemed to fall into two camps: those with their mother's dark hair and eyes and those with fair hair and eyes.

"You girls are so pretty," Edna complimented as she found a spot on the blanket to sit. Their expressive eyes brightened with appreciation. "How old are each of you?"

"I'm thirteen," Bonnie, one of the fair-haired children, answered.

"I'm nine," Ruby replied. She, too, had Sherman's and Bonnie's light features.

"And how old are you?" Edna asked the dark-haired little one.

"I'm five." Edna Mae held up her small hand with the fingers extended. "You're pretty," she added, taking a strand of Edna's strawberry blonde locks between her fingers.

"Why, thank you!" Edna smiled and the little girl climbed onto her lap.

"Edna Mae, let Miss Springfield get some food, now," Sherman's mother scolded.

"She's all right," Edna folded her arms around the little girl. "I'm not that hungry yet."

"Gordon's fifteen," Ruby volunteered. Edna smiled at Gordon, who gave her a little wave and took a bite of his sandwich. "And Sherman's seventeen," Ruby continued. Sherman's gaze met Edna's with a reassuring smile. He opened a bottle of grape soda and handed it to her along with a sandwich. She thanked him, and he sat down beside her.

"Edna Mae, you need to come on over here and eat your sandwich." Nancy pointed to the little girl's abandoned lunch. When Edna Mae didn't instantly rise, Bonnie lifted it and handed it to her little sister. So the two Ednas sat together enjoying their sandwich and soda, which was fine with Edna since the little one's friendliness made her feel more at ease.

The Mortons were definitely a much quieter bunch than Edna was used to. They barely said a word as they ate, and she wondered whether they were always this way or whether they were just uncomfortable with her. Milling around them were hundreds of people laughing, joking, and pitching horseshoes.

After finishing their food, Sherman's little sisters ran off to jump rope with some other girls, and Gordon headed toward the lake with his friends.

This left Sherman and Edna with his parents. The minute little Edna Mae left her lap, Edna felt uneasy. Edna could usually laugh and join in conversations with anyone. But, knowing about Sherman's stern upbringing made her wary. What if she said or did something his parents deemed unacceptable?

Edna reached for her soda, and pressed it to her lips. Just as she did so, little Edna Mae returned. "You never told us how old you are, Miss Edna."

Edna choked on her drink and nearly spewed grape soda on her lap.

Sherman patted Edna's back. "Are you all right?" he asked.

Edna knew her face had turned three shades of red. She nodded and patted her chest. "I'm fine, thanks." Once she'd cleared her windpipe, she decided to be herself. After all, she was a Springfield, and a Springfield could always hold her own.

Edna looked at Edna Mae with a smile. "I'm twenty-three." When her gaze turned to Sherman's parents, any trace of a smile faded from Mrs. Morton's lips and a single dark eyebrow lifted. Edna smiled. "I know what you're thinking. You're thinking Sherman's lucky I haven't been snatched up by now. I know it's hard to believe. But, truly, I'm the lucky one. Your son's a wonderful man."

Edna smiled at Sherman and then turned her pleasant expression toward his parents' stunned faces. After about twenty seconds, a grin lifted Mr. Morton's lips, and he started to laugh. He looked at his wife and pointed his thumb toward Edna. "I like her." Mr. Morton looked back at Edna with humor dancing in his eyes. He extended his hand toward her. "I admire a woman who can hold her own." Edna took his hand in hers, and he continued, "I believe you're right. Sherman *is* lucky you haven't been snatched up."

He gave Edna's hand a vigorous shake and then leaned back on his elbows, still chuckling. Mrs. Morton's face never changed. It was as stunned as ever.

"Well," Sherman rose to his feet and extended his hand to Edna, "I believe I'll go show Edna around the lake."

Mr. Morton stood when Edna did. "Enjoy yourselves," he said. Edna heard him chuckling as she and Sherman walked away.

Once they were out of earshot, Sherman threw back his head and laughed. "You sure won my Papa over."

Edna's insides were still a quivering ball of nerves. She smiled, but couldn't laugh as heartily as Sherman and his father had. "I don't think I impressed your mother."

Sherman put his arm around Edna's shoulder. "Oh, she'll come around. Mama's not as stern as she seems. She's really a sweetheart."

Edna didn't tell Sherman that she seriously doubted that. Instead she said, "I hope you're right."

~*~

Sherman drove back up the mountain after taking Edna home and parked his car in front of the shanty. He stepped out and looked up at the twinkling stars and moon. On a crisp fall night like this, everything seemed right in the world. Things had gone well today, he thought. Edna liked his family and they seemed to like her. His mother had been a bit quiet, but she wasn't a big talker, anyway.

As he stared up at the moon he offered a little prayer of gratitude and then the thought occurred to him he'd gone a whole day without the Bakers or the murder crossing his mind. He'd been praying for the ability to get them off his mind ever since Edna suggested he make a space for forgiveness. He wasn't so certain he was required to forgive murderers, but he did want to stop thinking about them. Days like today gave him a glimmer of hope.

He stepped into the shanty to find his mother and father seated at the tiny kitchen table. His mother's stern eyes met his, and her frown unsettled him.

He greeted his parents. His mother's matter-of-fact tone twisted his stomach into a knot. "Sit down, Sherman. We'd like a word with you."

Sherman's heart started to thump like a gypsy's drum. Why hadn't he gone for a walk and come in after they'd gone to bed? Why had he thought things had gone so well when obviously his mother was upset? He pulled out a chair. It squeaked across the hardwood floor.

Once Sherman had sat down, Nancy stared at her husband and nodded for him to speak. Will's reluctant eyes met Sherman's. "Your mama is wonderin'..." Nancy poked Will's leg with her finger, and Will stared at her with creased eyebrows. "We... we're wonderin' what your intentions are with Miss Springfield."

"How serious is this?" Nancy added.

The expression on her face made Sherman's mouth go dry. He rose to his feet. "Mind if I get a drink? I'm awfully thirsty." He went to the counter and poured a glass of water from the ceramic pitcher and then sat back down to drink it.

His mother glared at him as he slowly sipped and then set the drink on the table in front of him. Sherman's thumb trailed along the outside of the glass, and he stared at the water instead of his parents' faces. "I aim to marry her if she'll have me."

Nancy leaned her forehead on her hands and stared down at the table. She took deep breaths, and Sherman wondered if she was crying. He certainly didn't mean to make his mother cry.

Will put a hand on his wife's back. "That's what I figured," Will said, more to Nancy than to their son.

Nancy lifted her gaze to Sherman, and he realized his mother wasn't crying. Controlled anger simmered in her dark eyes like a pot of boiling coffee. She rubbed her hand to her mouth and then let her arm fall to the table. "She's too old for you, Sherman. Twenty-three! You're not even eighteen!"

Sherman shrugged, "I know."

"You know?" his mother stared at him as if he'd lost his mind. "Is that all you have to say for yourself? You know?"

"I know there's an age difference, but you've said yourself I'm mature for my age. I know how to work. I know I can support a family. I'm ready." Sherman folded his arms across his chest.

Nancy scoffed. "You're not ready! You don't know the first thing about what it takes to support a family!"

"Nancy, the boy's been workin' full-time since he was twelve. Surely you aren't doubting his tenacity now." Will rubbed his hand along his wife's back trying to calm her down.

Sherman gave his father a grateful nod. At least someone was on his side.

"But why her?" Nancy persisted. "Why not someone closer to your own age? Or someone more like us?"

His mother's remark caught him off guard. He knew Edna was entirely different from his family, but how could his mother tell after only a few hours with her?

"I don't think the age really makes much difference in the long run. Who even thinks about age when one person's forty and the other's forty-five? And as for her bein' different, that's what I love about her," Sherman answered. "She's smart too. Did you know she graduated from high school at the very top of her class?"

"You may think you love her differences now, but wait until after you're married a while and those differences tear you apart," Nancy warned.

Sherman looked to his father for support. Will said, "I don't know about that, Nancy. Differences can be a good thing. Two people can complement one another. Sherman's kind of reserved and Edna's outgoing. It makes a good balance, I think."

Nancy looked at her husband as if he'd turned traitorous. "You aren't a lick of help."

Will shrugged, "It's Sherman's life, Nancy. If he's man enough to work and buy his own car, then he's man enough to decide what kind of woman he wants to marry."

"Thanks, Papa." Sherman took another sip of water and hoped this interview had come to a close.

"Well, you're not gettin' married until you're at least eighteen." Nancy pounded her forefinger on the table. "I'm puttin' my foot down about that."

"Yes, ma'am," Sherman nodded. "I haven't even asked her yet, and I hadn't aimed to marry until the spring anyway. Her daddy said the spring would be best."

"You've already spoken with her father?" Will's eyebrows lifted.

"Yes, sir," Sherman answered.

"And he gave his permission?" Nancy countered.

"Yes, ma'am."

"Does he know how old you are?" his mother asked.

"Yes, ma'am, he does."

Nancy shook her head and rubbed her forehead as if she were tired of the whole subject. "All right then, get to bed. We've got church in the mornin'."

Sherman gladly went toward his cot. As he did so, he heard his mother whisper, "Maybe it won't last 'til spring."

Chapter 30: Heaven's Gifts

Hinkle, Lookout Mountain, Walker County, Georgia
Sunday, October 29, 1922

Sherman pulled out a chair for Edna to take a seat at Grandma Josie's dining room table. Edna sat down and Sherman sat beside her. She looked across the table at the unfamiliar faces. Sherman's parents sat together on the right end of the table.

"Edna, this is my aunt Mary Ann, my aunt Josephine, and her husband Ief. Then this is Uncle Howard and Aunt Rannie, Uncle Thea and Uncle Granville." Sherman pointed to each person at the table. "Of course, you know Grandma, and I won't bother trying to introduce all the youngins." Sherman motioned toward the passel of children crowded around the kitchen table. "The grownups are overwhelming enough to remember," he chuckled.

Edna grinned. "Nice to meet you all." The adults each responded with cordial greetings.

Josie asked Will to say the prayer and then everyone started ladling food onto their plates and passing platters and bowls around the table.

"Aunt Mary Ann made the potatoes." Sherman winked as he handed them to Edna. Edna smiled, realizing that was his way of saying his grandmother hadn't made them. He'd told her about the elderly woman's inability to cook.

Edna scooped some potatoes onto her plate and handed the bowl to Sherman's mother. Edna had grown to like the woman a little better. Yet she had the distinct impression that Nancy was still weighing her opinion about whether Edna was a proper match for her son.

"So when are you moving to Kentucky?" Will asked Mary Ann.

"The children and I are taking the train up Wednesday. Gordon's already found us a house." Mary Ann replied as she took the fried chicken from Josephine.

"How do you feel about moving?" Howard asked.

Mary Ann put a piece of chicken on her plate and passed the platter on. "I'm going to miss everyone." She looked around the table with a sad smile. "But I think it's for the best. I need a fresh start."

Her siblings bobbed their heads in agreement. Edna could tell from the expression on each of their faces that they were sad to see her go, but agreed that leaving would help her find some peace.

Mary Ann took Will's hand on one side and Josephine's on the other. "I don't think I'll ever forget that day at the Durham depot. I still feel like it was all just a nightmare and that one day I'll wake up and Papa will be right here with us."

They each bowed their heads and Josephine brushed a tear from her eye. "But I think going to Kentucky will help me not think about it every single day," Mary Ann added.

"We understand." Josephine patted her sister's hand. "But we sure are gonna miss you!"

Mary Ann nodded and brushed a tear from her own cheek. Straightening her posture and smiling she suggested, "Let's think about happier things. Edna, tell us how you and Sherman met."

Edna smiled at the memory. "Well, it was my birthday, and I'd just made my wish for a handsome, hard-workin' man." Everyone chuckled and Edna continued. "It's true, I tell ya. I'd blown out the candles on my birthday cake and wished for a handsome, hard-working man. Then, a couple hours later, I went to the spring to draw water and whom did I meet, but this handsome, hard-working man."

"How could you tell?" Mary Ann leaned in with a smile.

"Well, the handsome was evident from the start." Edna winked at Sherman and everyone laughed. "But I knew in an instant he was hard-workin' because he had his bundle of coal mining clothes with him. Everybody knows how hard coalminers work."

Everyone nodded their heads in agreement. She could tell she was winning points with the men at the table. Edna continued. "I'll be honest with you, though—at first, I thought he might be a little young for me, but he did fit my wish, after all." Edna sighed. "My, he was handsome, all cleaned up and smilin' at me." Edna winked at Sherman again. "I knew in an instant he was the answer to my wish."

Everyone chuckled and Josie prompted Edna to continue, "What happened next?"

"Well," Edna looked straight at Josie's friendly face. "He offered to carry my water for me. He carted it all the way to my house." Edna smiled at Sherman, whose cheeks had turned rosy. "And then he asked if I'd mind if he came back again." Edna shrugged, "Of course, I said yes. It's not every day you blow out your birthday candles and receive your wish within hours."

Josie clapped her hands together, delighted with Edna's retelling. "See there, Will and Nancy, you've raised him well. Such a fine young gentleman." Josie reached and patted Sherman's hand.

Sherman shifted his other hand under the table, laced his fingers with Edna's, and pulled her hand to rest on his leg.

"So tell us about yourself," Josephine prodded.

"Oh, there's nothin' much to tell. Just a farm girl from Daisy." Edna winked.

"Edna graduated from high school—top of her class," Sherman said proudly. Each of them expressed their admiration of her accomplishment, and Edna could feel her face turning red. Sherman continued, "She had to live with some friends in Soddy while she went to high school because it was too far to walk every day."

"Really, now?" Grandma Josie exclaimed.

Edna nodded. "I came home on weekends and the summers. But it was the only way I could go."

"You're to be commended for that kind of determination," Josie expressed approvingly.

"Thank you, Mrs. Morton."

"Oh," Josie said with a wave of her hand. "Call me Grandma Josie like everyone else."

"Yes, Ma'am." Edna took a bite of potatoes.

After everyone had eaten, Nancy rose from the table and returned with a cake. One candle topped it in the center, its flame flickering. In unison, the family broke into song, wishing Sherman a happy eighteenth birthday. As the singing concluded, Sherman closed his eyes for a moment and blew out the candle. Everyone clapped and congratulated him.

After eating cake, Sherman suggested Edna go for a walk with him. He took her hand and they strolled past the barn, out into the fields. Edna's eyes lifted to the colorful foliage. Fiery red, brilliant orange, and sharp yellow leaves combined as if nature were trying to show off her best colors in one last fireworks display.

"Isn't it gorgeous out here?" Edna's eyes scanned the horizon. "I love autumn."

Sherman agreed and then asked, "So what do you think of my family?"

"They're nice. Quieter than mine," she chuckled.

"Just a little bit," he agreed. "But the children are rowdy enough."

"There's so many of them. I don't know how I'll ever keep them all straight." She shook her head.

He squeezed her hand, "You've got plenty of time to learn their names."

They walked into a thicket of trees where a large log had fallen. Sherman checked around it, making sure no varmints lingered nearby.

He motioned for Edna to take a seat and then instead of sitting beside her, he knelt at her feet. Edna's heart hammered, knowing what would come next. He'd never actually asked her before, but he often indicated he intended their relationship to be of a permanent nature.

"I asked your Daddy some time ago for your hand, and he said if I proved I could keep you happy and that I could provide for you, I could ask you to be my wife."

Sherman pulled a ring from his pocket and held it up to her. Edna swallowed the lump forming in her throat.

"I believe I've proven those two things to your Daddy. The question is, have I proven them to you?" Sherman asked, his blue eyes pleading with hers.

She nodded her head.

"Then, if I have, would you do me the honor of being my bride?"

Speechless, Edna nodded again. Sherman slipped the ring on her finger. She threw her arms around his neck and kissed his cheek. Taking her hands in his he asked, "Your daddy said spring would be all right. Does that sound good to you?"

"It sounds wonderful to me, but what about your parents?" As thrilled as she felt, she still held lingering doubts about his parents' acceptance of her—especially his mother.

"My parents are fine with spring," he answered, caressing her cheek with his thumb.

"Do they really like the idea of you marrying me?" she pressed.

He nodded. "They know how much I love you."

"Do they know how much I love you?" she winked, putting her hand to his cheek, and sifting her fingers through his dark hair.

He smiled, pressed his lips to hers, and Edna melted against him. In the beginning, he'd been her last best chance at a family of her own, but now she knew she loved the man who held her in his arms. He'd walked into her life on her birthday and here he was proposing to her on his. Heaven always did send the best gifts.

Chapter 31: A Chance for Clemency

Rome, Georgia
Thursday, March 15, 1923

"Boys, the Governor has agreed to a clemency hearing," Stephen Chambers announced as he approached the Baker boys in their jail cell.

Ralph and George rose from their cots and stood to face him.

"What does that mean?" Ralph felt his heartbeat accelerate. Chambers looked optimistic, but Ralph felt wary. "Is that a good thing?"

"It means the Governor is considering the possibility of reducing your sentences."

Chambers words still weren't registering completely. Ralph glanced at his brother for an indication of what this meant.

"It means we may not hang," George said to his brother.

"That's right, there's a good chance neither of you will have to hang." Mr. Chambers smiled and put a hand through the bars and patted Ralph's shoulder.

As realization dawned, Ralph raised a triumphant fist in the air and shook it high above his head. He broken into laughter and grabbed his smiling brother and tossed his arms around him. "We're gonna live, George! We're gonna live!"

George lifted his head toward the cracked ceiling. "Thank heavens!"

"Do Ma and Pa know?" Ralph asked.

"What about Lulu?" George interjected. The two brothers released one another and turned toward their attorney.

"They know." Mr. Chambers shook his head. "But remember, I don't want you to get your hopes up too much. It all depends upon what the governor says, but it seems that reporter friend of yours has been writing articles. His articles have been wired to newspapers around the country and people have been writing the governor. They've put so much pressure on Governor Hardwick that he's agreed to this clemency hearing to decide whether he'll waive the death penalty."

Mr. Chambers slipped a rolled up newspaper through the bars. George took it and opened the *Atlanta Constitution*. He held it wide so Ralph could read along with him. George finished reading first and lifted his eyes toward the attorney. "What's our plan?"

"We're going to get some people to talk with you two and sign affidavits that Ralph is too young and couldn't possibly be held accountable for his actions. And you, George, we'll have a doctor come in and declare you mentally deficient because of both medical and hereditary factors. Under the influence of alcohol, your condition was made worse and you aren't accountable for your actions."

"Mentally deficient?" George's eyebrows furrowed. "What's that supposed to mean?" Ralph glanced at his brother. He looked mad. Ralph couldn't say he blamed him.

"Well, it means you're not..." Mr. Chambers paused.

"You mean you're sayin' I'm not right in the head! That I'm dumb!" George shoved the paper at Ralph and gripped the bars. "You're sayin' I'm crazy."

"No, no, now settle down, George." Mr. Chambers eased back a little. "Nobody's sayin' that, but...well... Do you want to live, George?"

George's eyes widened and he took a deep breath.

"We're tryin' to keep you from hangin' George. If you want to live, then that meningitis you had messed with your nerves. It made you a little deficient mentally so that your judgment isn't always the best. Then there's that aunt of yours with a mental problem. Add liquor on top of it and, well, you didn't know what you were doing, now did you?"

George loosened his grip on the bars and shook his head slowly side to side, "No, I didn't know what I was doing. I never wanted to hurt nobody."

"Good boy." Mr. Chambers looked from George to Ralph and back. "There's hope, plenty of hope boys. The hearing's on April tenth. So anyone who comes to see you from now on, you're mentally deficient, George; and, Ralph, you were too young to know what you were doing."

Chapter 32: You Can't Believe Everything You Read

Mowbray Mountain, Tennessee
Saturday, March 17, 1923

Sherman drove through the little mining community with the top down on his Model T. His mind was on Edna and the cabin they'd be looking at today. He was so intent on his thoughts that the man standing by the commissary had to shout Sherman's name several times before he turned and looked.

"Hey, Sherman!" the man called, waving a folded newspaper in his hand. "I've got somethin' for you."

Sherman pulled to the side of the road and backed his car in front of the commissary.

"How do, Fred?" Sherman greeted the stocky coalminer.

The man trotted toward Sherman's car. He raked a hand across his bald head and then leaned against the door. "I've got somethin' for ya." He extended the rolled newspaper to Sherman. "When I was up North visitin' my sister, I saw this article in the *New York Times*. It's a story about those boys that shot your grandpa."

"Thanks," Sherman said, but he didn't mean it. He took the paper from his coworker and set it on the seat beside him.

"Where you headin'?" Fred asked.

"Down to Daisy to see Edna," Sherman replied.

"Ah," Fred nodded. "The weddin's comin' up perty soon, isn't it?"

"April eighth," Sherman smiled.

Fred patted Sherman on the back. "Well, good luck with everything."

"Thanks." Sherman waved at Fred and pulled his car away from the curb.

He drove through the little community, turned to head down the mountain, only occasionally glancing at the rolled paper beside him. He was looking forward to a relaxing day with Edna and had no desire to read one more article about how people wanted to let those Baker boys off.

The local papers ran enough articles about the collections for the Baker family and the write-in campaign to save Ralph and George. Sherman didn't care to read another. Community do-gooders clamored for mercy. They claimed Ralph was too young to be executed and that George's guilt was questionable. Sherman supposed both counts were true to some extent, but the Baker boys were old enough to get drunk, carry a gun, pick a fight with a deputy sheriff, and kill him. Weren't they old enough to pay the price?

Sherman pushed the newspaper to the floorboard of his automobile, sick of thinking about it all. He looked up at the clear spring sky and took in a deep breath of fresh air as his car bounced along the mountain road like a ball down a flight of stairs. He inhaled and exhaled slowly calming his nerves and clearing his head. The rest of his journey down the mountain, he'd think about Edna and the life they'd have together.

Sherman had barely driven onto the Springfield property when Edna stepped outside carrying a picnic basket. He got out of the car, greeted her with a kiss, and took the basket from her.

"I thought if we hurried, we could get on down the road before Thadda and Dot could spot us and come runnin' from the fields," Edna chuckled.

"Good idea," he winked, opening the door for her. She got in, picked the paper up from the floor, and put it in her lap so they could put the picnic basket at her feet. Once Sherman climbed behind the wheel and backed out, Edna saw that Thadda and Dot had started in their direction waving.

She waved at them and instructed Sherman to keep on going. He did as she said and soon they were riding down the road toward the creek. He didn't mind the little ones tagging along sometimes, but today he and Edna had some decisions to make.

Edna took the newspaper in her hands and unrolled it. "What's this?"

Sherman glanced over at it. "Oh, just some article about the Baker boys a friend gave me."

Edna read the headline aloud. "'Seek to Save a Boy from the Gallows. Leaders of Millions of Youths Telegraph a Plea to Georgia's Governor for Baker. Lad Shot Sheriff.'"

"Probably another one of those articles about how Ralph's too young to pay for his crime," Sherman grumbled.

Edna continued reading. "Pleaded that he was trying to protect his brother at whom the officer was firing."

"I'm so sick of hearin' this stuff." Sherman shook his head.

Edna read in silence for the next few minutes then stopped. "Have you read this?" The appalled tone of her voice caught Sherman's attention.

"No, why?" he asked, slowing the car down a little.

"Listen to this." She cleared her throat and began reading the article. "'Millions of boys in the United States, through executive representatives of their organizations in this city, joined yesterday to telegraph Governor Thomas W. Hardwick of Georgia, urging him to prevent the hanging next Friday of 15-year-old Ralph Baker. Ralph—along with his 23-year-old brother, George—was convicted of shooting and killing Deputy Sheriff J.W. Morton in Durham, Georgia.'"

"Right," Sherman nodded. "I heard about that. The governor has postponed the hangin' 'til next month."

Edna nodded. "Yes, but listen to this." She continued, "'Evidence at the trial of the brothers in Walker County revealed that the Deputy Sheriff was killed by the younger boy after George had been shot by the officer and while they were struggling for possession of the Deputy Sheriff's pistol.'"

"What?" Sherman exclaimed. "I've heard 'em twist this thing up one side and down the other, but this takes the cake!"

"Can you believe this?" Edna's voice was incredulous. "George wasn't even shot, was he?"

"No," Sherman growled.

"You've got to hear the rest of this." She continued reading the article to him, "'It was shown that Ralph, who was alleged to be mentally deficient, had wrenched a pistol from his brother a few minutes before the killing when he found George brandishing it at the Durham railroad station.'"

"'Mentally deficient'?" Sherman chuckled. "Now, that's a new word for meanness. He had enough smarts to know how to read and write. But he would have to be stupider than a stick to shoot a deputy sheriff! Besides it was George they claimed had mental issues, not Ralph. The reporter didn't even get that right!"

Edna agreed, and then kept reading. "'George, an athletic youth, attacked the deputy sheriff, who drew his pistol and fired several shots at George.'"

"What?" Sherman slammed on the brakes and pulled his automobile over to the side of the road, letting it idle. He took one end of the paper while Edna held the other. Together, they read the remainder.

> "Ralph testified that he thought Morton was intent on killing his brother and that he crept up behind the deputy and shot him through the body. The prosecution tried to show that Ralph, who was only 14 years old at the time, had also been drinking.
>
> Soon after the brothers were sentenced to be hanged, movements began in several parts of Georgia to save at least the younger Baker from the gallows. Petitions were sent to Governor Hardwick to commute the sentences of both boys to life imprisonment. Governor Hardwick announced a short time

ago that he would consider all these petitions before the scheduled executions.

The governor was awaiting the report of the State Prison Commission about a hearing on the case brought about by R.D. Baker, the father of the condemned youths. Representatives of numerous local bodies in Georgia attended the hearing and advocated commutation, many of them declaring that a 14-year-old boy, and especially one whose mental faculties were impaired, could not possibly realize the enormity of his crime.

Reports that have reached boys' organizations throughout the country in the last week have indicated that Ralph may have to pay the extreme penalty. Hence, petitions from boys' organizations across the country were sent to the National Boys' Work executive organization here.

The subject arose yesterday during a monthly meeting in the Madison Square Hotel. Philip D. Fagans, president of the executives' organization and of the Woodcraft League of America, urged action, especially on behalf of Ralph. The body voted unanimously to send the following telegram to Governor Hardwick:

March 12, 1923

Hon. T.W. Hardwick, Governor, State of Georgia, Atlanta, Ga.

At a meeting held today of executives representing national movements engaged in work for boys throughout all parts of the United States, including Boys' Club Federation, Community Service, Playground Association, Boys' Work Department International Y.M.C.A., Big Brother's movement, Jewish Welfare, Woodcraft League of America and Boy Scouts of America, reaching millions of boys throughout all parts of the United States, it was voted that a petition be respectfully presented to you on behalf of the boys of America that some way be found to avoid the hanging of Ralph Baker, fifteen-

> year-old boy in your State, because of his extreme youth and that consideration be given to development of some plan whereby this lad may be given a chance to make good. We are confident that the boys of America, if they but had the chance, would speak as one in support of this earnest plea.

Sherman shook his head. "I've never read such a crock of twisted nonsense in all my life!"

"It's bizarre," Edna declared. "Where in the world did they get this cock-eyed version of the story? Aren't reporters supposed to check their facts?"

"The state's attorney told Uncle Howard that there's a big-shot New York reporter who's stirring up all this mess." Sherman pointed at the name on the byline. "Yep, that's him." He tapped his pointing finger at the paper. "What makes me sick is they're trying to make it sound like Grandpa was at fault, and those pitiful Bakers are the victims."

"Well, I guess this goes to show that if people can't get what they want the legal way, they'll use the press to twist facts and sway public opinion to suit their own ends," Edna shook her head. "If it works, and they let Ralph off, I don't see how they can justify hanging George. Ralph openly admits he did all the shooting. If they aren't going to hang the one who admitted to murder, how are they gonna hang the other?" Edna asked.

"Mr. Rosser, the state's attorney, says there's this 'but for test' they use in the law. You say, 'But for George, Grandpa would be alive,'" Sherman explained. His voice rose with the irritation he felt inside. "They call it being 'at cause.' George caused it—if it hadn't been for him and what he did, none of it would have happened. So he's just as guilty in the eyes of the law as his brother who pulled the trigger. Besides, Aunt Mary Ann says George *did* shoot. And I believe her, not that lyin' Ralph Baker."

"Hmmm. Maybe, but what if Ralph's telling the truth and George didn't shoot? I don't see how they can hang a man who didn't actually fire a weapon," Edna countered. "It doesn't seem right to me."

"But he caused it, Edna. Don't you see that? If George hadn't started that fight, Ralph wouldn't have shot, and Grandpa would be alive right now. He's gotta hang—they both do. It's justice. It's the only fair thing. 'An eye for an eye and a tooth for a tooth,'" Sherman quoted.

Edna's eyes widened and her mouth dropped a little. "You don't really believe that do you?"

"Of course I do," he nodded. "God's vengeance demands that those two pay for killin' Grandpa. It's all in the Bible, Edna. If you ever read it, you'd know that."

Edna twisted in her seat, staring at him with an expression of hurt in her eyes. Her face was red and splotchy and her anger evident in the way she hissed out her next words through clenched teeth. "I read my Bible, Sherman. And I resent the fact that you think I don't."

"Well, you evidently haven't read the Old Testament, because it's very clear on these matters. Capital punishment is right there in the law." Sherman thumped his forefinger on the seat between them. "They even had a guy called the revenger who executed people who were guilty of murder."

"You clearly haven't read the New Testament, or you'd know we don't go by the Law of Moses anymore!" Edna barked.

"What do you know about the Bible?" Sherman scoffed.

"Evidently more than you do!" Edna reached for her purse and pulled out a small New Testament. She opened it to a place she'd put a ribbon in Matthew 5. "You need to read this." She pointed to where she'd marked verses 38 through 44.

Had she planned this all along? Had she hunted up Bible verses to prove him wrong? "I don't need to read anything," he growled. "I've been to more church than you and your whole family put together. And I've memorized more Bible verses than you've probably ever even read in your whole life!" Sherman folded his arms across his chest and stared forward, refusing to look at Edna or her little New Testament.

Edna inhaled and exhaled several times and then began reading in a calm, clear voice, "'Ye have heard that it hath been said, An eye for an eye, and a tooth for a tooth: But I say unto you That ye resist not evil; but whosoever shall smite thee on thy right cheek, turn to him the other also. And if any man will sue thee at the law, and take away thy coat, let him have thy cloke also. And whosoever shall compel thee to go a mile, go with him twain. . . Ye have heard that it hath been said; Thou shalt love thy neighbor and hate thine enemy. But I say unto you Love your enemies, bless them that curse you, do good to them that hate you and pray for them which despitefully use you and persecute you.'"

"This is different." Sherman pounded his fist on the dashboard. "This is murder. Do you understand that, Edna? Murder! Those two shot down my grandpa in cold-blooded murder! They've *got* to die. Jesus wasn't talkin' about murder."

"I feel sorry for you, Sherman." Edna shook her head and began twisting the ring he had given her.

"You don't need to feel sorry for me. Feel sorry for my grandma who has no husband to take care of her." Sherman's voice cracked with emotion. "Feel sorry for my aunt and my little cousin who'll probably have nightmares for the rest of their lives!"

"You don't get it, do you, Sherman?" Edna remained surprisingly calm and it was making Sherman madder by the second. "You don't have to hold onto the hate for justice to be served. God's laws are just. Actions reap consequences. The Bakers will pay somewhere along the line whether you hate them or not—whether they're hanged or not. But you're ruining your own life sowing these seeds of hate in your heart. Those seeds affect you, not the Bakers."

Sherman shook his head. "Edna, you don't have a clue what you're talkin' about. Your grandpa wasn't murdered. You don't know how hard it is to have all this drag on and the whole world wantin' sympathy for the men who killed the person you love."

"They may have killed your grandfather, Sherman, but you're killing us." Edna pulled the ring from her finger and put it on the dashboard in front of him.

Sherman's eyes darted toward Edna. "What are you talkin' about?"

"I can't live with someone who's filled with hate." She swallowed hard. Her voice softened. "You're not who I thought you were."

"What?"

Edna opened the car door and stepped out.

"Get back in the car, Edna!"

She shut the door behind her and looked at him through the open window. A tear trickled down her cheek. "Good-bye, Sherman." She started walking down the road.

Sherman's heart hammered and he grabbed the ring. He slung open his door and started after her. "Edna!" His boots sloshed through a puddle, splashing mud on his starched white pants.

She didn't turn to look at him, just kept walking. "It won't work, Sherman. We're too different."

"But I love that we're different!" he said, running after her.

She turned to face him with her hands on her hips. "No, you don't. You don't respect me. You don't respect my family, and you are the most holier-than-thou boy I've ever met in my life. My brother is right—who died and left you God? You think you know so much about God. You and your pious, perfect, saintly family. But you don't even know the basic teachings of the God you claim to worship!"

Sherman's face flushed beet red and in that moment he wondered why he'd asked her to marry him. Her words sliced through him like a razor blade.

He growled through gritted teeth. "You're right. This'll never work." Without another word, he turned on his heel and marched back to the car.

Chapter 33: An End to Dreams

Rome Jail, Rome, Georgia
Saturday, Mach 17, 1923

The instant George heard his wife's voice, he rose to his feet and went to the bars of his jail cell. "Lulu! So good to see you! You look beautiful, sweetheart!" He leaned his face against the cold bars and kissed her lips.

"I've missed you too," she said, putting her arms inside the bars and hugging him the best she could.

Beside her stood Stephen Chambers, George and Ralph's defense attorney. Mr. Chambers shook Ralph's hand. When Lulu released George, Mr. Chambers extended his hand to George. "Good evenin', boys, how you holdin' up?"

George looked at Ralph and shrugged, "Bored out of our minds."

"Any word on the clemency hearing?" Ralph asked.

"It's looking good, very encouraging." The attorney smiled. "The people have really been pressuring the governor to let you boys off with a lighter sentence."

George grinned at his wife, elated at the hope being extended to him. "Where'd you get the red dress, Lulu? It's new, ain't it?"

"Do you like it, George?" she asked.

"Yeah," he said cautiously, "But how did you afford it?"

"That's what Mr. Chambers and I are here to talk with you about," she said, pointing to the attorney.

George didn't realize they'd come together. He thought they happened to arrive at the same time. A wave of jealousy swept over him. Was the attorney buying his wife dresses? He shot the attorney an angry glare.

"We found a buyer for the house!" Lulu rushed on. "I just need you to sign the papers."

Mr. Chambers retrieved a set of documents from his briefcase and started shuffling through them.

"What do you mean, found a buyer for the house? I don't want to sell the house. We just got those taxes paid off with the money the women raised for us," George protested.

"I know, George, but, well..." Lulu brushed a hand through her perfectly coifed hair. It was so unlike her usual unruly curls. She hadn't looked this good since before they married. "The house is lonely without you, George. So I've moved back in with Mama and Daddy. Daddy found a buyer for the house, and the man gave us a down payment already."

"So that's how you got the dress?" George deduced.

"It was on sale, and I haven't had a decent dress in so long." Her lower lip puckered into a pout, but her lips next transformed into a radiant smile. "I wanted to look nice for the hearing."

George shook his head. "But I don't want to sell the house. We'll need somewhere to live when I get outta here, and I don't wanna live with your parents!"

Lulu gave Mr. Chambers a pleading look.

The attorney cleared his throat. "George, even if the clemency hearing goes well, you won't be getting out of jail anytime soon."

George shrugged. "Okay, so it may take a few years, but I want to come home to my wife and our house. Not her parents."

"George, I don't think you understand." Mr. Chambers clarified, "The best you'll get will be life in prison."

A wave of nausea knotted George's stomach and he stepped back, fumbling for his cot. Ralph reacted similarly, reaching for his. Simultaneously, they sat down and stared at Mr. Chambers. "If you're good—*very* good—in prison, you might come up for parole in twenty years or so."

"Twenty years!" Ralph explained.

George felt as if the blood drained down his body and puddled at his feet. His mouth dropped.

"I'm sorry, boys, but that's just the way it is. Our primary goal here is to save your lives."

"But what kind of life?" George exclaimed. "Day in and day out in a cell like this! I'm gonna go stark-ravin' mad!"

Lulu stepped toward the bars and reached through, extending her hand. "I'll be here for you every step of the way, George. I'll visit you, I promise."

He rose to his feet and embraced her through the bars. After several minutes of consolation, Mr. Chambers held out the documents and a pen.

George stared at the papers for a few moments. He looked up at Lulu, who nodded at him.

"You sure this is what you want?" he asked.

Lulu nodded.

George looked to Mr. Chambers for assurance.

"It's the best thing, George. Your wife will be able to take care of herself with the money from the sale and you won't have to worry about her."

George felt numb. What else could they take from him? He reached for the pen and the paper and signed on the line. It was done, and with the signature went all hope for his future.

Chapter 34: From Bad to Worse

Daisy, Tennessee
Saturday, March 17, 1923

Sherman put up the top on his Model T, got inside, and slammed his boot on the gas pedal, driving the vehicle as fast as it would go. The wind from the open windows whipped through his hair and his eyes burned. What right did Edna have to judge him? How dare she say those things about his family? She didn't know what they'd been through. She couldn't begin to fathom the pain and suffering his family had experienced. How dare she quote scripture and expect him to lie down like a doormat and accept the injustice of it all?

Was he supposed to be happy that the Bakers could get off free as birds? "You don't turn the other cheek with murderers," he growled to himself as he sped down the road toward Chattanooga. "They'll just kill somebody else. She wouldn't think it was simple if it were someone she cared about who'd been murdered."

Sherman's car bounced along the dirt road that wound through thick foliage and trees. The sky started to darken to an ominous gray. "Rain," he grumbled to himself and rolled up his window. As if on cue, droplets splattered on his windshield. One, two, three, then hundreds—, within seconds, a deluge of water covered his windshield, making it nearly impossible to see where he was going. He held the steering wheel with his left hand while he reached over and tried to roll up the passenger window with his right.

Sherman didn't see the white dog until it was too late. He swerved and slammed on the brakes, but it was no use. There was a horrible thump as the car ran over the body. His wheels skidded across the mud until the driver's side of the car was completely off the road and almost into the ditch.

The car lurched to a halt and rumbled at a low idle. Sherman swore and slammed his fist on the steering wheel. Putting the vehicle in park, he flung open the car door and stepped into the downpour. The rain soaked his white shirt and clung to his skin. He went toward the dog. Crimson blood stained the white fur around the dog's head and neck. It lay limp and lifeless, its neck broken and head crushed. It had suffered an instant death.

He cast his eyes aside. He couldn't look at it. Then, he thought of the Bakers. Would he watch them hang when he couldn't even look at a dog? He turned back and forced himself to look at the animal for a full minute. Then, closing his eyes to shut out the sight, he walked several paces away and bent over. He leaned his hands on his thighs. Looking at the ground, he tried to swallow the constricting lump in his throat, tried to dispel the image of the white fur stained crimson.

"What next?" He shook his head and then looked up, directing his words toward the blackened heavens.

He stood there on the side of the road, letting the rain flow over him, wishing that somehow it could wash away the feeling that his life was falling apart.

It was nearly thirty minutes before the rain subsided, and Sherman cranked the engine on his car. His boots slipped and sloshed as he made his way back inside to put the automobile in gear. His wheels spun a little, and at first he thought he'd never make it out of the ditch—but finally he had enough traction to get back on the road.

Sherman started to head back to Daisy, but decided against it. He didn't feel like going home to that cracker box or having his parents ask him why he wasn't with Edna. Instead, he kept driving toward Chattanooga. Better yet, he'd keep going and visit his grandmother.

When Sherman reached the part of Chattanooga that skirted the base of Lookout Mountain, he looked ahead and saw a commotion in the middle of the road. A crowd of people were milling around with signs held high. Drivers were hanging their heads out car windows and talking to what Sherman now realized were a few dozen women clad in their Sunday dresses and hats. Sherman eased his foot on the brake and prepared to stop.

An older woman in a matching blue dress and hat held a mason jar toward the driver in front of Sherman. The man reached out and dropped in some change.

"Thank you, sir. It's very Christian of you to contribute." She smiled and waved as the man eased his car forward.

Sherman inched his car toward the woman in the blue dress. He kept his eyes forward, refusing to look at her.

"What's goin' on here?" Sherman grumbled to himself. It was getting late and he wanted to get up the mountain to spend some time with his grandmother before having to turn around and drive back to Daisy.

It was then that he made out the words on the signs: "Save the Bakers." "Don't let 'em hang a boy." "End the death penalty!" "God is merciful—we should be, too!"

Sherman shifted his car into park and threw open his door, almost knocking down the woman in blue, who held a mason jar of change toward him. She backed up a few steps and nearly fell into a puddle of mud.

"You people go home!" Sherman growled. "The Bakers are murderers and you have no business collectin' money for 'em!" He marched toward the clump of women of varying ages—some in their teens, some in their twenties and thirties, but most of them about his grandmother's age.

"How would you like it if they murdered your grandfather?" He screamed at a young woman in a green dress. Her eyes widened, and she backed away from him as if he were a leper. "Or you?" he yelled at an older woman in a frumpy yellow dress. "How would you like it if they murdered your husband? I bet you wouldn't be carryin' that sign and collectin' money for murderers then!"

"Now, settle down." Harriet Lock took Sherman by the arm while her sister, Abigail Montgomery, took his other. "We're just doin' the Christian thing and helpin' out a poor family in need."

"You must not know the Lord, son," Abigail cooed in a calming voice. "God is love and kindness and mercy and he would have us help those in need."

Her words flew all over Sherman like a flock of crows on a possum carcass. He wrenched his arms free of the women's grip and bellowed, "If you're so all-fired eager to help someone in need, then help Joseph Morton's widow! Or take up a collection for his daughter, who had to watch him murdered before her very eyes! If you really want to help, mind your own business and let justice send those fellas to hell where they belong!"

Abigail and Harriet gasped and a simultaneous expression of alarm spread over the crowd of women's faces. "You don't mean that!" Abigail cried.

"I sure do mean it!" Sherman grabbed the jar full of change from Abigail and slammed it to the ground, shattering the glass and sending coins clanging all over the dirt road. "Now get out of my way and let me drive through!"

Sherman marched back to his car and climbed behind the wheel. As if the Red Sea had parted, the women scurried toward either side of the road. Sherman drove through the opening. "Put your do-gooder energy into somethin' more worthwhile, like takin' care of the victims instead of fightin' for the criminals!" he yelled out the window.

He slammed on the gas and sped toward the mountain, up the winding roads, toward his grandmother. Angry, hot tears rolled down Sherman's cheeks and he swiped them with his sleeve. He had to get up the mountain. It was his heart's one desire, to be in a place where he could feel close to his grandfather again. He felt as if the earth were crumbling beneath his feet, leaving him nowhere to stand. Surely atop Lookout Mountain he could find a spot of solid ground.

After winding up the mountain, Sherman parked his car in front of his grandmother's house. Taking a couple of deep breaths, he tried to calm himself before seeing his grandmother. He pulled a comb from his pocket, raked it through his hair, and stepped out of the car.

"Grandma!" he called as he rapped on the door. "You in there?"

"Come on in," she called.

He opened the door to find her standing in the kitchen washing dishes. She dried her hands on a towel and called his name. "How wonderful to see you! Did you bring the rest of the family?"

"No," he replied, shaking his head. "Just me. I was out driving and decided to come for a visit."

"Why, you're soakin' wet!" she cried. Josie hobbled toward him and handed him her towel. He rushed to her and gave her a kiss on the cheek. He inhaled his grandmother's familiar scent. He put his hands on her arms and embraced her, relieved to have someone who knew how he felt, someone who would be on his side.

Grandma Josie looked up into his face, "Are you all right, Sherman?"

"I'm fine," he nodded.

"You don't look fine. You look upset." She motioned for him to sit at the kitchen table.

Sherman helped his grandmother into a chair and then sat down across from her. "It's just been a rough day is all." He ran the towel over his arms and torso.

"Didn't you bring Edna with you?" Josie looked toward the door as if she were expecting Edna to come in at any moment.

"No, ma'am. I'm by myself."

"What's wrong, Sherman? Did you two have a lover's spat?"

Sherman rubbed the towel across the back of his neck and muttered, "Somethin' like that."

"Oh, I hate to hear that. She's such a likeable young woman." Josie reached across the table for Sherman's hand.

"Yeah, that's what I thought," Sherman grumbled and looked down at the table.

"All right then, out with it," Josie demanded. "Tell me what happened."

The way she said it made Sherman's lips curl into a slight smile. She had such a unique way of making you come clean with whatever was on your mind—tough, but loving. There was no point in trying to hide it from her. She was too perceptive.

"We got in an argument over the trial," he said.

"The trial? Whatever for?"

"She thinks I'm full of hate 'cause I think the Bakers should be executed for their crime." He shrugged. "I guess she'd be happy if they walked away unpunished so they could go kill somebody else. She said all kinds of cutting things about me and the family and gave back the ring."

Grandma Josie's forehead seemed even more pronounced when she was confused or fretting. "That doesn't sound like Edna."

"You don't know her like I do." Sherman shook his head. "I don't think I even knew her 'til today." He leaned his head in his hands and massaged his temples. "She had the nerve to pull out her New Testament and start quoting Jesus to me, as if I'm supposed to just forget all about what the Bakers have done."

"What did she read?" Josie asked.

"Oh, something in Matthew about turning the other cheek and loving your enemies and praying for them. Impossible stuff like that." He shook his head then rose to his feet. "Do you want a drink of water, Grandma?"

"No, thank you, dear."

Sherman poured himself a glass and leaned back against the counter sipping it. When he finished it, Josie pointed toward the coffee table. "Fetch my Bible, please."

Sherman did as he was asked and set the Bible on the kitchen table in front of his grandmother, then sat down again.

Josie turned to Matthew 5. She, too, had the same passage marked. Sherman felt a strange sense of dread as his grandmother read aloud the same verses Edna had read to him earlier in the day.

Before she could comment, Sherman put in his opinion. "See there, it doesn't say a thing about murder. It talks about lawsuits and arguments, but murder's a whole different animal."

"You think so?" Josie's eyes narrowed a bit, as if she really wanted to know the answer and respected his thoughts on the matter.

"Of course it's different. You can't bring back a life. You can return a stolen item. You can make amends and say you're sorry for a lot of things, but a life is gone once it's taken and it can't be given back. It's different."

Josie nodded, "You may be right about that, Sherman."

"Thank you!" He tossed his hand in the air, relieved that someone seemed to see his point.

Josie spoke slowly as if she were pondering carefully her choice of words. "You know, I've read this passage over and over since you're grandpa's death, tryin' to decide what it's tellin' me." She leaned her chin on her fist and stared down at the Bible.

"Joe and I had a lot of good years together." She nodded and her lips tightened into a quivering line. "He was always the one I went to when I needed to understand matters of this sort. He knew the Bible backwards and forwards. But now that he's gone, I've been left alone to try to figure this out for myself."

A painful lump formed in Sherman's throat and moisture gathered in his eyes.

Josie continued in subdued tones, "I read this over and over again, prayin' for some understanding. God says vengeance is His and He will repay. So if He's takin' care of vengeance, then maybe this passage here in Matthew tells me what my part is." She read the last verses again, "'Ye have heard that it hath been said; Thou shalt love thy neighbor and hate thine enemy. But I say unto you Love your enemies, bless them that curse you, do good to them that hate you and pray for them which despitefully use you and persecute you.'"

She continued, "So that's what I'm supposed to do—and I must say, it's been a very hard thing to do." Josie shook her head. "Love the Bakers, bless the Bakers, do good to the Bakers and pray for them. That's my part."

"How can you make yourself love someone you hate?" Sherman's heart ached for his grandmother. How could she, of all people, be expected to love the Bakers?

"That's what I wondered, too. Such a difficult thing to do, Sherman." Her sympathetic eyes met his. "You know that as well as I do."

Sherman nodded and reached for his grandmother's hand. He put his palm over her arthritic fingers that rested on the table between them.

She continued, "And then I tried it. I tried what Jesus said to do. I started praying for the Bakers—not just the parents of those boys, but the boys themselves. It was a bitter pill at first, but I kept on makin' myself do it. I've prayed for 'em every mornin' and night for the last few months. I pray for the Lord to bless them and be merciful to them." Josie's expression lightened. "The odd thing is, over time, I really began to mean it."

Moisture gathered in her eyes. "I really do want the Lord to be merciful to those boys. I really do feel sorry for them, and I believe I feel a small measure of the love Jesus has for them. Just think how sad He must be, knowing the suffering they'll endure for what they did to my Joe!" Tears trickled down Grandma Josie's wrinkled cheeks, and her dark eyes met Sherman's with a light he'd never seen sparkling there before.

A warm feeling spread over him, and he knew his grandmother's words were true, but then he shook his head. "I can't do it. You're a better person than I am. It would take a miracle..."

"You don't think it took a miracle for me?" she countered. "I'm not that good a person. Nobody is."

"Then how?" Sherman felt so confused. How could it be possible? Was his grandmother only deluding herself, telling herself that she'd forgiven the Bakers when one day all the hate and anger would come rushing back?

"It wasn't me, Sherman. It was God. God took my feeble efforts of tryin' to forgive and made a miracle of it. I prayed for those boys and heaped blessings on their heads; and He turned it into a forgiveness I never thought possible."

Sherman leaned his head in his hands. "I don't know. It's too hard." Sherman fought back the tears that threatened.

"It's a leap of faith, Sherman—a token sacrifice. Sacrifice your pride and your hate, and God will fill you with His love. He's done it for me. He will do it for you, too." There was a look of promise in her eyes.

Sherman sat there leaning his chin on his fists, realizing that Grandma Josie had confirmed that Edna was right. She hadn't said it the way Edna had, but she'd said the same thing. God expected him to forgive the Bakers.

Grandma Josie seemed to read his thoughts. She reached over and patted his arm. "Now you just have to convince Edna to take that ring back."

Sherman shook his head. "She'll never forgive me. She thinks I'm self-righteous and hateful. She said I wasn't who she thought I was."

"Did you say anything to hurt her feelings?" Grandma Josie pressed.

Sherman shrugged. "Yeah, I said some hurtful things."

"Then you're gonna have to apologize for that and set things right between you." She patted her fingers to the table. She made it sound so simple, but Sherman knew it wouldn't be.

"It's probably for the best all of this happened now. Better to work out these differences before you marry," Grandma Josie observed.

Sherman indicated that he understood. But he still had no idea how he could convince Edna to forgive him. Besides, he still didn't feel all that wrong—no matter what Edna, Grandma, or Jesus said. He knew Edna would see right through a forced apology. He'd have to mean it before he said it, and who could say when his feelings would change? So much for a spring wedding...

After several silent minutes passed between them, Josie rose to her feet. "Let's sit outside a spell. The air's always clearer after the storm."

~*~

Sherman pulled his car in front of the Springfield place and turned off the engine. It was dark and he could see the lamps burning downstairs. He sat there gripping the steering wheel. "Please, Lord, please give me the words to make her take me back. I just need a little more time. Please make her give me a little more time..."

He stepped out of the car and walked up the steps. Just as he lifted his hand to knock, Maude Springfield stepped out on the porch and shut the door behind her. Sherman backed up a little to give her space.

"She doesn't want to talk with you right now."

"But, Mrs. Springfield, I need to tell her I'm sorry."

"You can tell her another day, when you really mean it." The little woman stared at him like a bulldog.

"But I do mean it," he insisted. "I'm terribly sorry about the things I said. Please let me tell her and make things right."

"You don't mean it. You may think you do, but nobody changes in a day."

"But I want to."

Maude Springfield shook her head in frustration and turned toward the door. She opened it and then looked back at him. "Did you think because she's older than you, or 'cause you're better than us, that Edna had an unbreakable heart?"

"No ma'am, and I don't think I'm better than..."

Maude interrupted him, "'Cause that's one thing God don't make, Mr. Morton. He makes a lot o' things, but He don't make unbreakable hearts. You, of all people, oughta know that better than most."

Sherman shook his head. "I didn't mean to hurt her, Mrs. Springfield."

Maude paused for a moment with her back to him. "But you did, didn't you?" she said softly before entering the house and shutting the door between them.

Sherman lifted his hand and started to knock, but instead called through the door, "Please tell her I'm sorry. Tell her I love her."

No reply came from the other side. Sherman got in his car and drove home.

Chapter 35: Pleading for Forgiveness

Mowbray Mountain, Tennessee
Sunday, March 18, 1923

Sherman sat in the little mountain church beside his father and thought about his grandmother's words. He still found it hard to believe she could have forgiven the Bakers. How could it be possible? He leaned his head in his hands as the preacher droned on.

Please help me forgive them, Lord. Grandma says I have to pray for 'em. I have to ask you to bless 'em. I can say it, Lord, but I don't know that I can mean it. Sherman gritted his teeth and continued to pray in his mind, forcing himself to think thoughts he didn't mean. *Please bless the Bakers. Please bless their parents. Please help those boys to have a quick, easy death. Is that what I should be prayin' for? I'd rather pray for Edna. Please forgive me for treatin' Edna that way. Please forgive me for screamin' at those ladies yesterday and breakin' their jar. Please help Edna to forgive me...* These were words he really meant.

Sherman felt his father's hand on his back. "Wake up, Sherman," Will whispered into his ear.

Sherman sat up and looked at the preacher, forcing his thoughts back to the present.

"'Why look ye at the mote in your brother's eye and considerest not the beam in thine own eye?'" the chubby minister in the black suit asked. "Many times, all we can see is other people's faults, and we're blind to our own. When we're tempted to look down on someone else, thinkin' we're better than they are, it's a good indicator there's something inside us that's amiss. It's times like these when we need some self-reflection, because the flaws we see in others are often a reflection of the flaws inside ourselves."

The minister's eyes met Sherman's, and he wondered whether the preacher was talking directly to him. No, there was no way the minister could know about him and Edna. Sherman hadn't told a soul about what happened other than his grandmother. And she couldn't have told anyone way out there on Lookout Mountain.

But God knew, didn't He? God knew Sherman's self-righteous heart. He knew that Sherman looked down on the Springfields and exalted himself so much that he'd hurt the woman he loved.

"'Pride goeth before a fall,'" the minister continued. "Remember that—thinkin' we're better than others will only lead to misery in the end."

Ain't that the truth! Sherman was miserable. His face burned with shame. It seemed as if everyone in the congregation might turn and stare at him. For months, he'd been using Old Testament verses to justify his hate. He'd told himself he was better than the Springfields because they drank, dipped snuff, and played cards. But it was Edna who understood God's word better than he did! She'd been right, and he'd been wrong. She was the saint and he was the sinner.

When the minister said the final "Amen," Sherman rose to his feet and darted toward the chapel door. He had to see Edna. He had to apologize and let her know how wrong he'd been. He wouldn't rest until they'd set things straight between them.

~*~

Sherman knocked on the Springfield's front door. Maude answered the door again, and Sherman was relieved it wasn't Edna's father. After the lecture Mr. Springfield had given him about never breaking Edna's heart again, he wondered whether he would even let him marry Edna now.

Maude stood in the cracked doorway. "Not today, Mr. Morton."

"But I'm so sorry, Mrs. Springfield. I was wrong. Edna's right. I have been self-righteous. I'm sorry I hurt you and Edna and your family."

"Thank you, Mr. Morton. I accept your apology." Maude nodded and started to shut the door.

Sherman put his hand to the door, "Please Mrs. Springfield. Please let me tell Edna how sorry I am."

"Maybe another day. She isn't feelin' well today."

"Is she all right? She isn't sick, is she?" Sherman pressed, still holding his hand to the door.

"She'll be all right. Go for now. You can come back another day."

"But..."

Maude Springfield shut the door. Sherman hung his head and moped back to his car.

He drove down the road and started to go back up the mountain, but he had another idea. He wouldn't give up so easily. He had the whole day to find a way to see Edna. He drove his car down the road and parked it where none of the Springfields would see it. He trekked toward the spring. The Springfields would get thirsty sooner or later, and when they sent Edna to the spring, he'd be able to approach her.

~*~

Maude stepped into the kitchen, where Edna sat sipping a glass of iced tea. Her bloodshot eyes lifted to meet her mother's gaze.

"Thanks for sending him away, Mama." Edna raked a hand through her hair. "I'd hate to have him see me this way."

"I didn't send him away 'cause of the way you looked," Maude said as she took a seat beside her daughter. "I sent him away 'cause that boy needs to learn a thing or two."

Edna nodded. "He does, and I'm still too upset to talk to him. But I sort of feel bad preachin' forgiveness to him and then not forgivin' him when he came to apologize." Edna paused. "Seems rather hypocritical, doesn't it?"

"Forgiveness is all well and good, but there's a point at which you have to stand up for yourself. Don't let him get away with treatin' you this way. If you do, he'll be runnin' over ya all your married life." Maude made a fist and pressed it to the kitchen table. "You gotta stand your ground. Make him work for your heart. I know you feel like you're older and all, but it won't serve you to cave so easily."

"But what if he changes his mind and decides I'm not worth fightin' for? Or that we're too different?"

"Oh, believe me, darlin'—there's nothin' that gets a man's heart to pumpin' like an unobtainable woman. Make him wait, make him work through some of this mess inside him. Then, when he's humbled himself, you can let him know you've forgiven him."

Edna nodded and took another sip of tea. But she knew deep in her heart she'd cave if he held her in his arms. He had some kind of hold over her that she couldn't explain. Some kind of physical magnetism she couldn't escape. Besides, how could she set an example of forgiveness and not forgive him?

"Now you get on upstairs and take a nap. He loves you. He ain't goin' nowhere. Let him get a little sorrier so he'll learn his lesson." Maude patted Edna's hand and winked. "It'll be all right."

"Thanks for not tellin' Daddy about all this. He'd be furious and never let me marry Sherman."

"Just stay out o' your daddy's way. If he sees you all bleary-eyed, he'll know somethin's up. You're lucky he decided to go huntin' after church."

~*~

Sherman sat in a thicket near the watering hole. He checked his watch. He'd been sitting here for four hours. It would be just his luck if the Springfields had gathered enough water on Saturday not to need more on Sunday. Being alone with his thoughts, he'd had plenty of time to rehearse what he'd say to Edna should she come to the spring.

He was about to get up and stretch his legs when he heard rustling on the path. His breath caught when he saw Edna's strawberry blonde curls and her slender figure. She approached the spring and knelt down to fill the buckets.

Sherman stood up and debated on whether to wait until she turned around and saw him or to speak up. He watched her gather the water and sent one more silent plea toward the heavens to be given the right words.

"Edna," he said.

Her head turned toward him. "Oh, it's you," she said coolly and went back to filling the last bucket. She rose to her feet and smoothed her skirt.

"Can we talk?"

"I don't think there's anything to be said," she shrugged.

His eyes narrowed. "But I want to tell you how sorry I am."

"Yes, Mama said you claimed to be sorry." She lifted the buckets and started to carry them around him.

"Please, Edna." He put his hands on her shoulders to stop her. "Please, let's work this out. Please forgive me."

"I forgive you, Sherman," she said, but there was no sparkle in her eyes, no look of love or admiration for him like he usually saw there.

"You're just sayin' that."

"No, I really do forgive you. But I also know how you feel now. You feel like I'm not good enough for you. That's a pretty pathetic way to start a marriage, don't you think?"

"I don't. I don't think I'm better than you. You were right, Edna. I've been wrong, terribly wrong, about you and your family and the Bakers and—about God. You were the one who showed me that. Please don't give up on us now," he pleaded.

"Are you tryin' to tell me that you don't think we're sinners because we dance, play cards, and drink?"

"I'm tryin' to say I'm not perfect, and I've been too quick to judge other people when I'm nowhere near perfect myself. I've been proud and arrogant. Worst of all, I hurt you and made you feel like I thought you weren't good enough for me. If anything, Edna, you're too good for me. But I love you, Edna, and I want to do better." He paused and shook his head. "I haven't forgiven the Bakers yet, though. I want to. I want to be the man you can respect. I talked to my grandma and she's told me how she's forgiven 'em and how I can, too. I'm tryin', Edna. I'm really tryin'. I'm prayin' for 'em. That's what Grandma did and I'm doin' it, too."

Edna nodded. "That's good, Sherman. I'm glad."

She tried to step around him and be on her way, but Sherman grabbed the two buckets from her and set them on the ground. He put his hands on her face and directed her gaze to his. He ran his finger along the contours of her cheek. "You do still love me, don't you?" he asked.

She closed her eyes.

"You will still marry me, won't you?"

"Of course I still love you, Sherman, it's just that . . . don't you think we should take some time to think things through?"

"We can work things out. I know we can," he assured. He gathered her in his arms and kissed her. At first she didn't respond, but within seconds Edna melted into his embrace and returned his kiss.

She hugged him and whispered into his ear. "I'm sorry I said those mean things about you and your family."

"But you were right, Edna. I have been a self-righteous hypocrite. I know that now."

She put her hands to his face and the loving expression returned to her eyes. "See there, I told you to remember that I'm always right."

Sherman chuckled, "Yep, that's where I went wrong."

Chapter 36: Wedding Bells

Daisy, Tennessee
Sunday April 8, 1923

Sherman stood in the Daisy Methodist Church, watching his bride walk down the aisle on her father's arm. He glanced at his mother and grandmother on the front row. They dabbed little lace handkerchiefs to their eyes.

His attention returned to his bride. With every step Edna took toward him, he thought of the events that brought him here. He remembered that misty morning chopping wood and talking to Grandpa Joe about the move to Mowbray.

"This move..." Grandpa Joe had said. "It's just the beginnin' of bigger things for you, Sherman. It's your chance to be the man you were born to be. The trick is lookin' at it as an opportunity, instead of a trial."

What a beautiful opportunity this was. Grandpa Joe would have approved, and Sherman had the distinct impression that his grandfather's spirit was near, watching and pleased with Sherman's choice.

Edna took his arm, and they turned toward the minister. The ceremony began and Sherman promised to love, honor, and keep her throughout life. In turn, she made the same promises to him.

In his mind, Sherman saw his grandparents sitting at their kitchen table—Grandpa Joe reading his paper after a hard day's work and Grandma Josie telling her stories. He contemplated the future. He saw himself and Edna doing the same with grandchildren gathered around their kitchen table, dunking cornbread into their milk—better-tasting cornbread, at that! Sherman smiled at the thought. It was then that he realized how similar he and Edna were to his grandparents. He was the quiet worker and she was the lively storyteller.

Sherman kissed his bride and he knew without doubt that he and Edna would have many years of happiness together.

Chapter 37: Power of the Pen

Atlanta, Georgia
Tuesday, April 10, 1923

State attorney James E. Rosser stepped into the Senate chamber where the clemency hearing for George and Ralph Baker would be held. His gaze traveled over the crowd that had gathered in either morbid curiosity or in a meddlesome attempt to sway justice. Rosser shook his head and caught the serious expression on his partner, Ed Taylor's, face.

"The power of the pen," Ed said in a sarcastic tone, letting his hefty briefcase thump onto the counsel table.

"Hmmm," James groaned in response to his associate's comment. He knew as well as Ed did that they wouldn't be here today if it hadn't been for Rupert Merewether. James couldn't figure out what had motivated the city slicker reporter to venture from his cushy New York City nest to pry into their small town affairs. Merewether hadn't been content to stir up local sympathy for the Bakers. He'd gone a step further and planted erroneous information in the *New York Times*, evoking a national outcry. What was his objective? He didn't seem to be the typical do-gooder out to promote leniency and mercy. Merewether was up to something—something self-serving.

James stepped between the two counsel tables assigned to the defense and the state. He stopped a moment, and scanned the Senate chamber. His attention traveled from the curiosity seekers to the family of the convicted, who sat directly behind the defense table. Their apprehensive faces did not lift to meet his gaze.

Nodding politely at the defense attorneys, James took a seat next to Ed Taylor at their counsel table. James checked his pocket watch and noted the governor wouldn't arrive for at least five more minutes. He opened his briefcase and pulled out the March 12th edition of the *New York Times*, which had marked the start of the national write-in campaign. Boys' organizations across the nation, including the Boy Scouts of America and Big Brothers, had written Governor Hardwick, attempting to sway him toward leniency with Ralph because of his age. The media circus was making justice uncertain.

After a few minutes, James heard a chorus of "Onward, Christian Soldiers" coming from the hallway. The Senate door opened and the governor entered, followed by a number of women from charitable organizations. Among them, head and shoulders taller than the lot, was Rupert Merewether. His eyes were closed and his derby was clutched dramatically to his heart. His tenor voice bellowed the chorus, "Onward, Christian soldiers, marching as to war with the cross of Jesus going on before."

James frowned. Hearing that slippery manipulator sing the words bordered on blasphemy in his opinion. Merewether and the women formed a line. They came in and slipped behind the Baker family.

James' eyes caught Howard Morton's. The only representative from the Morton family who'd been able to make the long trip from Lookout Mountain to Atlanta sat there with his arms folded across his chest.

James approached him and extended his hand. Howard returned a firm handshake and offered a simple greeting. James wanted to promise Mr. Morton that justice would be served today, but he wasn't prepared to predict what the governor might do in the face of so much public outcry.

A flurry of female voices captured both men's attention, and they looked over to see the group of women chatting amongst themselves and settling into their seats.

Howard Morton shook his head in disgust, and James could only say, "We'll do our best, Mr. Morton. I promise you we're prepared for today."

"Thank you," Howard said.

As Governor Hardwick entered the chamber, everyone rose to their feet. He approached the bench at the front, and the voices died down. The governor motioned for everyone to be seated.

James continued to observe the women for a few more moments. He recognized Harriett and Abigail, the ringleaders of the movement to save the Bakers. Clad in bonnets, hats, and lacy attire, they fanned themselves like a flock of hens perched on their eggs. The scowls they turned in his direction let him know they were ready to claw anyone who so much as peeked at their eggs. The objects of their protection, Ralph and George Baker, were clad in neat suits and seated at the counsel table. Rupert Merewether scrunched in among the women, like a sly old fox who'd weaseled his way into the henhouse. He caught James's gaze for an instant, and a knowing smirk flickered across his face before he pasted on a pious expression.

James gritted his teeth and rolled his eyes, then turned his attention toward the front of the chamber.

Governor Hardwick straightened his tie and cleared his throat. "While I've allowed this hearing to take place in the Senate chamber to accommodate the large numbers of people who have become interested in the Baker case, I want to make it clear that no manifestations of approval or disapproval from the audience will be permitted. Also, no one will be allowed to speak except counsel for either side, and no others will be heard except at the request of counsel.

"The time will be divided equally between the prosecution and defense, and because the onus of proof is upon the defense, I will allow them the opening and closing arguments."

Mr. Chambers, one of the counsel for the condemned youths, rose to his feet. "It is our intent to show that Ralph Baker is too young to be responsible for his actions. His extreme youth interfered with his proper assessment of the situation." Chambers paused before continuing, "During the altercation with Mr. Morton, Mr. Morton pulled his weapon and pointed it at George Baker. Ralph, a mere lad, felt that his brother was being attacked and, in his defense, returned fire after Morton had fired his weapon at George Baker." A slight murmur rippled through the chamber, and Governor Hardwick issued a stern warning with his gaze.

Mr. Chambers cleared his throat. "Also, it has come to our attention that George Baker is mentally deficient due to medical and hereditary factors. Under the influence of alcohol, this condition was exacerbated, making George unaccountable for his actions."

Mr. Chambers stepped toward the governor. "We have here a petition from a number of Floyd County citizens, and a letter from a Rome minister who has visited the condemned youths while they have been held in the Floyd jail."

After the Governor scanned the documents, he had his assistant take them to the state attorneys' desk. Together, James and Ed read the letter from the minister. The statement expressed the view that Ralph Baker was a kindhearted boy and that George was mentally deficient. James looked at his partner with a single raised eyebrow.

"How convenient," Ed muttered so only James could hear.

Mr. Chambers continued for the defense, "I also have here a number of affidavits from physicians, stating that George Baker is of unsound mentality, a result of both nerve trouble brought on by meningitis and inheritance." Mr. Chambers placed the affidavits on the governor's desk and then handed him more papers. "And these are certificates from the United States Census Bureau showing that, according to the age given in the census returns for 1920, Ralph Baker was only fourteen years old at the time the murder was committed."

The governor reviewed the documents and passed them to the state's attorneys. James read them over while Mr. Chambers made his concluding remarks. It looked like a last-ditch effort to him. He studied the governor's dispassionate face, trying to deduce whether or not he was buying it.

When it was his turn to present the state's position, James Rosser rose to his feet and addressed the governor. "The state shall base its argument entirely on the record." He started by relating the events of the killing in detail, referring frequently to the case record.

"The Bakers boarded the train to Durham at a lonely station, over a mile from human habitation in either direction. George Baker then offered a drink to a total stranger, a traveling man who was also a passenger on the train. When the man refused this proffered drink of whisky, George Baker threatened to shoot him. George Baker also stole the fuses that are used for signaling from the train, and then threatened the conductor with his gun when he attempted to stop George from harassing the passengers. It's obvious from these events the Bakers had, with forethought, intended to cause trouble aboard the train."

"Finally, the conductor was able to get the Bakers to the back of the train, and they were put off in Durham. It was there that they encountered Joseph W. Morton, an elderly deputy sheriff who was at the depot to meet his daughter coming in on the same train. They went up to this old man and asked if he had a warrant for them. He informed them that he did not have a warrant.

"Then," continued Mr. Rosser, "one of them cursed and contradicted him, saying, 'Yes, you have got a warrant and now try to serve it.'"

"George Baker then struck the old man and knocked him down, whereupon Ralph Baker shot him three times. Morton then drew his own gun and emptied it, but in his dying condition, all his shots went wild." Mr. Rosser turned for effect and, aiming his finger like a pistol at the floor, continued from the trial record. "George Baker then drew a gun and also fired at the old man. Morton died within four minutes, his head in his daughter's lap, while the Baker brothers walked away."

Mr. Rosser paused and then faced the Governor once more. "As they turned away, Ralph Baker turned around and said, 'Is that hot enough for you? If it is not, then damn you, we will give you some more.'"

Shaking the trial transcript in his hand, Rosser summarized, "There never was a more deliberate, cold-blooded murder committed by Jesse and Frank James. And I might add the first hold-up and murder committed by those two infamous characters occurred when they were seventeen and fifteen years of age." James was quiet for a moment, letting the impact of his words sink in.

"Nothing was ever said about Ralph Baker's age or George Baker's mental condition when they were tried, convicted, and condemned. It is only since then, when the cases reached the prison commission and governor, that these angles have come up," he said.

James held up the offending March 12th *New York Times* article. "It is appalling and incomprehensible that organizations of all sorts and conditions from Maine to California have deluged the governor of this state with letters requesting clemency for these two. When Walker County begins to take upon itself to try all the murder cases between Maine and California, it will be time for these people to interfere, and not before!" James shook the newspaper in his hand.

"And as for the people of Atlanta who have worked for clemency, I must say that Walker County did not try to interfere to prevent the hanging of Frank Dupre, a 'boy bandit,' recently convicted and hanged in Fulton County!"

Turning toward the defense counsel's table, James Rosser's eyes met Mr. Baker's. The father of the condemned men tightened his arm around his wife's shoulders. James swallowed hard as his gaze went next to George's wife and the younger Baker siblings. Their stolid faces showed little emotion. Their set expressions seemed to indicate a spirit of heartbroken resignation to whatever fate might bring.

A twinge of sympathy needled James' heart as he returned to his table and sat down, still breathing heavily from his vehement presentation. Yes, he felt sympathy for the family, but he had to protect the citizens of Walker County. There was too much at stake with this case. He couldn't afford to relent when peace and order in Walker County hung in the balance.

Clearing his throat, defense attorney Glenn rose to his feet. "In answer to the charge that the age and mentality questions were not brought up at the trials, the defense would like to make it clear that, at that time, we had not received information regarding a streak of insanity in the Baker family. This newly discovered evidence could not be used legally as the basis for a new trial. Also, the age of Ralph Baker was conceded at the trial to be 14 at the time the crime was committed. As the age of accountability in Georgia is 14, it was not necessary to belabor this point."

Mr. Glenn straightened the lapels of his suit and drew closer to the governor. "I will raise an entirely different version of the fatal encounter with Mr. Morton. This was a mutual affray. Morton fired the first shot and George Baker had no gun. He had already given it to his brother upon disembarking the train."

"Have these questions of fact not been covered by the jury?" Governor Hardwick interjected.

Mr. Glenn lowered his head a little. "Yes, they have," he admitted.

"Then," said Governor Hardwick, "the sole question before me is whether or not the death penalty would be too severe in these cases."

"Would the state wish to add more to their presentation?" asked the Governor.

Solicitor Ed Taylor, for the state, rose to his feet. "I would like to draw attention to a series of other murders which have occurred in Walker County during the twelve months prior to the killing of Mr. Morton. Three deputies were killed shortly before Mr. Morton's murder. Also, about one year previous, the sheriff of Walker County was murdered and his slayer was not hanged."

"This final crime, committed by the Bakers, has aroused such intense feeling in Walker County that, when George Baker was caught and arrested, a mob had formed for the purpose of lynching him. It was only the intervention of a justice of the peace that quieted the mob and allowed George Baker to go to jail and stand trial for murder."

Mr. Taylor continued his plea to the governor. "This conduct by the mob shows its willingness to abide by the law." He waved his hand toward Rupert Merewether and the women with him. "This other mob, moved by hysteria and sentiment to prevent carrying out sentencing, is little better than the first one!"

The Governor motioned toward the defense. "You may make your closing argument."

Attorney Chambers stood up and straightened the lapels of his suit. With an impassioned plea, he began, "Shall we hang a child,

Governor? Shall we hang his mentally deficient brother and send the entire nation into an uproar, looking upon Atlanta as a city so backward and savage that we now execute children and mentally impaired individuals?" He gestured toward his clients. "Will slaughtering these youths bring back Mr. Morton?"

"This case is not like others we've seen. There are extenuating circumstances that must not be ignored. We're dealing with two unusual young men. The first, Ralph Baker, who did all the shooting, is a mere child—incapable of understanding his actions at the time of the shooting. The anxiousness to defend his brother is understandable in one so young and inexperienced. The second young man, George Baker, who is clearly mentally deficient, was under the influence of liquor when he started an argument with the deceased. That was George Baker's crime: starting an argument. Shall he die for that?

"Where do we draw the line, Governor? Would we hang a ten-year-old if he fired a weapon that killed someone? A twelve-year-old? What's next? There must come a time when we realize that some people are not accountable for their actions due to youth or mental deficiencies. This is such a time."

He stood squarely before the Governor and, with heartfelt sincerity, pleaded, "I think you know as well as I do, Governor, that these young men do not deserve to die. The District Attorney would have you execute them because of other crimes committed in Walker County. I plead with you, Sir. Do not make these boys an example. Do not make them pay for other men's crimes. I trust you will not sacrifice their lives just to prove a point."

Chapter 38: Startling News

Rome, Georgia
April 25, 1923

George lay on his cot, hopeful that good news about his fate would come soon. The governor had commuted Ralph's sentence to life in prison. Surely, he'd get the same reprieve or something even better. After all, it was Ralph who admitted to the shooting. George hadn't even fired his weapon.

He closed his eyes and enjoyed a peaceful slumber, hopeful that things were looking up. Rupert Merewether's articles had helped Ralph. The people would help him, too. He had to believe that.

He wasn't aware of how long he'd slept before he felt Ralph's hand on his shoulder shaking him awake.

"George, there's a reporter here from the *Constitution*. He's got a dispatch." George opened his eyes and began to realize what this meant. He roused himself, rose to his feet, and approached the reporter who held a yellow piece of paper between his fingers. George searched the man's face for any indication of the outcome, but could discern nothing.

The man slipped the paper through the bars so that George could take it, but didn't say a word.

George could tell by the heading that it was an Associated Press dispatch with the governor's announcement in Sandersville.

Slowly, George waded through the typewritten message. Unaccustomed to reading press dispatches from which unimportant words were omitted, it was a full minute before the import of what he was reading filtered through his mind.

> Governor declares outcome clemency hearing. Young man deliberately filled mean corn liquor, murder in heart, threatened, without slightest provocation three men before Morton killed. Request clemency denied. George Baker receive full penalty. Hanging date set. April 27, 1923.

George's face went fiery red and then a ghastly white. His fingers released their hold on the yellow slip and it fluttered from his trembling fingers to the floor. His whole body sagged against the bars.

He felt sick, as if he might faint, and a moan escaped his lips. Grasping the bars of his cell for support, he made his way back to his bunk, where he cast himself face-down, his body shaking with sobs.

"I've got to die," he cried so loudly that his voice echoed through the prison. "I'm not guilty," he sobbed over and over again.

Ralph reached through the bars and grabbed the reporter's arm. "They can't kill him and let me live. I did it! I'm the one who shot the deputy. Not George. George didn't even have a gun. How could they hang him and not me?"

The reporter shook his head frantically and wrenched Ralph's hand from his sleeve. "I don't know, son. I'm sorry. I just don't know." The reporter stepped back out of Ralph's reach.

Ralph rushed to his brother and put his arm around his shoulder. "I'm so sorry, George. We'll tell 'em to hang me instead. I did it. It's all my fault. They'll have to hang me if I tell 'em to hang me instead."

George shook his head. His poor, naïve brother. He really didn't understand how things worked. "It's no use, Ralph. They won't change their minds now. It's me. They're gonna kill me. They're going to hang a man who never killed anybody. I've got to die. Oh, God, I've got to die!" George's voice rang out through the grim prison until every prisoner in the jail knew the fateful news.

The entire prison fell into eerie silence as the other prisoners stood in awestruck groups, saying nothing.

Suddenly the silence was broken by a woman's sobs. Lulu Baker ran to the cell and reached her hands through the bars, "Oh, George! I heard. They can't take you from me, George! They can't! You didn't do it! We'll make them understand you didn't do it!"

George rushed toward his wife, and slipped his hands through the bars, clutching Lulu the best he could. Her body shook as she pressed her face against the bars and clung to her husband. "What will I do without you, George? What will I do?" she sobbed.

Chapter 39: Peace at Last

Daisy, Tennessee
April 27, 1923

Sherman draped his arm around his bride's waist and kissed her cheek. He stared at her sleeping face and marveled at her resemblance to an angel. They'd only been married nineteen days, but in a way it felt like the first. This day would mark the end of the most painful year of his life.

In a few hours, he would attend the hanging of George Baker. He wouldn't be allowed inside the jail, but he would stand on the jailhouse steps with his father and uncles and see this through. Then he'd come home and build a life with Edna here in Daisy—a life of which his grandfather would be proud.

Sherman thought about his parents. He missed them now that they had moved back to Lookout Mountain, but he'd be seeing them today at the courthouse. Thinking about the hanging brought Governor Hardwick's words to mind. The governor had commuted Ralph Baker's sentence only two days earlier because of his age, but his brother George would die today. The governor ignored the pleas of those who took up Baker's cause, saying, "This young man seems deliberately to have filled himself with mean corn liquor and then, with murder in his heart, to have threatened without the slightest provocation at least three other men before he and his younger brother killed Morton."

Sherman felt mixed emotions about George's execution. On one hand, it would help his family put the past to rest and give them a sense of justice. Yet, Sherman couldn't get past the nagging feeling that it should be Ralph on those gallows instead of George. Ralph kept insisting that it was he who fired the fatal shots. Then again, if George had been sober and not picked the fight, Grandpa Joe would be alive today.

Sherman closed his eyes and thought about his grandfather. He could see his face clearly in his mind. The wrinkles around his eyes, the way he smoothed down his mustache. He remembered cutting wood with him at the sawmill, helping him patch roofs on the Durham shanties, and working alongside him in Grandma's garden. Sherman smiled as he recalled the swats he'd received on occasion for riding the barn. He could hear Grandpa call, "Put it up!" when he and his cousins snuck back to the croquet course on a Sabbath afternoon. Sherman's smile broadened and he bit his quivering lip as a tear trickled down his cheek.

The memories came flooding back, and with them came an indescribable peace that swept over Sherman's entire body. It tingled up his spine and drizzled down his limbs like hot chocolate on a cool spring morning. He knew the long-anticipated moment had arrived and the warmth intensified. Gratitude brought fresh tears.

Sherman knew his prayers had created this space for forgiveness. All this time, the protected chamber of his soul remained vacant. The gates of his heart had held back the tide for so long. He had asked himself a thousand times in the last few weeks why forgiveness wouldn't come. He'd despised the unyielding fortress that held forgiveness at bay. But now he understood. God had been clearing a place big enough to hold all the emotions this moment would bring.

Peace tumbled over the collapsing walls and filled every crevice of his heart. Along with the flood of gratitude came compassion for the man who would die today and for his brother, who would spend his life in prison. Sherman could see it all so clearly now, and with the clarity came sorrow for the waste of human life. These young men hadn't been taught as Sherman had. They had not had his parents, had not had his grandfather to guide them like a northern star.

He traced the contours of Edna's cheek and brushed aside a strand of her strawberry blonde hair with his finger. She'd been right about making a space for forgiveness. She'd also been right when she'd assured him that the memories would return when he needed them most. This day would mark the end of his happiest and saddest year; how fitting that today would be the day his prayers would be answered.

Edna rolled over and her eyelids fluttered open, her green eyes meeting his. "Good morning." She smiled up at him. He put his hand to her cheek and kissed her.

"Are you ready for today?" she asked.

"With you beside me, I'm ready for anything." Sherman winked, pulled her into his arms, and kissed her. In that moment, he resolved to do whatever it took to provide for and protect the woman he loved, and to raise their children to have faith in the things that mattered most. Joseph Morton's legacy would live on.

Chapter 40: A Time to Die

Walker County, Georgia
April 27, 1923

"I'd be happy to offer you an opiate, George." Dr. Coulter reached through the jail cell and put a hand on George's shoulder. "It'll help ease the tension on your nerves."

"No, I don't need anything." George gripped the bar a little tighter. The doctor had been watching George all morning as visitors came and went. Dr. Coulter was amazed at his composure. Only once had he cried a little: when some of his buddies came to tell him good-bye. But even then there was no sign of breaking down.

"You look exhausted, George. Please let me give you a little something," the doctor pleaded, feeling helpless tending to a man headed for the gallows.

"Ah, I'm just tired 'cause they brought me up from Rome around midnight. Haven't had much sleep."

"I thought they were gonna bring you on the morning train." Dr. Coulter glanced behind him at Deputy Sheriff Mullins, who sat on a wooden chair against the wall.

"We changed our minds," Mullins answered. "I brought George with me. The other officers drove up in a separate car. And John Horgan from the Salvation Army brought George's parents and their youngins up from Rome."

George clung to the bars for support. The long imprisonment had made him weak. Dr. Coulter pointed to a chair inside the cell, where a plentiful breakfast sat. "You've hardly touched your food."

"I'm all right. Don't feel like eating."

At around ten-thirty, Rupert Merewether entered the jail and approached the prisoner. He reached his hand through the bars. George stared at it several moments before finally taking it in a firm shake.

"How are you holding up, George?" Rupert asked.

"I've seen better days," came George's dry response.

"I'm sorry to see it come to this. You know I did the best I could," Rupert insisted.

"Well, you can finish the story, Mr. Merewether. You can tell 'em they are hangin' an innocent man," George said. "I didn't even have a gun. I was drunk on poisoned liquor. I remember vaguely that I had a disagreement with Morton, and that I slapped him." George's voice lowered and he seemed to be talking to himself. "It was Ralph, it must have been Ralph who fired the shots."

The doctor watched Rupert Merewether jot down what George said in his notebook.

"How is Ralph taking things?" Rupert asked.

"Ralph is down there in the jail at Rome, heartbroken. He offered last night to take my place." George looked from Rupert to the doctor. "He would gladly take my place. He wanted me to get the life sentence and him the death penalty. I haven't done anything to be hanged for, even if I may have been connected with Morton's death."

"And how do you feel?" Merewether asked, his pen hovering above his pad.

George spoke with the tired, patient voice and expression that had grown upon him since his confinement. "I'm ready to go. My great regret is for my people, my poor, heartbroken father and mother, my wife, who means more than my life to me."

"And what about Morton? Do you blame him for your being here?" Rupert asked.

"I'd had no previous trouble with Morton and bear no grudge against him. I'll admit it was the whisky. Drinkin' brought me to this place. If I could do it over, I wouldn't touch the..." George's voice trailed off and his eyes shifted toward the doorway.

Dr. Coulter looked in the direction of George's gaze. There stood the young man's wife, mother, father, and younger siblings. Mullins removed his hat out of respect for the family. The jail fell silent.

His wife and parents, along with a 13-year-old brother and two younger sisters, approached the bars. The reporter and Dr. Coulter stepped aside giving them privacy. Their conversation was subdued. George pressed his head against the bars that separated him from his family and tears gathered in his eyes. Again, he remained in control of his emotions.

The conversation wasn't lengthy. Mrs. Baker tottered away first, her body shaking with sobs. George's father left a few moments later, a solemn expression on his brave face as he led the two little girls. The brother, red-faced and heartbroken, seemed to take it worst. With tears streaming down his cheeks, he clutched George's hand and then followed his grieving family.

For the next few moments, Lulu and George clung to one another the best they could through the bars. George kissed his wife and brushed the tears from her cheeks. His own eyes misted as she turned from him. She clutched her handkerchief to her face and fled the chamber.

Deputy Sheriff Tom Tarvin entered the cell area. Directing his words toward Dr. Coulter and Merewether, he said, "It's time. We need to start making the final preparations. If you folks would step outside..."

~*~

Tom Tarvin unlocked George's cell. Together, he and Deputy Sheriff Mullins escorted George into the area where the scaffold had been erected.

"Would you like to make a statement to the crowd outside?" Tom asked him.

George nodded. "Yes, sir."

They accompanied George to the east window. It had been opened to let in the air. George stepped closer and began to speak. As George reiterated his innocence anew and invited all to profit by his example and keep out of bad company, Tom couldn't help but feel a wave of remorse. Would a guilty man handle his demise with the same composure as this man? Would he continue to claim his innocence to the bitter end if he were guilty? What was the point in it?

After George spoke from the east window, Tom suggested the other part of the crowd might not have been able to hear him.

"Let's go over to the north window and let you speak to the people over there," Tom suggested.

George agreed and they made their way to the window. Calm and self-possessed, George spoke a few words of farewell to several hundred people within earshot of the jail. He didn't speak loudly, but there was no tremor in his voice. Tom knew he would never forget George's words, and he doubted anyone who heard him ever would either.

"I wants to tell everybody good-bye," George said. "I want to tell all you boys to keep away from trouble and from bad associates. That's what brought me to this. I'm payin' the death penalty for a murder I never committed."

At this point, George saw a Floyd County deputy sheriff who had been kind to him in the jail at Rome in the crowd below. "Good-bye, Buck," he said. Then, seeing another friend, he called, "Tell the woman you board with I'll never forget her kindness to me." He recognized several men in the crowd and waved good-byes to each, some of them calling "Good-bye, George" in return.

"Stay away from liquor boys. It brought me to this. I never should've taken the first drink." George's voice grew clear and steady. "Folks, I am going away. I hope to meet you in a better world."

Tom nodded toward Deputy Acknow for him to start clearing the jail. Only a few invited officers of the law from Walker and other counties, the newspapermen, and a few others were permitted in the narrow space, above and below, which was to be the scene of the execution.

The officers allowed a few others holding permits to remain on the little porch where they could hear just the sound of the trap. The deputies ushered out the majority of the crowd who had been inside the jail. Once outside, they joined several hundred people. The throng was quiet and orderly, even subdued.

Tom and Aknow helped George to the gallows.

Three ministers—Reverend Howard of Rome, Reverend Tucker of Cassandra, and Ensign Horgan—each delivered prayers while George knelt on the trap. The condemned man breathed fervent "Amens" throughout the prayers with an especially fervent expression when Reverend Tucker asked that blessings be upon Sheriff Harmon as he performed his duty as an officer of the law.

Tom quickly dabbed a tear from his eye and began the final preparations. He tried to be as gentle as he could, tried not to think of the likelihood that George didn't deserve this fate. Instead, he tried to focus on the task at hand and his duty as a law officer. But no matter what he tried to think about, Tom knew this was a day he would never forget.

~*~

Sherman stood on the front porch outside the jail with his father and uncles. When he heard the snap of the falling trap, he closed his eyes and offered a prayer for George Baker's family. The hollow feeling in the pit of his stomach made him wonder if this was really necessary.

It was a full ten minutes or more before someone stepped outside the jail and addressed them.

"It's done. Dr. Underwood and Dr. Coulter have pronounced George Baker dead." A perfect silence fell over the crowd, broken only by the sobs of the grief-stricken parents seated in an automobile about a hundred yards away.

Just as the crowd started to disband, somebody started a collection to pay the funeral expenses. "Let's give him a decent burial, folks," a man called out, waving a hat in the air. "We can't have him buried by the county. Won't you help out these poor parents?"

The crowd was so thick that people bumped into Sherman as he followed his uncles toward their cars.

George's father stood with his hat clutched to his heart beside his automobile, while the women sobbed softly within.

"They have just made an example of my boy," the man agonized through his tears as someone paused to offer him sympathy. "George didn't deserve such a fate as this. Look at Douglas, who killed Sheriff Catron; he's in prison, but still has his life. Other men have killed and not paid the penalty with their lives, but my boy, little more than a child, had to be an example. It's hard! It's hard!"

A tear misted Sherman's vision. He let it remain. His uncles continued to nudge their way through the crowd, but Sherman lagged behind a few steps until people came between him and his family. As he reached the man taking collections in a hat, Sherman reached deep into his pocket and withdrew what change he had.

He slipped the money into the collection hat and continued on his way. When Sherman reached his car, he cranked the engine a few times until it rumbled to a purr. He stepped toward the driver's side door and paused.

"We've raised enough to bury him!" the man cried, holding up the hat.

A small smile curled Sherman's lips.

"You all right, Sherman?" he heard his father ask from inside the Model T. Sherman rubbed his sleeve to his eye and then tapped his hand to the roof.

"I'm fine," he answered. Taking one last look at the Baker family, he climbed behind the wheel and drove toward Daisy—toward Edna, toward life.

Epilogue

Mary Josephine Bradford Morton (a.k.a. "Josie") died on April 24, 1926, and was laid to rest alongside her husband, Deputy Sheriff Joseph Washington Morton, on Lookout Mountain in the Payne's Chapel Methodist Cemetery in Hinkle, Georgia.[2]

Mary Ann Morton Craig Phillips moved to Walton, Boone County, Kentucky with her second husband Gordon Phillips and only returned to the mountain for occasional visits. She never fully got over her father's murder. Many years after it, she could relate with clarity and detail the events of her father's death—always with the hope that one day, she would awaken to find it had all been a horrible nightmare. She died April 27, 1960, and is buried alongside her husband in Kentucky. She was 64. [3]

Sarah "Josephine" Morton Rogers was a mother to all but never had children of her own. Her husband, Ief, became deaf. While walking across the highway in Trenton, Dade County, Georgia, he stepped in front of a car and was killed. Josephine sold her property and lived with different members of the family. She died on December 25, 1954, at the age of 66.[4]

George Williamson "Plodding Will" Morton became a rock mason and helped lay the rock on Sherman and Edna's home in Daisy. He died July 17, 1964, and is buried at Payne's Chapel Methodist Church Cemetery. He was 84.

Nancy Jane Hixson Morton died on April 17, 1967, and is buried alongside her husband in Payne's Chapel Methodist Church Cemetery in Hinkle, Georgia. She was 85.

Sherman Joseph Morton became a railroad engineer and a land developer. He owned and developed the main strip of Daisy, Tennessee, with a complex of buildings that was used as a restaurant, furniture store, dental office, and office complex. He also developed several subdivisions in Daisy and an upscale trailer park. Sherman died of old age in Chattanooga on April 12, 1996. He was 91.

Edna Jane Springfield Morton gave birth to two daughters and three sons. Each of her daughters (Betty Jean and Sherma Jane) only lived a mere month. Sherman and Edna's sons are Austin, Jack, and Donald. Austin served during WWII aboard the Saratoga and became a railroad engineer. Jack became a dentist and developed land alongside his father. Donald holds legal and accounting degrees and served for many years as Chairman of the Fiscal Review Committee of the state of Tennessee. Edna got her first job in 1966 working alongside her son Jack in his dental practice as a receptionist and dental assistant. It was one of the happiest periods of her life. She died at home of a stroke on the morning of August 30, 1975 at the age of 76.

Thaddeus Luther Springfield (aka Thad) was a farmer and drove a school bus. He came in from a day of working in the fields, sat down and died of a heart attack on August 13, 1931, in Daisy, Tennessee. He was 58.

Maude Pearson Springfield lived with her daughters, Lucille and Thadda, during the Great Depression. Together they got by on Lucille and Thadda's employment and Maude made their dresses for them. She died suddenly of a cerebral hemorrhage on July 10, 1956, at the age of 79.

William "Frank" Springfield took over his father's farm for a time and then worked at the Post Office. He married Opal Coutta on October 22, 1925 and together they had one son and two daughters. Frank died suddenly on September 18, 1956, in Daisy, Tennessee of a heart attack caused by a blood clot. He was a month shy of 54.

Dorothy Maude Springfield (aka Dot) married Casper Hilliard on May 6, 1932. They had three daughters together. Dot died of pancreatic cancer on December 21, 1974, at the age of 62.

Thadda Springfield Moody joined the Women's Army Corp during WWII. She worked in an airplane factory and married five times—twice to one man, Paul Moody. Their second marriage stuck and she and Paul lived happily together on Daisy Mountain. Together they set out to serve a mission for the LDS church in 1985. While driving from Salt Lake City, Utah, to Chicago on the way to their mission, Paul died of a heart attack in Kimball, Nebraska, on May 30, 1985. After coming home to Tennessee for the funeral, Thadda continued to serve the mission on her own. She was never able to have children, but she is one of the author's favorite aunts. Thadda passed away on February 15, 2004, at the age of 88 and is buried in Hixson, Tennessee, alongside her husband.

Ralph Baker spent 20 years in prison and was then released. He stole a car and was sentenced again to prison, where he died of tuberculosis.[5]

George Baker's body was taken to Wann's Chapel. On the day before the burial, more than 2,000 people viewed the body at the funeral home. The next day, the funeral was delayed more than two hours while another 2,000 or more people filed past the coffin. In total, the burial attracted between 6,000 and 10,000 people. According to *The Chattanooga Times*, "More than 1,500 automobiles, most from Chattanooga but many from North Georgia, jammed all roads leading to the Morris Hills Baptist Church and Cemetery and hundreds who had no transportation attended by foot."

The majority of those attending the funeral were curiosity seekers. However, many were there out of sympathy. Hats were passed through the crowd and more than $500 was collected and turned over to Baker's parents.

Several weeks later, a marker was placed over George Baker's grave. The simple stone still stands in the Morris Hills Baptist Church Cemetery, bearing only the man's name, birth and death dates, and a message that reads: *The pearly gates are shining bright, weep not for me. I am all right, waiting for you who fought my fight. Your faithful petitions are answered in heaven.*

Bibliography

Morgan, Donna Morton. The Lookout Mountain Mortons and Their Descendants. Baltimore: Gateway Press, Inc. 1989.

Hollingsworth, Earnest. The Old Miner and His Guardian Angel. Collegedale, Tennessee: The College Press. 1977. pp 141-143.

"Seek to Save a Boy from the Gallows", New York Times, March 13, 1923.

"Boys Sentenced to Death Get Reprieve," Oakland Tribune, March 14, 1923.

"Respite Granted for Baker Boys," The Constitution, Atlanta Georgia, April 10, 1923.

"Older of Baker Boys Must Die," The Constitution, Atlanta Georgia, April 26, 1923.

"Last Effort Made to Save George Baker," The Constitution, Atlanta Georgia, April 27, 1923, pp. 1, 7A.

"Baker Boy Pays Supreme Penalty in Lafayette Jail," The Constitution, Atlanta Georgia, April 28, 1923, p. 1.

"Lessons of the Bakers," The Constitution, Atlanta Georgia, April 29, 1923.

"Will Bury Baker Boy Near Home in Walker County," The Constitution, Atlanta Georgia, April 29, 1923.

"Baker Will Be Sent to Floyd Chaingang," The Constitution, Atlanta Georgia, April 29, 1923.

Hays, Hamp. Georgia, Walker County, Supervisor's District 7, Enumeration District 186, Sheet No. 11A, Fourteenth Census of the United States 1920-Population.

Casteel, Bill. "Last Legal Hanging in Georgia Culmination of Bizarre Events," The Chattanooga Times, September 27, 1982, p. A2.

Endnotes

1 Gypsy Love Song, from the Broadway musical "The Fortune Teller" (1898), Victor Herbert / Henry Bache Smith

2 Morgan, Donna Morton, The Lookout Mountain Mortons and Their Descendents, p. 14

3 Ibid., p 76

4 Ibid., p 33

5 Ibid., p 3

About the Author

Marnie L. Pehrson was born and raised in the Chattanooga, Tennessee area. An avid enthusiast of family history, Marnie integrates elements of the places, people and events of her Southern family and heritage into her historical fiction novels. Marnie's life is steeped in Southern history from the little town of Daisy that she grew up in to the 24 acres bordering the famous Chickamauga Battlefield upon which her family resides.

Marnie and her husband Greg are the parents of six children. She is the founder of multi-denominational SheLovesGod.com which hosts the annual SheLovesGod Virtual Women's Conference in October each year. Marnie has served in many capacities within her church in presidencies of the women's, young women's, and children's organizations, as a Sunday School teacher and pianist. Service as family history consultant inspired her foray into historical fiction.

Marnie is also an internet developer and consultant who helps talented professionals deliver their message to the online world. You may visit her projects through www.PWGroup.com and www.IdeaMarketers.com.

You may also read more of her work at www.MarniePehrson.com and www.SouthernLit.com. Marnie welcomes reader comments and may be reached at marnie@marniepehrson.com or by calling 706-866-2295.

Other Books by Marnie Pehrson

The Patriot Wore Petticoats

Historical fiction, 224, pages, ISBN: 0-9729750-4-7

Daring "Dicey" Langston, the bold and reckless rider and expert shot, saves her family and an entire village during the American Revolution. Having faced British soldiers, rushing swollen rivers, the "Bloody Scouts," and the barrel of a loaded pistol, nothing had quite prepared this valiant heroine for the heart-pounding exhilaration she'd find in the arms of one brave Patriot. Based on a true story about the author's fourth great-grandmother. Learn more at www.DiceyLangston.com

Angel and the Enemy

Historical Fiction, 287 pages, ISBN 0-9729750-9-8

The War between the States is raging and Angelina Stone's world is falling apart. Her beloved father lies rotting in a Union prison and when her Georgia home is invaded by Yankee officers, Angelina knows she will never be the same again. One night will change her life forever... Will Angelina be able to overcome her fears, lay prejudice aside, and learn to trust? When the stakes are high, will she risk losing everything? Only by doing so can she face the demons of her past and win the battle that rages in her own heart - a heart that is eternally tethered to . . . the enemy.

Beyond the Waterfall

Historical Fiction, 136 pages, paperback ISBN: 0-9729750-7-1

Jillian's feet were precariously planted in two worlds: the Cherokee nation on the brink of extermination, and the world where Jesse Whitmore belonged. On her first meeting with him, the charming and handsome merchant had set her young heart ablaze. Yet, could she trust him? Or was he just like all the other white men she'd encountered? Would he stand beside her while she witnessed her nation ripped apart, or would he join the ranks of the powerful greedy to betray her? Based on family history and local legend.

Hannah's Heart

Historical Fiction, 162 pages, paperback, ISBN: 1-59936-012-8

Hannah Jamison is ready to give her heart away. Unfortunately, the man she's falling for shows no indication of ever reciprocating her feelings. When Mother Nature intervenes in her behalf, all Hannah's dreams seem to be coming true . . . until she discovers that following her heart means losing the ones she loves. Is Hannah willing to pay the price?

Savannah Nights

Modern Mystery, 140 pages, paperback, ISBN: 978-1599360256

Samantha Reynolds sets off for college to a Culinary school in Altanta leaving her best friend Sean Cooper behind just when their friendship had started to blossom into something more. Sean also leaves town on a basketball scholarship at a major university.

They lose touch of one another until ten years later when Samantha is prominent chef in an Atlanta restaurant. When her mother s untimely death shocks her world. Samantha heads home to Savanna, Georgia where she hopes to lead a calmer life. Instead, she ends up entangled in a mystery her mother was trying to solve.

In order to piece together the puzzle Marjorie Reynolds left behind, Samantha turns to her old friend Sean, now a city alderman in whom her mother confided. Together they must learn what Marjorie discovered before Samantha ends up sharing her mother s fate.

Waltzing with the Light

LDS Historical Fiction, 268 pages, paperback, ISBN: 0-9729750-6-3

Nestled within the valley of the Appalachian mountains, Daisy, Tennessee, seemed like a sleepy little town until depression-era drifter, Jake Elliot, entered it and knocked on the front door of the yellow farm house and met Mikalah, the oldest of the Ford children. Little did he know how his life and his heart would be affected from that moment forward.

Rebecca's Reveries
Historical Fiction, 224 pages, paperback, ISBN: 0-9729750-2-0
Rebecca Marchant had led a sheltered life until she found herself inexplicably drawn to the home of her father's youth. Surrounded by the historical landscape of the Chickamauga Battlefield in Georgia, Rebecca finds herself plagued by haunting dreams and vivid visions of Civil War events. As Rebecca walks a mile in another girl's moccasins through her visions and dreams she learns about compassion, forgiveness, temptation and the power of true love.

You're Here for a Reason: Discover & Live Your Your Purpose
Inspirational Nonfiction, 248 pages, paperback, ISBN 978-0967616278
Author, speaker and life coach Marnie Pehrson launched "Rejoice in 2007" to show her gratitude to God by helping thousands of Christians worldwide realize their divine purpose and better live life to its fullest. Her message: Don't let anything stand in your way. Not worry, not fear, not the adversary and, especially, not your own limiting beliefs about yourself! Marnie now shares these lessons about experiencing the true joy that can only be found in a close relationship with the Savior, Jesus Christ.

We must grow so close, she says, that our life purpose is in sync with what He created us to do. Just as an eagle is happiest when it's soaring through the air and a horse is happiest when it's galloping across a field, you are happiest when living the life you were born to!

Each of the fifty-two wise, honest, and profound lessons from "Rejoice In 2007" is designed to help you discover and live your own unique life of joyful purpose. Used consistently with scripture and prayer, they will indeed fill what Goethe described as the "God-shaped hole" in every human heart.

You Can't Fly If You're Still Clutching the Dirt: How to Stop Worrying and Achieve Your God-given Potential
Inspirational Nonfiction, 148 pages, Paperback, ISBN 0-9729750-8-X
Deep down, you know God created you for a reason. He's told you that you're a child of God. You're made in His image, and He has a plan for you. You sense in your heart of hearts that you have wings to fly, but worries, fears, and insecurities drag you down to earth, preventing you from spreading your wings and taking flight.

This book will teach you how to quit worrying and trust God; easily distinguish between what you control and what God controls; find freedom to focus on the two decisions that are yours to make – What you want and Why you want it. Find deliverance from the worry-inducing questions of Who? When? How? and Where?

Lord, Are You Sure?
Inspirational, 152 pages, Paperback, ISBN 0-9729750-0-4
A roadmap for understanding how Heavenly Father works in your life, helping you understand why certain problems keep repeating themselves, how to break the cycle and unlock the mystery of why you encounter challenges and roadblocks on roads you felt inspired to travel.

Packets of Sunlight for Parents
Compiled by: Marnie L. Pehrson
Inspirational, 144 pages, ISBN 0-9676162-4-7
Brighten your day with inspiration for parents of tots to teens! Inspirational quote book.

Packets of Sunlight for American Patriots
Compiled by: Marnie L. Pehrson
Inspirational, 108 pages, ISBN 0-9676162-3-9
Let the founding fathers reignite your love for freedom! Inspirational quote book.

10 Steps to Fulfilling Your Divine Destiny: A Christian Woman's Guide to Learning & Living God's Plan for Her
Inspirational, 124 pages, Paperback, ISBN 0-9676162-1-2
Have you ever said to yourself, "I'd love to do great things with my life, but I'm just too busy, too untalented, too ordinary, too afraid, too anything but extraordinary"? Inside this book you'll learn how to reach your full God-given potential.

To order call 800-524-2307 or visit
www.MarniePehrson.com

www.ingramcontent.com/pod-product-compliance
Lightning Source LLC
LaVergne TN
LVHW020539100826
845148LV00010B/1538

* 9 7 8 0 9 8 2 5 8 7 8 0 5 *